© Max Lamirande, 2024

Published by Max Lamirande

© 2024 Saguenay, Quebec, Canada

All rights reserved. No part of this book may be reproduced or modified in any form, including photocopying, recording, or by any information storage and retrieval system, without permission in writing from the publisher.

Cover image copyrights:
shutterstock_249573286 – *standard license*
Order CS-0CA09-11b8

Alamy - ERGPT2 – Standard Image
Order reference: OY95167147

ISBN: 978-1-0692800-1-5

I0604103

FOREWORD

Dear readers,

THANK YOU FOR READING MY WORK.

I welcome you back to the Pacific Alternate Series. Another very fun book to write! I have always imagined making my own alternate history of the Second World War in the Pacific. So now it's a reality and let me tell you that I am enjoying myself getting the story to you!

Nothing fancy, nothing crazy either. I try to keep everything I write within the realm of operational possibilities. I think that the Japanese could have achieved a lot more than they did in the real war, especially by using their battleship force when it mattered.

The state of the alternate war in Europe (see Blitzkrieg Alternate Serie 2nd Edition) opens a new set of possibilities for the Japanese Empire. The occupation of Oahu (rendered possible by the U.S. decision to send most of its naval forces to fight the Axis in the Atlantic) impedes the Americans from launching an immediate counterattack in the Pacific as they did historically. Yamamoto's new set of decisions to occupy more strategic islands in the Pacific also broadens the realms of options for the Imperial Navy.

The Grand Admiral's use of its battleship force is also a factor that changes the conduct of the early part of the war, bringing to bear a lot more firepower than the Japanese did in real history because they feared losing them.

As you will see in this second book, the new Japanese reality also comes with challenges, like supply and the Empire reaching its operational limit in the Pacific theater.

With a better start and an improved strategic position, Japan could have done a lot more in the war, but not to the point that it would offset its limitations, like its production capabilities, the incredible distances it had to defend, or the fact that it chose to fight the most prominent industrial power on earth and make it angry as hell with their Hawaiian Invasion.

I hope you enjoy the second book in the Pacific Alternate Series as much as you did the first. The story widens in scope and departs from the historical timeline followed by the first book. Burma, Southern China, Australia, the Coral Sea, and the American West Coast get a lot of action.

If you like naval battles as I do, you will be served, especially if you are a fan of big guns. The Japs using their dreadnoughts more liberally makes for some exciting stories.

Air battles are also aplenty as we follow the stories of our two pilots, Harry Bergman and Takashi Onishi. On the ground, you will be able to read the adventures of Imperial soldier Ishiro Tanaka (the dude's not a good guy, let me tell you that) while getting a little more historical stuff with MacArthur's book extracts or Tameichi Hara destroyer stories. Submarine warfare is also present with the Wahoo and skipper Jim Cloutier. And, of course, you get Yamamoto, Roosevelt, and other cool stories to make sure the strategic aspects and the decisions that affect the war are explained.

In short, now starts the real fun. Happy reading.

PROLOGUE

Battleship Yamato
Pearl Harbor, Oahu, June 11th, 1942

Still feeling tired about his round trip to Imperial Headquarters, Yamamoto paced inside his cabin, trying to find some sense of the war to date. It had been another long set of flights to come back from the Dai Honei meeting (Imperial HQ meeting) he'd been called to a few days ago.

He flew back on the same sturdy Nakajima G5N Shinzan four-engine bomber. It was a prototype long-range heavy bomber that Japan had developed but had not yet decided to launch into full production, as other war priorities took precedence over a weapon that wouldn't be so useful to wage a Pacific campaign. By June 1942, only three prototypes were built. For the Grand Admiral's taxying needs, however, it was perfect. The aircraft had an incredible range of 2650 miles (4260 kilometers). He flew back to Wake (20 hours), then Midway (11 hours), and finally from there to Hickam Field, near Pearl Harbor.

During most of the voyage, he'd been deep in thoughts about the Empire's future and its continued plans for conquest and expansion. The Army was not being realistic, in his opinion. The victories of the last few months had been so sudden, so easy, and so completely one-sided that it blinded several people in the Japanese high command to the dangers of over-extension and of "*going a battle too far.*" But it seemed that he was the only one still wary of what the Allies could do to Japan. Pretty much everyone else in Nipponese command circles had thrown caution to the winds and believed that the war was already won.

The Grand Admiral believed that the crucial battle would be here, in the Hawaiian Islands. Japan needed to concentrate all of its might and power in Oahu to prevent the Americans from retaking it and breaking out in the Pacific. Their fleet needed to be destroyed, and then their coast needed to be bombarded until they wanted to talk peace.

The Empire could not win a long-term fight against the United States and needed to defeat it so thoroughly that they would lose heart and sue for peace. The Grand Admiral believed he knew America. In a sense, he knew them well enough. But he under-estimated their deep resolve and anger toward Japan for the cowardly attack on Pearl Harbor. The Nipponese commander could plan and scheme all he wanted; they would not stop attacking the Empire until they destroyed it.

But at that point in time in 1942, flush from all the great victories enjoyed by the Imperial Navy, Yamamoto had not yet come to that conclusion. It was a time of enthusiasm for the Empire. Its flag towered from Pearl Harbor to Singapore and all the Pacific Islands between those two points. In fact, it looked invincible.

He walked back to the small desk in his cabin. The captain's quarters on battleship Yamato were spacious by any naval standards of the day. The ship was large and designed to be an admiral flagship, so it had been furnished with a large area for the Combined Fleet's commander.

The large steel-encompassed room possessed a large mahogany desk for the Admiral to work, a long table capable of housing over twenty guests, and even a couple of nice couches in the center that acted as a "*living room*" of a sort.

On the large table where he usually entertained officers for diner (he did so several times a week, as most captains from the Combined Fleet came to visit and chat with its commander regularly) was a map of the Pacific theater, just beside a second one of the Hawaiian Islands.

The Grand Admiral first looked at Australia, where he hoped to dear god that things would go well for the invasion planned to be launched soon on the Port of Darwin in Western Australia. He'd reviewed the numbers, and while he did not doubt that the Army would be able to land and take the city, overrunning the entirety of Australia was another matter. Hell, the thing was as big as China, and Japan had been trying to subdue it for the better part of the last five years. Nonetheless, he supplied the Army with a powerful fleet to support the invasion. Raizo Ishaka's 2nd fleet would support the Darwin attack. It would then redouble back through the northern Australian coast and speed toward the Coral Sea. Ishaka's fleet (four battleships, one light carrier, five heavy cruisers, and over forty destroyers) needed to move to that part of the theater. According to Japanese naval intelligence (and some submarine sightings), the Allies had gathered a sizeable fleet.

To suppress the Allies in the theater, complete control of that Sea was required, and Port Moresby needed to be taken. The land assault failed miserably and was bogged down in the Stanley Mountain Range (on the Kokoda Trail), so Yamamoto had decided to plan an amphibious operation once they'd won control of the Coral Sea. In order to do so, he was going to plan several sea actions to get rid of the Allied Naval presence there.

The sudden appearance of U.S. capital ships in the area created some problems for the Imperial Navy. Possible difficulties, but they would undoubtedly have to sink the enemy ships before they could contemplate a landing in Port Moresby and have their transport ships adequately protected.

Ever since he'd received the reports on a large fleet arriving in Brisbane, Australia, the Grand Admiral had wondered how they got there. The Pacific Ocean was certainly large enough. With his recent conquests, he'd hoped to impede the Americans from sending ships to the southern seas (Hawaii, Samoa, New Hebrides, Gilbert, Fijis, and New Caledonia). Apparently not.

He put his hand on his chin, thinking while looking at the map. He'd extended the Empire's range and defensive perimeter all the way to the Fijis and New Caledonia, believing it sufficient to isolate Australia entirely from any reinforcements. Obviously, it was not the case; the Allies had simply gone around the Islands Japan occupied and sailed from the deep Pacific into southern waters. They'd probably used French Polynesia and its deepwater port (Papeete) to do so.

This brought up the matter of occupying those Islands. Hell, he wondered if Japan even could do so, as the faraway Islands of the outlying Japanese Empire were already hard to supply and reinforce. It was at least four thousand kilometers from Suva in the Fijis to the French Islands. He resolved to look into the matter with his chief of staff and see what could be done. One of the first reinforcement shipments was due soon to Noumea (Moselle Bay). From there, he would re-assess once he got the reports on the state of the defenses and logistical installations there. The Empire's resources were already stretched thin as they were. He could probably take Papeete, but he didn't know if he could hold it.

In the meantime, he had a battle to plan. A knock on his cabin door was heard. "*Enter,*" said the Grand Admiral. Kōsaku Aruga, the Yamato's captain, entered the room, walked to Yamamoto, and bowed in the typical Japanese gesture. He was followed by Minoru Genda, the Carrier strike leader and now commander of all air assets in Hawaii. The last to walk in was the Combined Fleet's chief-of-staff, Admiral Matome Ukagi, the man who helped plan it all. The two newcomers also bowed respectfully.

"*Gentlemen,*" started the Grand Admiral. "*Welcome. Let's sit down. We have an attack on America to organize.*"

According to Japanese strategic thinking, only a powerful navy could protect them from the encroaching of Western Powers like the United States, the Germans, or the British Empire. At the same time, a strong navy would help Japan fulfill its destiny and expand across the Pacific and Asia. While the Empire could never hope to match the United States' prodigious production capabilities, it certainly could build big and powerful ships designed to take on several enemy dreadnoughts at the same time. The Imperial Navy thinkers decided that they would win with quality and, most importantly, size and firepower.

So, the Imperial Navy had built a class of battleships that could intimidate the potential enemies of the Empire. Plan No. A-140F6 – the one that won over the rest, proposed a behemoth so big it wouldn't even fit through the Panama Canal. The naval strategists decided that it was the way to go since if America wanted to build the same, they would be denied the use of their own waterway and have to go around South America to transfer the ships to the Pacific or Atlantic.

The new class of ships was something to behold, with the thickest armor in the world, the biggest guns (460mm), and the most tonnage (72,000 tons at full load).

With men like Yamamoto in the lead, Imperial High Command decided that this was the way to go. The Empire might have been better served by building several aircraft carriers with the resources it sank into the mega-project, but it was not the decision its leaders took.

Many Japanese naval strategists (along with many others in America and Europe) still believed that big-gun navies were the weapons of decision to overpower the enemy in maritime war. Unfortunately for Japan, the superb and powerful vessel of the new class was twenty years too late. But notwithstanding their overall usefulness, the new ship class made for a great story and would prove helpful, as well as quite powerful in the coming Pacific conflict.

The first ship in the class, Yamato, was already operating in the Hawaiian Islands theater and had proven its destructive power in the duel with the Diamond Head fortification, giving the Japanese Naval command a high level of enthusiasm for the super battleships and their usefulness in the conflict. And now the second of four planned super-battleships was about to be launched.

On that sunny day of June 10th, 1942, the ship was finally ready to sail. Most of the important people in Japan (including the Emperor and Prime Minister Tojo) gathered near Nagasaki Harbor to see the ship slide into the beautiful, mirror-like water of the Pacific Ocean facing the city. Amongst them were also many of the imperial nobles, Marshal Hajime, the Army commander-in-chief, and a throng of other naval officers who had come just for that occasion.

Ships don't slide quietly into water. As all the wooden planks and moorings were removed, the Musashi moved into the harbor, followed by the enthusiastic yells of the gathered crowd. The ship was so big that, unplanned by the supposed genius engineers who built it, it created a powerful tsunami almost four feet high.

The giant wave rolled menacingly until it pounded the shallow harbor, forcing water up the narrow rivers and capsizing boats, even sinking a submarine moored not far from the ship's launch. The water even gushed up to street level, pouring into homes and shops. Panicked residents rushed out of their homes, only to be forced back inside. The gathered officers and nobles were unaffected by the event since they were higher up on the pier, but the whole scene gave everyone a sense of how big the new super-battleship was.

As the Musashi sped toward the harbor's exit, everyone privy to the minor disaster, wondered if it was a sign of its power or a bad omen for the ship's future.

After its sea trials, the ship was expected in the Coral Sea in order to help the Imperial Navy crush the Allies there. It certainly would make its mark, and soon at that.

Northern Thailand
The Japanese campaign in Burma, June 11th, 1942

Soldier Ishiro Tanaka basked in the warm sun, sitting on top of the a wagon on a moving train, hairs in the wind. The scene before him was magnificent. Lush jungle, mountains dotted with greenery, rice fields, and a pleasant, warm summer odor. A breeze also gently rubbed his face, created by the train's movement. He appreciated it since the typical weather was hot and humid. But from his vantage point and with the wind in his face, he felt good. From a distance, it looked like the rolling wagons bristled with guns. Tanaka was not alone on the roof and neighboring trains since he was only one man in a 16 000 strong division called the 18th Imperial Division.

The unit, one of Japan's elite ground units, rolled toward Northern Thailand, where the invasion of British Burma was about to take place. The unit had successfully taken part in the Malaya campaign that culminated in the conquest of the famed Singapore fortress. The Empire now controlled all of French Indo-China, Thailand, Malaya, and the Dutch East Indies.

Japan was, by June 1942, flush with resources and also with success. So much so that its ambition had grown tenfold, and now the Imperial Army wanted to have a go at Southern China and India. Ishiro didn't really care where high command sent him along with the Division. In fact, it did not matter to him one bit as long as he was allowed to continue to fight and live the soldier's life he loved so much. He'd known little else since he enrolled in the armed forces a while back in the 1930s.

He wondered wat awaited him in this so-called Burma place. Looking over the horizon, he decided that all would be allgiht.

(...)

Lieutenant General Thomas Hutton, the commander of the Burma

Army with its headquarters in Rangoon, only had the 17th Indian Infantry Division and 1st Burma Division to defend the country. It was a ridiculous force with which to hold an enormous expanse covered in jungles and rough terrain. The British had not sent anything else to the theater, as they were busy enough rebuilding after their disaster in the United Kingdom. It was expected, in time, that the Indian Army would shoulder much of the load in the area. The big country had a decent industrial infrastructure and was gearing up for war. But in June 1942, none of that mattered to the Allied commander. He would have to fight the Japanese forces with what he had.

Facing the weak Allied forces was Japan's might. The Imperial Army's plans for a campaign in Burma appeared on their conquest agenda because of the country's own natural resources (which included some oil from fields around the city of Yenangyaung near the capital, Rangoon) and minerals such as cobalt and large surpluses of rice). The Imperial Army was also flush from its incredible victories in the Dutch East Indies and in Malaya in particular. Many in the high command, starting with Marshal Hajime himself, believed that the Japanese forces were vastly superior to the decadent Western Powers. And besides, the divisions used for all the southeast Asian conquests had suddenly become available and without enemies to fight. So why not find new ones?

An additional reason for the Nipponese leaders to conquer Burma for the Empire was the so-called Burma Road, the only external link for the Chinese Nationalists. Having been at war with China since 1937, the Japanese naturally wished to cut this link, as they also sought to finalize their conquest of China.

General Hisaichi Terauchi was the commander of the invading forces called the Southern Army Group. More specifically, the invasion of Burma would be executed by the Japanese 15th Army, commanded by Lieutenant General Shojiro Iida (headquartered in Bangkok). The army was composed of the 57th, 33rd, and 71st divisions, reinforced by the elite 18th Division and two armored brigades (Type 94 tanks).

The campaign was set to start in the last week of June 1942.

Fleet gathering
San Diego Harbor, June 12th, 1942

Before the rise of tensions between the USA and the Japanese Empire, San Diego had been the U.S. Pacific Fleet's home, along with the other main navy base at San Pedro, near Los Angeles.

President Roosevelt's decision to transfer several of the battleships and carriers from Pearl Harbor to the Atlantic to face the Axis forces in Europe and support Operation Torch ended up being quite a bad one since it created a unique opportunity for the Imperial Navy.

Sensing the potential gain that the possession of the Hawaiian Islands could give Japan, Grand Admiral Yamamoto convinced the Emperor and the commander of the Imperial Army, Marshal Hajime, and Prime Minister Togo to invade Pearl Harbor.

The rest was now already history. The bold attack swept the only useable base with which the Americans could have started their counterattack. From nowhere else could it attack the Japanese, as the distances involved were too great and the logistical needs too important. The Grand Admiral followed through with complete occupation of the most relevant deepwater ports (or suitable areas to make one) with the conquests of the Gilbert Islands, American Samoa (Pago-Pago Harbor), New Caledonia, New Britain, and the other multitudes of Islands now within Japan's realm. In fact, the entire Pacific was lock strategically locked against the U.S. forces. The only place they could realistically operate from was the U.S. West Coast, or else sail around the Japanese-occupied areas and go to Australia to bring the fight there in the Pacific Southwest.

For the defenses of the United State mainland itself, the Japanese blitzkrieg aftermath left the U.S. Navy with only its San Diego, San Pedro, and Seattle Naval bases. The three were powerful instruments of war and were even better at supplying war fleets than anything Pearl Harbor or any other Pacific Islands could provide. But their main weakness was that they were too far from the action to be of any use.

Thus, in typical fashion, America made do with what it had. Two large ports and plenty of ships, with more coming down the line in the construction docks all across the United States of America.

The newly constituted U.S. Pacific Fleet, under the overall command of Admiral Chester Nimitz and flanked by aggressive Admirals Frank Fletcher and William "Bull" Halsey, was not yet the immensely numerous ships gathering it would become later in the war. Still, it was a mighty instrument to wage naval battles.

Over the last two months before June 1942, the U.S. Navy had sent everything that could be spared from the European theater (Atlantic and North Africa) toward San Diego Bay. While not yet up to the Japanese Combined Fleet's numbers, it would, however, be able to hold its own against Yamamoto's sailors. It was centered around three main fleet carriers (to Japan's six), namely the USS Wasp, Yorktown, and Hornet. The flattops were followed by five battleships that could also slug it out with the Jap dreadnoughts; the South Dakota, California, Maryland, Colorado, and West Virginia. Five heavy cruisers and over thirty other support ships (light cruisers and destroyers) completed the line-up.

A powerful relief fleet under the commander of President Roosevelt's friend and former overall Naval commander Admiral William Leahy (recently brought back from retirement) was sailed to Australia in order to try and keep the tenuous Allied hold in the Southwest Pacific and support General Douglas MacArthur, the new commander in the area, with the defense and eventual reconquest campaign.

As he overlooked the harbor's entrance from his vantage point on the battleship Maryland, Admiral Nimitz could not help but be happy. The French fleet had finally arrived in San Diego. Marshal Petain and General de Gaulle (the two French leaders) promised some reinforcements to the Americans since the Allies were strapped for ships everywhere. And they also wanted to protect what was left of their Pacific possession, French Polynesia. The five ships were great additions to the U.S. Pacific fleet. They included modern battleships Lorraine and Bretagne. Both were World War One dreadnoughts that were remodeled and refitted in the 1930s. Following in their wake as they entered San Diego Bay were three heavy cruisers, the Duquesne, Tourville, and the Foch. Some smaller support ships also flanked them.

While without any aircraft carriers, the French fleet nonetheless made an excellent firepower addition to the Pacific Fleet. The Allies were ready to sortie and challenge the Imperial Navy's might if Yamamoto chose to come to the West Coast for a visit.

CHAPTER 1

USS Wahoo
Brisbane, Australia, June 10th, 1942

Submarine skipper Jim Cloutier was standing on his boat's deck, supervising some gun maintenance (the ship was equipped with a 76mm deck gun) when he heard a booming noise from warning klaxons. Then, the harbor alarm sirens started to be heard. He first thought it was an enemy attack but soon discovered the reason for the commotion. A large fleet was entering Brisbane's harbor. *"Look, captain!"* said Beatie, his deck gunner, who stopped working on his weapon and pointed toward the harbor's entrance.

Several large ships were making their final approach into the protected Brisbane area. The Australian relief fleet had arrived. *"Finally,"* said Cloutier, adding a smile to Beatie. Several other men climbed out of the submarine's hatch to observe the American vessels' arrival.

The much-anticipated fleet was finally in Australia, which meant that the Wahoo would be able to go about its new mission: merchant shipping attack at the heart of the Japanese Empire. The submarine had been ordered to stay in Brisbane until the Americans arrived, for Australia didn't have a lot of vessels with which to protect itself. Jim wondered what his tiny sub could have done if the Japanese Navy had decided to show itself on the country's eastern coast, but that didn't matter one bit. The brass in high command had wanted everything available in case of an enemy attack. But apart from a battle in the Coral Sea between the Royal Australian Fleet and a Jap task force, everything else had been pretty quiet.

The Wahoo's voyage after Samoa had been pretty uneventful, apart from a few run-ins against Japanese convoys near the New Hebrides and New Caledonia, where they'd hoped to stop to replenish their supplies. In the end, they'd been lucky and stopped at a deserted British station in the northernmost area of the Hebrides and found a sheltered bay where they hid the sub and went ashore. There, they found remnants of a seaplane base and some diesel that they could use for their boat. Fruits were plentiful on the beautiful island and helped restore some form of morale to the crew.

The damned Japs were far and wide across the Pacific, and Cloutier had felt discouraged by the lack of Allied presence. But then they finally got to Australia and were ordered to Brisbane, where a semblance of a naval presence was being gathered to resist the Axis forces. There, they'd stayed until that day of June, enjoying some downtime on firm ground.

Cloutier let all of his men go ashore on leave. They'd deserved it; the last few months had not been easy on them, and besides, they'd sunk two ships, so it wasn't too shabby.

As he looked at the outline of one of the American battleships sliding into the harbor, he thought it made for a magnificent scene, as the day's bright sunshine was outlining it.

He anticipated his orders to sail would come the very next day, and he was happy to think that the USS Wahoo would be on the prowl soon.

Strategic Naval dispositions - 1
The Combined fleet (Oahu), Mid-June 1942

In Pearl Harbor - combined fleet	Grand Admiral Yamamoto		
CVL Hosho	BB Yamato	Ca Tone	10 X CL
CV Akagi	BB Nagato	CA Myoko	27XDD
CV Kaga (torpedo damage July 21st)	BB Hiei	CA Chikuma	
CV Shokaku	BB Kongo	CA Maya	
CV Zuikaku	BB Mutsu	CA Kinusaga	
	BB Fuso (in transit to Pearl		
CV Hiryu	Harbor, June 4th)		
CV Soryu (in transit to Pearl Harbor June 6th)			

The Combined fleet rested in Oahu, Pearl Harbor (in the Hawaiian Islands). Its purpose was to make sure the area wouldn't fall back into American hands. Grand Admiral Yamamoto knew that as long as the Imperial Navy held the strategic base, there would be no American reconquest campaign in the Pacific. The enemy had to come for Oahu, and that was the beauty of it: it was predictable, and the Japanese Grand Admiral packed it with everything he could find in terms of guns, men, and aircraft.

He equipped the enormous fleet with the best Japanese naval units and had plans to bring more ships once the rest of his Pacific objectives were reached. It first had the pride of the Navy, the Kido Butai. The experienced carrier strike force was led by the large Akagi and Kaga; they were former battlecruisers converted to aircraft carriers in the 1930s following the Washington Naval Treaty. The two mighty ships were flanked by the modern Shokaku and Zuikaku, the largest Japanese flattops, that each embarked over seventy-five aircraft. After some campaigning in the south seas and involvement in the Battle of the Coral Sea, the last two main fleet carriers, Soryu and Hiryu, were on the way to Pearl Harbor (from Truk Base in the Carolina Islands) to bolster the fleet for Yamamoto's planned second raid on San Diego, set for July 1942.

Being a big gun believer, Yamamoto did not neglect the battleship component of the Combined Fleet. First and foremost, it sported the super-dreadnought Yamato with its 460mm guns. It was followed by the mighty and modern Nagato with its 410mm guns and its sister ship, the Mutsu. Former battlecruisers now battleships (after their modernization in the 1930s) Kongo and Hiei were also part of the fleet. A 7th battleship was sailing from the Kure Naval base in Japan to Pearl Harbor (Fuso).

The fleet was then flanked by five powerful heavy cruisers that almost counted as battleships by themselves. Nipponese models packed a lot more bite than their Allied counterparts, most even having torpedo tubes to add to their large guns (from 180mm to 220mm). Twenty-seven destroyers and ten light cruisers completed the lengthy order of battle.

Strategic Naval dispositions - 2
Japanese 1st Fleet (Timor), Mid-June 1942

In Java/Timor- Australia invasion 1st Fleet		Raizo Ishaka
CVL Shoho	CA Takao	12XCL
BB Yamashiro	CA Aoba	20XDD
BB Ise	CA Nachi	
BB Tosa	CA Furataka	
BB Hyuga		30XDD gone to shipping escort

Raizo Ishaka's 1st fleet's position within the Japanese realm by mid-June 1942 resulted from the hard campaigning of the previous three months. Several fleets had roamed the Dutch East Indies and other Allied possessions and ended up in Timor, facing Australia.

Following the Empire's lightning successes, the Imperial High Command (Dai Honei) decided to invade Western Australia and take the major port of Darwin. Ishaka was thus left with a powerful fleet to ensure that the landing would succeed. The invasion would be led by the Japanese 52nd Division and several SNLF elite marine battalions. Several additional divisions from the Kwantung Army were en route to the south seas to reinforce.

Finally, the Japanese order of battle for its invasion of Australia would be supplemented by the enormous force that had subdued Java a few months before. 14th Army, coming off of four long years of war on the Chinese theater and now flush from its Dutch victory. The soldiers were well-trained, well-equipped, and led by determined commanders. Their forces included the 2nd, 55th, and 64th divisions, some of the best in the whole of the Japanese military. And then the last unit was its most fearsome—the Imperial Guard Division. Fifteen thousand strong, with the best equipment (including Type 95 tanks), double artillery compared to standard Japanese units, and the best men the country could offer: A posting to the Guards Division was a reward and a promotion, so the unit tended to gather all the best from the Army into one unit.

The fleet itself would be sufficient to escort and successfully shrug off anything MacArthur could throw at it. It sported four modern battleships that would help shore-bombard the Australian defenses: Yamashiro, Ise, Hyuga, and the powerful Tosa. Four heavy cruisers, twelve light cruisers, and twenty destroyers closed the naval order of battle. At the same time, thirty of the destroyers that helped take over the hundreds of Dutch Islands were detached from the fleet to go back toward the shipping lanes to escort the transport ships that would bring all the newly conquered resources and oil to Japanese factories.

Strategic Naval dispositions - 3
Japanese 2nd Fleet (Rabaul/Truk), Mid-June 1942

TRUK / RABAUL 2nd fleet	Shigeyoshi Inoue	
CVL Zhuiho	BB Haruna repair until july	15XDD
CVL Ryujo	BB Kirishima	
CVL Taiyo (transit from Japan june 4)	CA Atago	5 X CL
CVL Unyo (transit from Japan june 4)	CA Haguro	
	Ca Suzuya	

The Japanese 2nd Fleet was the smallest of the operational fleets by Mid-June 1942. It wasn't because it had the least responsibilities. In fact, it had the most daunting task of the three active fleets within the Japanese realm. Its mission was to destroy the Allied naval presence in the Coral Sea and control the area all the way up to the Fijis and New Caledonia. In short, its job was to make sure that Australia stayed isolated.

Yamamoto knew that he would have to reinforce Admiral Inoue's fleet at one point and fully intended to do so once the landing in Darwin was a success. In the meantime, Inoue had what he had. The plan for the 2nd Fleet was to organize a landing on New Guinea's southern coast near Port Moresby to take the vital harbor and complete the encirclement and isolation of Australia. From there, more landings would be possible on the enemy's northern coast.

The fleet had a powerful carrier force, even if they were only escort or light carriers. Ryujo (30), Zhuiho (25) (Taiyo (35), and Unyo (20) represented 110 embarked planes, so together were a force to be reckoned with, especially given Allied theater weakness in that category.

The 2nd fleet had the Haruna and the Kirishima in terms of big guns. While the former sustained damage in the Battle of the Coral Sea and was under repair at Truk base until July 1942, the Kirishima was no pushover with its eight 356mm guns. It was also flanked by three modern heavy cruisers (Atago, Haguro, Suzuya), fifteen destroyers, and five light cruisers.

The 2nd fleet was more than a match for the Australian relief fleet.

Raid on Noumea gone sour part 1
New Caledonia, June 12th, 1942

The mighty 356mm shell landed on the USS Utah's superstructure, blowing up spectacularly shaking the old American battleship to its core. The Japanese ordinance exploded on hitting the armored shell, scattering in a star-like fashion and blinding everyone looking directly at the blast. The torrential rain that battered the ship didn't bother the catastrophic fire and explosion one bit. The American task force was sailing thru churning waters, heading almost due south.

Admiral William D. Leahy, commander of the Australia relief fleet, more formally known as the 2nd Allied fleet, stood on the bridge, struggling to keep his balance. The ship shook through the heavy gale, waves, and the hits it was receiving from the enemy ship. He kept his eyes focused on where the enemy shell had landed. The area was still shrouded in fire and smoke, so the vessel's status was unknown. "*Report*" yelled the American commander, struggling to keep his balance through the ship's shaking and rumbling. "*Still awaiting news, Admiral,*" said one of the bridge officers nervously.

Battleship Utah had been on a shore bombardment raid to attack the newly conquered Japanese base of Moselle Bay in Noumea, New Caledonia. The stronghold was not completed yet as an airfield was being built and expanded. Leahy, the Admiral in command of the American relief fleet, had decided to organize an attack on the island to test the enemy perimeter defenses.

Noumea was located on a small peninsula jutting out from the New Caledonian southwest coast about 30 miles from the island's southern end. Moselle Bay (Leahy's intended target) was an excellent deepwater port at the very tip of the peninsula. Sitting on a direct line on the map between the Hawaiian Islands and Australia, the island was a truly strategic area to control in order for the Allied to keep their convoys lines open, while for the Japanese, it was about to shut them down.

After the 2nd Fleet arrived in Auckland, New Zealand, the Admiral sent most of its ships toward Australia's foremost military harbor in Brisbane. After some radio communication with MacArthur, they'd both agreed to make a quick stop in Noumea to test the Jap defenses in the area. Their strength was undetermined as of yet. The plan was to sail by the island and shell the harbor and the construction works near it with Utah's big guns.

USS Utah was an old Florida class of battleships built just before the Great War (1911). The ship had pretty thin armor compared to modern standards but still had 12-inch guns (10 of them in five turrets).

In 1931, the battlewagon was retired and converted into a target ship. But with the increase in tensions with the Japanese Empire and the obvious need for more warships, the U.S. Navy had rearmed the ship with its guns (kept in the San Diego mothballed fleet arsenal), and the boat had been sent back into service. It wasn't the most modern U.S. ship afloat, but it would have to do with the state of affairs in the Pacific; The Allies needed ships everywhere.

Making the thousand kilometers journey from New Zealand to New Caledonia in a few days, Utah, flanked by the cruiser San Francisco, arrived in the range of Moselle Bay early at dawn on June 8th. Leahy had expected light resistance, but unknown to him, the Imperial Navy had dispatched battleship Kirishima as escort to a supply convoy (after the Battle of the Coral Sea near Australia), along with a few destroyers and heavy cruiser Atago.

The U.S. plan would have been relatively simple if not for the lucky arrival of Haruna on the scene, as the Japanese had not yet reinforced the island with planes. But as luck would have it, the Yankees were met with a powerful Imperial Navy task force.

Kirishima was built as a battlecruiser during World War One (1915).

Eleven years later, the Imperial Japanese Navy upgraded the ship to battleship status by increasing its armor thickness and placement, making it faster with new engines and power capabilities. Again modernized in 1933, it was, in 1942, a modern, fast battleship equipped with eight 356mm guns. In short, it outclassed Utah by a large margin.

So as the first shell from Utah had landed on Noumea (Moselle Bay) proper, inflicting catastrophic damage on several port facilities (also sinking a small Imperial Navy minelayer), one of Kirishima's floatplanes detected the small American task force and sped toward it.

Leahy had planned to attack and retreat immediately, not fight a gun duel with one of Japan's top-of-the-line vessels. So, from the moment the first large water geysers towered near Utah (the Haruna advanced at its maximum speed and was trying to find the range on their U.S. enemy), the U.S. commander turned his two ships around and sped at best speed southward.

And the game of cat and mouse had been going on for several hours ever since. Its Nipponese counterpart utterly outclassed Utah. Range, gun size, armor protection, everything. At first, the American Admiral had hoped he was facing Japanese heavy cruisers, but after the first hit on his ship that destroyed its forward gun turret, he knew that something packing a lot more punch than a mere 250mm gun was shooting at Utah.

Fortunately for the beleaguered U.S. sailors, the weather was worsening by the minute, and a gigantic wall of water approached the battling fleets. Leahy had ordered his men to sail directly for the massive storm brewing up due southwest. The goal was relatively straightforward. Reach the area where the Japs would not see them anymore. In 1942, most Imperial Navy didn't have radar technology except the most modern ones like Yamato and Musashi. Once they lost visual contact with Utah and San Francisco, the battle would be over.

As his ship burned from the inside, took waters by the hundreds of gallons every minute, the American Admiral wondered if he hadn't been too bold in his move. Perhaps he should have known better.

Strategic Naval dispositions - 4
U.S. Pacific Fleet (San Diego) Mid-June 1942

U.S. Pacific Fleet – San Diego Admiral Chester Nimitz

CV Wasp	BB South Dakota	CA Atlanta	19 DD
CV Yorktown	BB California	CA San Diego	10 CL
CV Hornet	BB Maryland	CA San Juan	
	BB Colorado	CA Juneau	
	BB West Virginia	Ca Reno	

San Diego Fleet – French Vice-Admiral Émile Muselier

BB Bretagne	CA Duquesne
BB Lorraine	CA Tourville
	CA Foch

PALMYRA TASK FORCE

CVL Long Island	CA Pensacola
BB Tennesseee	Ca Wichita
CA Vincennes	8XDD

By the middle of June 1942, the U.S. Pacific fleet was slowly taking shape in San Diego Harbor. The United States had been caught with its pants down by the Japanese Navy in Pearl harbor and by the fact that most of its ships had been busy fighting in the Atlantic. And they'd paid dearly for the strategic blunder of losing Pearl Harbor and most of the Pacific in only three short months.

By the end of 1941 (after the disaster in the United Kingdom), President Roosevelt had pushed the USA into war against the Axis in Europe. The conflict soon sucked more and more resources, and it didn't take long for many of the Pacific Fleet's ships to be transferred to the other theater. The Hawaiian Islands had thus been mostly undefended if Japan chose to attack it with strong enough forces.

Grand Admiral Yamamoto obliged and invaded Oahu along with the rest of the island chain in a lighting attack that destroyed many ships and gave the Imperial Navy a base to control the strategic entrance into the Pacific. With it, Japan could hold the Americans out of the theater for an undetermined period.

The United States Navy was powerful in its own right but had obligations on both sides of the country. Several of its heavy units were already engaged in the Atlantic against the powerful Germano-Italians. The European Axis had many ships, and intelligence reports also pointed to the Kriegsmarine (Germany Navy) building heavy units at a fast pace. They occupied the United Kingdom and controlled Gibraltar and Suez, giving them access to the Atlantic and the Indian Ocean with the Italian Fleet.

Roosevelt and his two top military commanders (General Marshall and Admiral King) had to tread lightly and send ships to both sides. The Allies thus concentrated the force that would retake Hawaii in the large San Diego Naval base. It was not yet the powerful fleet it would be a couple of years in the future, but it was strong enough to start thinking offensively against the Combined Fleet anchored in Pearl Harbor.

The U.S. Pacific Fleet had three main fleet carriers by mid-June. Namely, the USS Wasp (60), Yorktown (60), and Hornet (60), for a total of 180 embarked planes on its carrier strike force. Attacking the Combined Fleet directly in the Hawaiian Islands was consequently a daunting task for Admiral Nimitz since he would, in all likelihood, face six main fleet carriers and an estimated 400 to 500 land-based planes.

The good old battleships South Dakota, California, Maryland, Colorado, and West Virginia represented the fleet's big guns. Five heavy cruisers (Atlanta, San Diego, San Juan, Juneau, and Reno) and nineteen destroyers completed the order of battle for the Americans in San Diego. At the same time, they had a small fleet sailing in the vicinity (the Palmyra Task Force) that included the small light carrier Long Island (20 planes), the battleship Tennessee, the heavy cruisers Pensacola, Vincennes, and Wichita, plus an additional eight destroyers.

The recently arrived Free French fleet (headed by Vice-Admiral Emile Muselier) had battleships Bretagne and Lorraine and three heavy cruisers (Duquesne, Tourville, Foch) added to Allied might that would soon try to challenge Yamamoto in his lair.

Raid on Noumea gone sour part 2
New Caledonia, June 12th, 1942

Battleship Utah was a war too late in its design. It had not been built or modernized to face something like the Kirishima. The Imperial Navy dreadnought continued its headlong charge, intent on destroying its enemy. Admiral Leahy was overwhelmed with catastrophic messages about flooded compartments, fire on decks, and severe damage. Fortunately for the Americans, the Japanese had not yet hit anything vital in the engine compartment.

While the water it was taking in slowed the ship down (it had been hit at least four times by the Kirishima's 356mm shells), it still made a good 20 knots. The U.S. admiral hoped to reach the menacing wall of water that was the major storm brewing directly in front of his ship.

"Enemy ships now behind us about twelve kilometers," reported the deck officer in contact with the lookout and the radar room. *"Visibility is worsening by the minute,"* added the man, still listening to the watchmen at the other end. *"Sighting officers say that in ten minutes, visibility will be to zero. The storm is getting worse, and the rain is pouring down on the deck, Sir."* Leahy looked at the officer and nodded. It wasn't difficult to believe the claim, looking outside. The sea was but a churning boil of foaming water. It seemed that Utah was in a boiling soup. Rain battered the observation viewport, and it poured so hard that it even extinguished some of the fires on the battleship. *"At least one advantage of braving the maelstrom,"* thought the Admiral. *"Thank you. Helm, stay the course and keep dodging."*

As he looked at the dark, menacing wall of water that was the storm system that his ship was heading directly into, a towering geyser of water rose just to Utah's portside. Another close encounter with a Japanese shell. Leahy wondered how many of them the old lady would take before sinking. The damage had already been catastrophic, and he wondered if the vessel wouldn't only be suitable for a dockyard and several months of repairs. If it survived the current ordeal.

The running naval battle included other ships also dueling. San Francisco was doing better against its counterpart, the Japanese heavy cruiser Atago. Both ships shelled the other, but no hits had been reported yet on any side. Occasionally, Leahy could see the flashes of the American cruiser firing away at the enemy.

The range was still great, and the ships were a lot more agile than Utah (both vessels were modern and could do 30 to 32 knots), so they dodged the other side's ordinance easily.

The rain pouring down on the battleship got so heavy that it even muffled the sounds of battle, which were indeed quite loud. The booming noise of Utah's guns firing was something to behold, but even they were overwhelmed by the water falling down like a waterfall on the ship. The American Admiral wasn't certain that it was the best of ideas to enter such a big storm. But it was either chance it with the weather or die at the end of the damned Japs.

The ship somehow made it to the mighty storm, and the minute it was fully engulfed by it, Leahy felt like a giant hand took hold of the vessel and battered it from side to side. Utah rolled over truly gigantic waves, tipped over them, or slashed thru the impossibly high walls of waters.

More damage, injuries, and countless other problems were reported to the bridge for the next six hours. Several solid sailors, generally used to the rigors of a rough sea, became seasick. Many more got injured, hit by flying objects, or simply fell over and hit the decks or walls.

But the Admiral's main objective was reached. The Japanese ships didn't follow and turned tails toward their Moselle Bay harbor in Noumea.

The next day, after a terrible night, the stricken American battleship finally weathered the worst of the storm and limped at 6 knots toward Australia. On the 14th, MacArthur ordered to get the Admiral out and back to Brisbane, so a couple of the fastest destroyers (nothing great since the 2nd fleet only had older ones) sped toward the broken ship to pick up Leahy and his senior staff.

The Noumea Operation had been a dismal failure, and both American commanders took note of the fact that the Allies were not yet ready to go on the offensive.

The Utah would eventually get back to Australia, but only ten days later, and it wouldn't be fit for duty before spending a long time in drydocks.

Strategic Naval dispositions - 5
Allied Second Fleet (Australia) Mid-June 1942

Australian 2nd Fleet Admiral Leahy	
CV Ranger	Ca San Francisco
CVL Charger	Ca Chicago
Bb Utah	BB Iron Duke (British)
BB New York	CA London (British)
BB Washington	5X CL
	10XDD WW1

RAN (Royal Australian Fleet) FLEET
CA Canberra
Ca Australia
CVS Albatros
3 CL

By June 1942, the Allied 2nd Fleet was not the most up-to-date naval force in the World. In fact, it was the opposite. For the most part, its ships were outdated or in need of urgent modernization. Led by American Admiral William D. Leahy, it was a scratch force that included everything the beleaguered United States had been able to send to Australia's help. Formerly called the Australian relied fleet, it had been renamed upon its arrival in Brisbane the 2nd Fleet. The new designation better reflected that it was a multinational force with American, British, and Australian ships. After they rebased to Australia following the defeat, some Dutch submarines also fell within its area of responsibility.

The fleet was led by the USS Ranger, the first U.S. carrier built from the keel up between the two wars. The plan had first been to keep the ship in the Atlantic since it was deemed too slow to face the fast Japanese flattops. It carried forty-five planes. Its little brother, the light carrier Charger, also considered unfit for service in a modern naval war, was sent to Australia anyway. It had fifteen embarked planes. Three battleships also came with Admiral Leahy. The first, Utah, an aging and over-the-hill dreadnought, would not have been considered for duty if not for the desperate Allied situation. It had been recently rearmed with its old guns in storage in the mothballed fleet. As shown in the desperate battle of New Caledonia, it could not really do well against modern Nipponese battleships. The other two were more modern. New York, launched in 1915, packed a serious punch with its 356mm guns. BB-56 Washington was the most powerful of the trio, being one of the North Carolina class of fast battleships designed in the 1930s (356mm guns and 28 knots speed). The fleet was then flanked by two heavy cruisers, five light cruisers, and ten recently re-activated World War One destroyers that were damnably slow and still operating on coal for fuel.

Winston Churchill, the British Empire's leader and Prime Minister of the United Kingdom, sent two good ships to Australia's rescue. The mighty (but aging) battleship Iron Duke (343mm guns and 29 500 tons displacement) and the modern heavy cruiser London.

The Australian Royal Fleet, battered severely in the First Battle of the Coral Sea, completed the order of battle with two heavy cruisers (the Canberra and Australia), a seaplane tender (Albatros), and three light cruisers. All its operational destroyers had been sunk in the scuffle with the Japanese.

By any standard, the Allied 2nd Fleet would have been considered powerful. But it faced the might of the Japanese Imperial Navy that added up, with the combined numbers of the 1st fleet (Timor – Darwin Invasion force under Admiral Raizo Ishaka) and 2nd Fleet (Rabaul/Truk Coral Sea theater under Admiral Shigeyoshi Inoue) to a staggering total of six modern battleships (and one more sailing toward the theater) five light carriers, seven powerful heavy cruisers, seventeen light cruisers, and over thirty destroyers.

While no one doubted Allied courage to face such odds, few military experts believed in their chances to weather the Jap storm that threatened to engulf their country.

Raid on Darwin
Western Australia, June 16th, 1942

Japanese ace Takashi Onishi flew beside the Japanese twin-engine Mitsubishi G4M medium bomber he'd been tasked to escort. Not that high command expected a lot of resistance over the target. It was more or less simply customary to have bombers escorts, for a single fighter could wreak havoc in any air raid executed by the slower aircraft. The Zero fighter's engine purred nicely, and the weather was clear. The airstrike flew into a blue sky devoid of clouds. Visibility was also perfect, so Onishi wasn't worried about enemy aircraft; they would see them coming from a long distance.

The G4M packed a decent punch with nearly 2000 pounds of explosive ordinance or naval torpedoes. They also bristled with guns and had great speed for a bomber.

The Japanese flight of attack bombers was headed for Darwin, in Australia, where the Imperial Army was soon to land to start the conquest of Australia. Onishi and his men had been tasked with protecting the G4Ms if the Allies decided to show up. But Takashi highly doubted they would.

In 1942, Darwin – while it was the capital of the Northern Territory – was a small town with limited civil and military infrastructure. Due to its strategic position in northern Australia, the Royal Australian Navy (RAN) and Royal Australian Air Force (RAAF) constructed bases near the town in the 1930s and 1940-1941. The city's population was only 5,800 souls.

During the Allied defense of the Dutch East Indies, Darwin had become a substantial Allied naval base, used for supplies and as a crucial airbase. The Japanese had captured Ambon, Borneo, Celebes, and Timor (facing Australia's west coast) between March 1942 and early June 1942.

Once the Netherland East Indies were secured in their entirety, the Japanese high command decided to have a go at Australia, with amphibious landings in Darwin proper. The place had everything the Imperial Army needed to conduct a decent campaign. Airfields, large modern harbors, oil facilities, and civilian areas.

Scheduled to arrive in a few days was the 14th Army, which included the 2nd, 55th, 64th divisions, and the Imperial Guard Division. A couple of tank brigades (Type 95) would also participate in the coming fight against the Aussies. In all, over 75,000 soldiers would participate in the Empire's bid to conquer a continent.

Starting June 1st, several Japanese reconnaissance flights overflew Darwin and identified the areas where the troops would land. They also spotted over twenty merchant ships in Darwin Harbour, as well as thirty aircraft at the town's two airfields. Several coastal guns and other defensive areas were also spotted. The raid objective on Darwin (only the first of many in the following days) was to smash the airfields to smithereens and then start softening up the defensive positions. Japanese intelligence believed that only a battalion-sized unit defended the Australian base. Still, the Army had nonetheless decided to soften them up as much as possible before the troops arrived. The battleships of Raizo Ishaka's 1st Fleet could have taken care of leveling the town to the ground, but the Japanese commanders wanted to use the place, so it was not good to destroy it too thoroughly. Just a little to make the landings possible.

The Japanese raid arrived over Darwin by mid-morning. Onishi and several squadron comrades dove down toward the airfields and strafed the runways with several Allied planes (Brewster Buffalos) neatly parked in rows on the ground. The town's air raid sirens were belatedly sounded at about the same time.

The Japanese bombers executed their bombing runs on the harbor and the vessels within it, sinking ten merchant ships and damaging nine more.

After their strafing run, Takashi and his comrades were surprised by several Australian Air Force P-40s of the RAAF 33rd Pursuit Squadron, stationed in an airfield a little further from Darwin, so untouched by the initial Jap attack.

A sharp and intense dogfight followed that the Japanese Zero fighters easily won. All but one of the fifteen Warhawks that tried to intercept the Japanese air raid met a fiery end, including two at the hands of Onishi himself.

Once all Aussie aircraft in Darwin were vanquished, Nipponese aircraft bombed and strafed the base, civil airfield, the town's army barracks, and oil store at leisure.

All these facilities were seriously damaged. By the time fighter pilot Takashi Onishi turned tail with his comrades to fly back to base in Timor, the town he had left behind his canopy's view was a smoking, burning wreck. More attacks would follow in the next two days, finishing the preparations for the invasion.

Second Battle of Palmyra part 1
Pacific, June 20th, 1942

After the first raid on Palmyra at the end of April, the Americans had taken note of the light Japanese presence in the area. The atoll and the other similar bits of islands near Palmyra were at the extreme limit of the Japanese perimeter. A submarine (USS Archerfish) was posted near the island to report enemy ship movements. Several small convoys landed anti-aircraft guns and some equipment to build an airfield by mid-May. The submariners noted the event, prompting Admiral Nimitz to do something about it. A few days later, a Japanese destroyer also dropped an Imperial Engineer unit and the rest of the 12th Sasebo Special Landing Force (12th SNLF).

The Japanese then proceeded to fortify the island and make it impregnable. Worried about the last US raid, Yamamoto ordered the defenses to be beefed up and the airfield to be built as soon as possible. Palmyra was an atoll, so it couldn't be the deepwater seaport that the U.S. Navy would need to have a real base in the Pacific. Still, if re-occupied by the Allies, it could become a problem for the Combined Fleet that was 1800 kilometers away on Oahu. An atoll was no protected harbor, but it was possible to anchor ships and build supply facilities to operate a fleet.

On June 20th, 1942, that was precisely the idea the Americans had in mind: Attack Palmyra again and land some Marines to reconquer the island. The operation was entrusted to the so-called *"Palmyra Taskforce,"* which had successfully executed the first attack in April. The fleet had a light carrier (the Long Island with 20 aircraft), a battleship (Tennessee), two heavy cruisers (Pensacola and Vincennes), and eight destroyers. They had been roaming the general area that skirted the extreme extent of the Japanese Empire, with some success for the whole month of May and the first half of June, attacking some shipping, playing cat and mouse with Jap submarines, and even sinking one.

This time around, they also came back with the 4th Marine Regiment and about a third of the first armored battalion (Shermans). The landing was set for June 21st after the Navy struck the base with the Long Island's planes and then a little shore bombardment by the battleship and the cruisers.

The sheer distance from the main Japanese base in Pearl Harbor meant that the Americans believed that they could act with impunity in the area.

But Yamamoto was far from being a stupid man and had put some measures in place. First, a seaplane base had been rapidly set up in the Palmyra lagoon (the seaplane tender Chitose was moved to the atoll in mid-May), enabling several planes to be used for search operations. The Chitose was nothing more than a ship equipped to refuel, rearm, and repair seaplanes and flying boats. Once the airfield was built in Palmyra, it would be possible to use conventional reconnaissance aircraft. The Chitose operated the planes that took off and landed from Palmyra until it was ready. It was using a giant crane and a refueling apparatus to efficiently support the fifteen Kawanishi H8K2 recon planes that searched the area beyond Palmyra (to the east) daily to look for American ships.

A small but powerful task force was also detached from the main Combined Fleet in Pearl. The fleet was centered around the modern carrier Shokaku, the battleship Mutsu, five destroyers, and the two heavy cruisers, the Tone and Chikuma.

The Japanese task force wasn't cruising anywhere near Palmyra. Still, it sailed about halfway between the Hawaiian Islands and the Atoll, ready to move southward if one of the flying boats detected anything or rush north if a battle loomed for the Combined Fleet on Oahu or near it. It acted as a fast-response reaction force and could also move if the Allies dashed toward Johnson Island.

Stalemate on the Kokoda track
Pacific, June 20th, 1942

The Kokoda track was not a nice place to have a stroll. On the contrary, it was anything but. It also was not a place to fight in. The track threaded fifty-nine miles across the Owen Stanley Range and was filled with hard, thick, disease-riddled jungles with high mountain passes and overall terrible weather.

A lone, well-equipped man would take at least ten days to get thru it—an army, weeks. Paths were steep, narrow, slippery, and a perfect ambush zone. Soldiers in coastal areas like Port Moresby or the northern beachheads of Lae, Gona, and Buna were also fighting in the world's most malarial, mosquito-ridden area.

General Harukichi Hyakutake, commander of the 67th Division (or what was left of it), hit the radio with the headphones in frustration. *"Damned high command!"* he said in a hushed voice. The radio operator who heard him pretended that nothing was amiss. But he'd listened to Rabaul command's answer for his reinforcement requests: denied. It did not bode well for the Japanese unit trying to hold on to dear life in the Owen Stanley Range.

The campaign had started well enough, and they'd fought their way thru the thick, sickness-infested jungle almost all the way to the southern coast, but the Allies had been able to land substantial reinforcements just in time to push the 67th back in disarray. Hyakutake had been on a defensive stance ever since. Some supplies were flowing from Buna, on New Guinea's northern coast, but no more soldiers were scheduled to come up. The losses taken by the 67th Division meant that it was impossible to go on the attack again. The General needed airstrikes, more troops, and plenty of artillery if Japan were to pierce the strong Allied forces blocking his way to Port-Moresby. *"Stay on the defensive and await further instructions"* had been the dry, negative response to his insistent requests. Hell, he wasn't even certain he could hold the enemy with his dwindling forces.

It wasn't just battle attrition. It was also about the damned jungle. It killed or incapacitated more soldiers than the Allies. He'd insisted and yelled at the operator on the other side of the line in Rabaul Base. Nonetheless, that enlisted soldier had had a high-ranking officer just above his shoulder, for the final answer came rapidly enough. *"You are instructed to hold in place and defend to the last man. Acknowledge the order or be relieved of command."*

And he did confirm his damned instructions. He just didn't understand why the higher-ups in Rabaul would not help him. He walked out of the makeshift earthen bunker that his men had made for him to act as a field HQ. The place was infested with bugs and rodents, but at least it sheltered him from the pouring rain that came almost every day (and several times daily at that).

Taking a deep breath, he looked around. Several soldiers were handling artillery guns (the ones they'd been able to haul up these god-forsaken mountains), and others were working on an additional bunker. The men seemed in a good enough mood.

He fished his Homare cigarette pack from his front pocket. Homare was a popular brand in Japan. The tiny packet bore printed decoration of an Imperial flag crossed over a laurel wreath with some Japanese characters. Looking at it quickly, he wondered how long he would be able to smoke. His division was still getting some food, but it seemed that the rest of the standard supplies only trickled in. It apparently had to do with some convoy that had failed to arrive in Buna, the city they were getting their logistical support from. Hyakutake suspected it was a different reason. The high command had probably re-directed it elsewhere.

Trying to feel the moment, he dragged a prolonged breath intake and took the satisfying smoke in his lungs. He turned to look at the towering mountains encircling them all and wondered what and how he would be able to get across the damned things. He exhaled his smoke and sighted.

What Harukichi didn't know was that Grand Admiral Yamamoto had already written off his force and considered it only as a holding action that kept the Australian 1st division busy and out of position in the Kokoda track. At the same time, he put the finishing touches on his new plan against Port Moresby. The Imperial Navy would try a landing directly on the southern coast, right beside the city itself.

But as fate would have it, General Harukichi Hyakutake's war was not over yet.

Second Battle of Palmyra part 2
Pacific, June 20-21, 1942

The Shokaku's commander, Captain Hiroshi Matsubara, launched his plane the minute that it was possible. Early on the 19th, he'd received a report from the Palmyra seaplane base that an American fleet approached the atoll.

An hour after that, another report had come in, giving the details on the result of an Allied air raid on the defensive installations. His task force, still out of position to the north, sped with all due speed toward the beleaguered island.

He'd nervously counted the minutes and hours that it took his force to get in range. *"Launch all available planes toward the enemy fleet's last known whereabouts."* The deck officer nodded silently with a respectful bow before relaying his captain's orders.

A minute later, the carrier's planes took off Shokaku's long (794 feet), teak wood-covered flight deck. 18 Mitsubishi A6M Zero fighters, 27 Aichi D3A ("*Val*") dive bombers, and 27 Nakajima B5N *("Kate")* torpedo bombers left in succession and took to the sky. The ship looked magnificent. Bristling with anti-aircraft guns and with a sleek design, it adorned a large rising sun painted on the middle of its yellow-painted flight deck. The airstrike rapidly sped off the Japanese fleet area to get to their intended destination.

Meanwhile, in Palmyra, things heated up significantly. The first U.S. Marines were ashore amidst heavy, suppressive fire from the 12th SLNF Battalion that awaited their enemy right on the beaches. The atoll was tiny, so there wasn't much space with which to hide or run away. The U.S. soldiers fought where they landed for the better part of a few hours. It took some time to get several Sherman tanks ashore, but they gave the Americans the upper hand when they arrived, and the U.S. Marines finally got off the beach.

The fight in and around the airfield was intense. Still, the Japanese were severely outgunned, with American planes attacking from above and some timely support from the destroyers and cruisers just offshore (the Tennessee Battleship did not fire after the U.S. soldiers landed for fear of killing troops from its own side.) By mid-afternoon, the Japanese forces were confined to a tiny part of the island and desperately trying to hold on.

At 4 PM, the Shokaku's plane decided to make an appearance and finally arrived on the scene. The Nipponese pilots did not give much attention to the fight on the ground but took to the American ships ringing the island. Their standing orders were to find and sink U.S. Navy ships.

Allied anti-aircraft guns opened fire as the Japanese torpedo planes and dive bombers commenced their attacks on the large, obvious Tennessee battleship and the Long Island. The sky around and over the vessels filled with red tracers shooting in every direction, and the American sailors put as much lead as they were able to in their enemy's paths. A Japanese dive bomber soon planted a powerful 1000lbs bomb right on the battleship's deck, penetrating two decks inside before catastrophically exploding. Sixty-five sailors were killed.

Moments later, a 242 kg high-explosive "land" bomb struck the Long Island's flight deck, detonating on impact to create an 11 ft (3.4 m) hole and kill 30 men.

Then, a third one slammed on Tennessee stern, penetrating three decks before exploding, causing severe damage and a mighty fire. The plane catapult was also destroyed by the blast. All the while, the anti-aircraft guns took their tool and shot down six Japanese aircraft.

A furious dogfight erupted over the atoll. The 18 Zero fighters engaged the Long Island's six fighters (the light carrier had a total of twenty aircraft, including fourteen bombers and five F4F Wildcats). The battle was short, and the tally was one Japanese plane shot down for all six Allied ones crashing into the ocean near Palmyra.

The Japanese planes also sunk two destroyers and the Pensacola with direct torpedo hits, losing some of their numbers as well in the fight. The final count when the Japanese strike force turned back to their carriers was a heavily damaged battleship, the light carrier Long Island crippled and not able to recover any planes nor conduct more air operations, and three ships sunk.

With the assistance of fire hoses from the six remaining destroyers, the infernos on Tennessee and the carrier were under control by late night. The whole time the sailors fought the raging vortex, the task force leaders worried that the light produced by the fires (seen from dozens of miles away on a clear sky and calm ocean) would be a beacon for the Japanese to find them in the dark. But the fast-reaction Jap force was simply too far to engage in any kind of surface action that night. Wounded personnel were evacuated from the stricken ship and brought ashore since, by that time, the Marines had taken control of Palmyra.

It was decided that the entire fleet would sail out of the area by midnight, leaving the Marines contingent in control of the island but isolated thousands of miles behind enemy lines. The U.S. Navy had not anticipated such a quick reaction from the Imperial Navy, so it had to make the hard decision.

Even though the Allied troops were now far and wide from the mainland, they'd given the United States their first real victory in the war. They also captured a partially completed airfield. The Chitose seaplane tender, stuck into the Atoll during the battle, was captured almost intact by the Marines.

Palmyra was back in American hands.

Washington D.C.
Oval Office meeting June 22nd, 1942

"Well, well, well," said President Roosevelt, harboring a large smile, as he dropped the piece of telegram that had just arrived on his desk. It was morning on the 22nd of June 1942. The message's timing was perfect; it arrived just in time for the daily meeting with King (Navy) and Marshall (Army and overall command). Given the time difference, the message had been transmitted in the middle of the night, but it didn't matter to the U.S. leader. Good news was good news.

"Indeed, Mr. President," answered a radiant Ernest King. The man was usually of a foul temper (pretty much all the time), so it was refreshing to see the old warhorse roused up about something. *"So, the japs aren't invincible after all, hey Ernest?"* added Roosevelt in a friendly tone. *"They certainly are not, Mr. President, and my boys are chomping at the bits to show the world that we can kick their ass to kingdom come."* *"Before we get too enthusiastic, Admiral,"* said General Marshall, *"We need to get a sense of the victory we have here. We didn't sink one Jap ship. We just took a small, isolated island in the middle of nowhere and took heavy casualties while doing it,"* finished the overall commander in a somber tone.

"Arghh, George!" exclaimed Roosevelt. *"Must you always be that serious! Can't we just enjoy our first, even if tiny, victory against our implacable foe for at least a minute before we shelve back into reality?"* finished Franklin. *"Yes, Mr. President."*

The U.S. leader continued. *"So, while this victory is meaningless in the overall scheme, it shows us that the japs can't be everywhere at once. We need to send more help to these boys in Palmyra. I want the atoll held and defended."*

"This might be quite a daunting task," started King. The President raised an eyebrow as an answer, putting his fingers together and under his chin. The Admiral continued. *"We are concentrating our*

forces in San Diego for the planned attack against the Combined Fleet in Pearl Harbor. Our radio intercepts are giving our decoding specialists a sense that Yamamoto is brewing up something and that the enemy has decided to try another raid on the U.S. Mainland."

"Interesting news, Admiral," said Marshall, whistling softly. *"So, the boys at the OSS are finally delivering on that Magic decoding thing you talked to me a few weeks back, Ernest?"* asked Roosevelt. *"Yes, Mr. President. So, I think we would be better keeping our naval forces close to San Diego and bunched up together since we are already numerically at a disadvantage with the japs."*

"Okay, but I still do not want these men abandoned in Palmyra, so make sure they have some supplies." "Yes, Mr. President, we'll do what we can. Some subs can be used and several fast destroyers."

"Good, good. So, what else is going well today, gentlemen?"

Kentai Kessen
The Decisive Battle Doctrine; Oahu, June 22nd, 1942

Several thousands of miles away, Admiral Yamamoto was pondering on the attack the Americans knew of with the breaking of the Imperial Navy's code. The Japanese leader was holed up in his spacious Yamato battleship cabin, which he rarely left, busy as he was running a fleet in Oahu and a naval campaign across the Pacific.

The Grand Admiral was sitting down on one of the large couches near his working desk and looked fixedly at the painting of famous Admiral Tōgō Heihachirō on the wall facing him. The man had achieved what Isoroku had only dreamed of to date. The conclusion of peace in a single, final, and glorious battle.

Grand Admiral Yamamoto knew it was the Empire's only chance for survival against the American industrial giant. He just didn't know how he would bring it about. He was desperately chasing his own Tsushima, the victory that ended a war in 1905, with one naval victory that won it all. The Kentai Kessen Doctrine was basically the Japanese trying to repeat the same kind of success, and the entire Imperial Navy's strategic thinking revolved around it. Japanese leaders weren't blind to their country's small size not enabling it to fight a long war. The Decisive Battle Doctrine was just that; keep the war as short as possible by annihilating the enemy's will to fight in one big naval battle.

Hence, the Grand Admiral had employed much of his planning to the maneuvers to bring about the battleship showdown he envisioned. In the battle plan, Admiral Nagumo's carrier strike force (Kido Butai) would play a central role in attacking the opposing U.S. Navy carriers. At the same time, the Imperial Navy's big guns, with Yamato in the lead, would flank the Pacific Fleet and bring about the battle that would end it all for Yamamoto.

The broad outlines of the plan were simple; he would sortie with the

Combined Fleet and head straight for the American Mainland. Secrecy or surprise wasn't his goal like it had been in the attack at Pearl Harbor a few months before. He wanted the U.S. Navy to notice his force so it would sail out of its protective harbor to challenge the Imperial Fleet in one mighty battle.

In his mind and his wargaming prior to sailing out of Pearl Harbor, all looked rosy and workable, so the Japanese strategic mastermind believed in his plan.

CHAPTER 2

Operation Mo
Japanese 2nd Fleet, June 24th, 1942

Following the defeat of General Harukichi Hyakutake on the Kokoda Track, the Army and Navy (following Yamamoto's instructions to do so) developed a plan that was titled Operation Mo. The plan called for Port Moresby to be invaded from the sea and secured by the end of June. The Japanese high command thus hoped to catch the Allies unaware and outflank the Australian Division that was deep into the Owen Stanley Range fighting against the Imperial 67th Division (Hyakutake). Upon the completion of Mo, further operations against the Northern Australian coast were also decided upon once it was completed.

Because of a damaging air attack by Allied B-17 aircraft on Japanese naval forces in Rabaul on the 3rd of June, where a couple of his ships had been damaged and the airfield almost destroyed, the Japanese decided to cover the naval amphibious landings with carriers. By now, events had clearly demonstrated that ships sailing in the Pacific without escorts in the aur to cover them was not a good idea.

Admiral Isoroku Yamamoto, commander of the Combined Fleet, planned an operation for July against the U.S. Mainland that he hoped would lure the U.S. Navy's carriers and battleships (most of which were now bunched up together in San Diego) into a decisive showdown near Hawaii. So, the Grand Admiral only detached some of his smaller carriers (all main fleet CVs were required for his operation) from the reserve fleet and new builds directly from Japan. The reinforcements had almost all arrived in Rabaul by the 16th of June, except for the giant Musashi battleship, which had recently completed its sea trials and was now sailing toward the base.

Admiral Shiyegoshi Inoue's 2nd fleet left the vicinity of Rabaul base on the 24th of June, laden with mighty ships and troops transports. The fleet was composed of 4 small aircraft carriers (CVL). Ryujo (30), Zhuiho (25) (Taiyo (35), and Unyo (20) represented 110 embarked planes, a lot more than what the Allies could provide in the same category. It was flanked by battleship Kirishima (Haruna was still under repair in Truk) and heavy cruisers Atago, Haguro, and Suzuya. Fifteen destroyers and five light cruisers completed the order of battle for the Imperial Navy.

Admiral Koso Abe, in command of the invasion fleet, had under his flag sixty-one transport ships carrying 16,000 men from the 27th and 66th Imperial Divisions, recently arrived from Manchuria (Kwantung Army). In addition, the ships transported 5,000 soldiers of the SNLF Marines Battalions (Kure Special Landing Forces).

Abe's forces left Rabaul along with the Japanese 2nd Fleet and proceeded south through the Vitiaz Strait between New Britain and New Guinea. The plan was to arrive in Port Moresby by June 26th. Allied forces in the Australian town were 5,500 strong, including some U.S. Marines and a couple of Australian regiments.

Unfortunately for the Japanese and completely oblivious to it, the U.S. Navy intelligence and the OSS (Office of Strategic Services) had broken the Japanese JN25 naval code. They were still working on ironing out the wrinkles (they were getting about eighty-five percent of what was sent by code), but in essence, they were aware of the Japanese plan and timetable.

By early June 1942 (after the Australian 1st Division repulsed the Japanese attack near Port Moresby), the U.S. first noticed mention of the "MO" operation in intercepted messages. On 13th June, the U.S. intercepted an IJN message directing several light carriers and other large warships like the Musashi to proceed to Inoue's area of operations. On the 18th, the British listening station in Cairns (on the Northern Australian Coast) deciphered an IJN message informing Inoue was about to sail out of Rabaul for a yet unknown destination. The British passed the message to the U.S., along with their conclusion that Port Moresby was the likely target of a Japanese operation called "MO."

The whole affair didn't take long to make its way to MacArthur's HQ and Admiral Leahy, commander of the Allied 2nd Fleet. The Anglo-Saxon ships scrambled out of Brisbane and sped away at full speed toward New Guinea's vicinity on the 19th, intent on trouble with the Imperial Navy.

Allied 2nd Fleet
To battle, June 24th, 1942

Admiral William D. Leahy was standing on the battleship Washington and was lost in thoughts. The deck officers who looked at him saw a man with unwavering confidence and stalwart bravery. Had he not braved Japanese might in New Caledonia and almost been killed? Battleship Utah had limped back to Brisbane on June 22nd, heavily damaged. In fact, it was mangled and would have to spend a lot of time in drydocks. And it wasn't even certain that the high command would decide to repair the old lady. There was a reason the ship had been disarmed in the 1930s. It was old and not up to modern standards. Only Allied desperation had put it back into service. Now that it had shown its glaring weakness against Japanese might, it wasn't sure it would fight again.

But the Admiral himself did not feel well. He was now raked with doubts. His encounter with the Kirishima had shown him that the U.S. Navy was wholly unprepared for this war. It wasn't that he didn't think he could beat them. He just wasn't certain he had the necessary strength to beat the Imperial Navy he was about to face in the Coral Sea.

The Allied 2nd Fleet was a very decent force on paper. In terms of air cover, it had the main fleet carrier, Ranger, with fifty planes, and the light Charger, with fifteen planes. Now that it had lost Utah, it was left with a very decent three battleships (New York, Washington, and the British Iron Duke), five heavy cruisers (including U.S., British and Australian ships), eight light cruisers plus ten destroyers.

So, while the Japanese enjoyed a decent superiority in terms of aircraft with their four light carriers, Leahy didn't need to worry too much. If it came down to a scrap, the Allies would be in a great position to maul Inoue's fleet. Yamamoto had sort of blundered strategically by not putting enough strength into the 2nd fleet and leaving too many ships out of position on Timor with 1st Fleet (for the

Darwin Invasion), where there were no Allied ships to challenge Raizo Ishaka's fleet.

Leahy's force sailed out of Brisbane about ten days prior and joined up with the Australian fleet (RAN) near Cairns. He proceeded northward with all due speed to intercept the Japanese task force near the New Guinean coast.

Thanks to the OSS and SIS, the admiral was well-informed of Japanese movements reported to be somewhere near Buna on the northern coast of New Guinea. Several air recons from flying boats and B-17s from Cairns had also spotted the enemy fleet, and the news wasn't so bad. They "only" had four carriers.

The Australian landings
Darwin, Western Australia, June 24th, 1942

The hundreds amphibious Daihatsu landing crafts (one of the first amphibious landing boats in the world) approached Darwin's beachfront under withering Allied fire that ricocheted noisily on the ship's steel hulls. The soldiers of the 55th Imperial Infantry Division were to be the first to get ashore. The unit was not the best out there. It lacked basic training and was only equipped with rifles and very few heavy ordinances like artillery. Japan raised several fresh troops for its conquest without necessarily having what it needed to make them decent units for war. They looked like light infantry or even right out of the First World War. They would have been well-suited for garrison duty in Manchuria or else fighting the under-equipped Nationalist forces in China.

Army command assigned the soldiers to the landings because while they did not expect to encounter a lot of resistance from the small regiment-sized force defending Darwin, they did expect losses, so they considered the 55th expendable. The other veterans' divisions that would follow the first amphibious attack were more seasoned and better-equipped (2nd, 64th divisions, the Imperial Guard Division, and the two Type 95 Tank brigades).

The men were extremely nervous since it was only their second time under fire in a landing (the first had been in the Batavia operation a few months before). Some officers and several sergeants were more experienced soldiers, having been transferred from other units when the 55th was formed. They kept the unsteady raw recruits' morale to a manageable level. The sailing from the ships (several transport ships, but also many of 1st Fleet destroyers that were designed to carry soldiers) to the Darwin shore was a difficult time for the Japanese forces. The Allies, not having any heavy defense in the city, still had a few coastal guns and artillery pieces, so they pummelled the amphibious landing crafts, destroying several with precise shots. Other crafts capsized under the heavy waves because the vessel's sailors driving them went at maximum speed and didn't react in time when explosions raked the waters around them.

The Nipponese infantry eventually made it to the shore, and the bow steel ramps were lowered down in the soft Darwin sand. The 55th men were again met with heavy machine guns and rifle fire, so many were shot down as they exited the Daihatsu. But their numbers alone overwhelmed the Allied soldiers, scattered all along the city's coastline. The Australian force commander had also opted to keep much of his force inland to avoid being shore-bombarded by the Imperial Navy just a kilometer or so offshore.

So, the raw imperial soldiers spilled into the neighboring port facilities, a small oil tank farm (the large petrol containers were just north of the small Darwin harbor), and into the city. In doing so, they lost an excessive number of men because of their inexperience and light equipment, but it was all the better for the Imperial Army. Trial by fire was a well-developed training technique in Japanese war philosophy. If they survived, it meant they were tough and good. If they died, well, it was just natural selection. Send them to the slaughter and keep only the ones that were good enough to survive.

Within another four hours, the first Type 95 tanks were ashore, along with the first detachment of the Imperial Guard Division, which expertly went about extinguishing any resistance the Aussies put up against the landings.

At the end of the day, on the 24th of June, Darwin was well on its way to being conquered by the Japanese Army, and the Allied retreated in disarray toward the south, along the Western Australian coastline.

Extract from General MacArthur's book, Reminiscences, 1964
The Coral Sea, Port Moresby and Darwin, June 25th, 1942

If one thing was sure at the end of June 1942, it was that the Allied position in Australia and the south seas was very precarious. Not many a betting man would have put his chips on our forces to win it all in the end.

The Imperial Army had just landed in Darwin, and there wasn't a whole lot we could do about it. Only the great distance of the Oceanic Continent gave us some sense of hope. There were thousands of kilometers between major cities in Australia, and the country's Western Coast was still relatively under-developed. The heart of the country was more on the other side, on the east coast.

Then, there was the Japanese offensive and the heavy Imperial Navy's presence in the Coral Sea and the New Guinean eastern part. The enemy entertained quantitative superiority many times over what we could field.

We only stood a chance in the naval category because we were the ones on the defensive in the Port Moresby area. It thus remained to be seen if the Japanese could transport their intended amphibious landings against our 2nd fleet and successfully land it, notwithstanding our forces.

At a meeting in Brisbane between me and Admiral Leahy, our naval commander, it was decided to continue the strategy I had set the month before: risk defending Port Moresby. William agreed that it was the only way to keep the Northern Australian coast safe. Also, a strong presence in Eastern New Guinea meant that the enemy could not have unchallenged control of the Coral Sea and the Solomon Islands (that we would bomb with our aircraft from the Port Moresby base). Furthermore, it put us in a great position to switch to the offensive once we survived the Japanese tide.

For if there was one unwavering belief in those dark days of 1942, it was in the fact that America and its Allies would rise to the challenge and vanquish its enemies. The Nipponese power was tremendous, and it would take us a lot of blood to destroy it. But America was stronger, and that was, in my mind, unchallengeable. It was good against evil, and we all know how every story ends.

The 2nd Fleet immediately set upon intercepting the Japanese task force headed for Port Moresby, and we both agreed Leahy and I, that nothing would be spared in stopping the damned Japs from landing their troops.

On the ground side of things, I ordered half of the Australian 1st Division back to Port Moresby and told the Aussie commander to put himself on a defensive stance. All the Marines were also brought back to the southern shore to prepare and handle the defenses in case the enemy succeeded in landing its troops. It would be a close thing, but I stayed confident that we would again weather the storm.

In Darwin, there wasn't much that could be done since there were no real defenses in the area apart from a regiment-sized unit, so I gave orders to prepare the protection of the western coastal towns of Wyndham(900km), Derby (1200km) and the major port city of Broome (1500 km away south). It was almost impossible for the Imperial forces to advance overland toward these cities, so I prepared for more enemy landings along the western coast.

The Australian Army sent the newly raised 6th Division toward Perth to set up a real town defense in case Yamamoto got too bold. However my primary strategy on the Western Coast was that Japan would face immense logistical difficulties if it chose to advance inland or go a lot further than Darwin. They would simply stay along the coast and try more landings in all strategic likelihood. It gave me time to prepare for the counter-attack.

The Second Battle of the Coral Sea Part 1
Carrier battle; June 25, 1942

At 06:25 June 25th, Leahy's Second Fleet was 115 nautical miles northeast of Rosel Island, entering Japan's defensive perimeter. At this time, the Allied admiral sent three cruisers (San Francisco, Chicago, and Canberra), three destroyers, and the battleship Iron Duke to the Jomard Passage. He designated the group of ships under the call tag Taskforce 1. It was led by British Iron Duke's captain Arthur Duncan.

Duncan's mission was to intercept the Japanese surface force and block the waterway where the Japanese fleet would need to cross to go toward New Guinea's southern coast. The Jomard Channel was located between the Louisiade Archipelago and New Guinea.

Leahy understood that Captain Duncan would be operating without air cover since his meager carrier force would certainly have its hands full battling the Japanese aircraft sure to be sent his way during the battle. Detaching Iron Duke and the six other ships weakened the air defenses of his two carriers. He decided to risk it regardless in order to avoid the enemy's amphibious invasion forces slipping through to Port Moresby while he fought the Imperial Navy carriers. He also could, in this way, force a surface battle with the numerically inferior guns of the Imperial Navy.

Correctly guessing that Admiral Inoue's task force was located west of his own ships (near the Louisiade), Leahy directed Ranger to send scouts to search that area in the early morning. By around nine, they'd found the Japanese fleet. The American Admiral thus scrambled all available planes and, by 1002, the planes from Ranger (twenty SBD and ten Grumman Wildcat F4F fighters). He kept the rest of his aircraft close to the task force for what he believed was the unavoidable enemy counter-strike.

The American planes sped toward the Japanese 2nd fleet and

eventually found it as it was sailing in the Normanby Island vicinity. Inoue's Zero fighter screen was dense with twenty guarding his ships, so they engaged the small American strike force. A furious dogfight ensued. But for the first time, the Americans didn't get the short-end stick of the battle. The Japanese flyers, a lot less experienced than their Kido Butai counterparts, did not do as well. In fact, it was the opposite. They performed poorly, like the rookie pilots they were.

One underlying weakness of the Imperial Navy was that before the war and still in 1942, the Navy pilot training program was very elective and, in doing so, produced only a limited number of pilots per year. Once out of the training regimen, they were already the elite of the elite, but the net result for Japan was that they were few and far between. Most of the top aces thus were assigned to the Combined Fleet's six main carriers (Akagi, Kaga, Soryu, Hiryu, Shokaku, and Zuikaku), so it didn't leave much to the newer carriers. Unfortunately for Japanese plans that day, the top flyers in the country were very far away in Pearl Harbor, preparing for their attack on Mainland America.

Losses were thus seven Japanese planes for three Grumman fighters, and most of the Dauntless dive bombers slipped through unscathed to face the flak gauntlet the Imperial ships fired at them. The sky lit up with red tracers as the anti-aircraft ordinances climbed straight through the air in an effort to shoot down the U.S. torpedo bombers lining up to loosen their weapons at their enemies. Eight of the remaining fifteen SBD were shot down and fell fierily into the sea, but the rest shot their torpedoes at the Japanese ships. They, of course, targeted the Japanese carriers. The weapons raced toward their target as the Japanese seamen tried to dodge frantically. A destroyer bravely put itself in one of the American torpedo's paths and exploded like a bursting egg but saved the carrier Unyo in the process. Two missed entirely; one more didn't explode, but three connected with Japanese ships. One struck the carrier Taiyo, right amidship, and created significant damage, which towered high in the sky in a catastrophic explosion. Another one hit the cruiser Suzuya right in the bow, almost sinking it outright, creating a severe list forward. The last one sunk the light cruiser Nagara in a hit that exploded right in the middle of the superstructure.

The ecstatic American flyboys sped back to their carriers, leaving a sea of fire, oily water, and damaged ships. Japanese pride was wounded.

Inoue, in turn, believed Leahy was south of him and had, before the U.S. strike, advised Taiyo and Ryujo's planes to send their aircraft to search that area. The Japanese 2nd fleet, approximately 300 nautical miles west of Leahy, launched several scout planes (Nakajima B5Ns) at eight in the morning to find the Allies. Simultaneously, cruiser Atago and three light cruisers also sent their own recon planes up (Kawanishi E7K2 Type 94 floatplanes) to search southeast of the Louisiade while they cruised south in search of surface ships.

At about midday, while his men still assessed the damage and tried to salvage the stricken ships, Inoue split his forces in two, sending Kirishima along with five destroyers southwest as escort to the landing fleet. At the same time, he reacted to the news of the floatplanes from Atago that had supposedly spotted Leahy's fleet.

At 1315, the Atago confirmed back to Admiral Inoue that it had located a large enemy task force: "*two carriers, two battleships, several cruisers, and destroyers.*" Another fleet was also spotted going southwest toward the Kirishima task force (and the landing ships) by the Ryujo's search planes. Admiral Inoue gave the go-ahead to every available plane to take off and strike the enemy fleet. A total of 57 aircraft (Zero Aichi D3A dive bombers and The Nakajima B5N) were launched from three flattops (Zhuiho, Ryujo, and Unyo) at 1345. After assembling above the Japanese fleet, they made their way by 1400 towards the reported enemy sighting.

At 15:15, the Japanese aircraft arrived over the Allied fleet and sighted some of Leahy's ships (they'd spotted the U.S. Task Force One heading for the Jomar Passage) but didn't find any of the enemy carriers. The Americans got lucky since their ship moved some distance from the time they got spotted and thus were not where the Atago flying boat had detected them when the airstrike arrived over the coordinates. They then decided to attack the surface force that was seemingly without escorts but only in a limited capacity, while the rest of the strike force headed back to their carrier to refuel and rearm.

Three Aichi D3A dive bombers attacked cruiser Chicago, and the rest tried to hit Iron Duke. The heavy cruiser was hit by three bombs, broke in half, and sank in a cataclysmic explosion, killing most of its crew (only fifteen survived). Two bombs hit Iron Duke. The dreadnought got away with damage that was serious enough, with several fires below decks and one of its main gun turrets destroyed. But its speed was unaffected, so it continued on its way. Once the Jap aircraft flew away, Duncan ordered the fleet to continue full speed toward the Jomar Straight, leaving a destroyer on-site to pick up Chicago's survivors.

Both fleets were scarred at dusk on the first day, but the Japanese admiral wasn't happy about the results. He had already sent Taiyo back to Rabaul under destroyer escort and was faced with a choice. He needed to decide if he wanted to destroy the surface fleet heading for the Kirishima detachment he'd sent toward the New Guinean coast or continue to try and find the Allied carriers.

Admiral Leahy, for his part, was pretty happy with the day's results and decided that he would concentrate on its primary objective: eliminate the landing threat to Port Moresby and disregard any more duel with carriers. He would thus focus his planes on covering Duncan and turn his fleet southward to get out of the danger zone.

As night fell on the 25th of June, the next day's battle would decide the Second Battle of the Coral Sea's outcome.

Battle of Sittang Bridge
Burmese invasion, 18th Imperial Division, June 26th, 1942

The Japanese looked unstoppable. The 15th Army had crossed from Thailand into Burma and, in ten days, had made serious progress toward Rangoon, their campaign objective, and the Burmese oil resources. The capture of the oilfields and severing of the allied supplies to China via the Burma Road looked like they would soon happen.

Private Ishiro Tanaka was running on the east bank of the Sittang River, rifle in hand, bayonet fixed, and he yelled at the top of his lungs. His unit had penetrated Allied lines during the previous night using the same infiltration tactics they'd used in the thick jungles of Malaya during their drive to Singapore. He was flanked by his comrades and fellow soldiers, also yelling the banzai charge. A few meters to Ishiro's right, captain Tidiko ran, samurai saber raised high in the air.

Several of the 18th Division detachments had gone across the Sittang on inflated boats and anything the Japanese had found locally. Wooden boats, fishing trawlers, and the like. Burma was a rugged country with very few infrastructures or decent roads. But the tough Nipponese soldiers were used to that type of terrain and didn't flinch one bit.

After they crossed the previous night, they'd found themselves across the river and outflanked most of the British brigade's defenses facing the destroyed bridge. Tanaka was amazed at the typical catatonic Allied response to Japanese moves. He wondered if they would one day learn or know better. It was rather straightforward. The Japanese forces always tried to outflank and infiltrate. So why didn't they do something about it? Tanaka was just a simple fighter, but he knew he would do it differently in the British's shoes.

His run ended in an enemy trench that was half-filled with water. He jumped in it, rifle in front, and hit an Indian soldier right in the chest, piercing it with his bayonet. His opponent died instantly in a blood-burbling sound. He turned around and fired his weapon, discharging it right onto another Allied soldier's face. It blew like a watermelon and spread blood and gore everywhere, including Ishiro.

The rest of his comrades were doing the same, and the whole enemy's defensive position had been taken within a minute. The officer quickly reorganized the man to face, rifles reloaded the other way. The trench they'd just stormed overlooked the destroyed Sittang Bridge and towered a little above the rest of the British and Indian forces below as it was perched on a high wooden hill.

Once they were all installed, the officer ordered them to fire down on the enemy. It took the British units, which were facing the other way (toward the other side of the river), several seconds to realize that something was amiss, with several bullets landing amongst their numbers, killing and wounding from a direction they did not expect. They turned around, only to find out that the damned Japanese had done it again. They'd flanked their position.

In under another ten minutes, the rest of the Allied troops retreated westward toward the large dirt road that continued into the Burmese immensity of a jungle.

The campaign was not going well for the Allies. The Japanese offensive had started around June 16th, and ever since then, the British forces under the command of Lieutenant General Thomas Hutton (commanding officer, 17th division) reeled back in disarray. About a week ago, the Allies had been badly beaten at the Battle of the Bilin River. They'd held on against superior forces for two days of close-quarters jungle fighting. But the Japanese outflanked them because they could and because they had more troops. Faced with the threat of imminent encirclement, Hutton decided to fall back.

And there, they'd made their stand and were now being annihilated by the powerful Imperial forces. They'd blown the bridge to try and slow down the Japs, but it was only a stop-gap solution, as Japanese troops were quite nimble and hoped over rivers easily and quickly, as was again proven by Tanaka and his comrades of the 18th Division.

The Southern Expeditionary Army Group, under the overall command of General Hisaichi Terauchi, was by any definition unstoppable with what the Allies had to put up against it. The army was composed of the 57th, 33rd, and 71st divisions, reinforced by the elite 18th Division and two armored brigades (Type 94 tanks). Since the British only had a division to try and defeat the Japanese, it didn't take long for their defenses to be overwhelmed. Furthermore, the Nipponese operated under total air supremacy, had ships offshore that could support the troops with their guns, and advanced helped by light tanks, while the Allies had nothing with which to counter them.

The Second Battle of the Coral Sea Part 2
The Milne Bay Gun Duel; June 26th, 1942

Heavy storm systems and turbulent weather started in the early hours of the 26th of June in the New Guinea area near Milne Bay. The heavy wind and rain seriously impeded aerial operations for hundreds of kilometers.

Consequently, both sides' carrier forces had no play in the unfolding events that day. They thus focused on finding each other in the worsening weather (the storm system was starting to envelop the whole Coral Sea area) but didn't find each other.

The action that would put an end to the battle happened near Milne Bay. The Iron Duke and its escorts intercepted the Japanese task force transporting the Imperial troops bound for the Port Moresby landings.

Battleship Kirishima and five destroyers had been tasked with escorting the transport vessels on their approach to the target. At the same time, Admiral Inoue continued his search and battle with the American carriers.

The Allies came down on the Imperial Navy fleet with the battered but still powerful Task Force 1, detached from Leahy's main fleet. The day before, it had been struck by a Japanese airstrike that sunk the heavy cruiser Chicago and left the battleship Iron Duke with moderate damage, including the destruction of one of its main gun turrets. The Allies were nonetheless numerically superior in strength to their opponent, with still two heavy cruisers (San Francisco and Canberra), two destroyers (one had been left behind to pick up Chicago's survivors), and the damaged battleship.

Of course, the powerful Kirishima and five destroyers led the Japanese task force. And then there were the transport ships. From the moment the Allied ships were spotted (visibility was poor, so the Japanese lookout only saw the enemy when it was too late), the

Kirishima's captain, Shima Takeshi, ordered the transport ship to turn back. He then called everyone to battle stations. The battlewagon would try to cover the troopship's escape.

The battle about to unfold would oppose two mighty dreadnoughts. The first one (British) was the Iron Duke, an aging English battleship built before the Great War. In the 1930s, it underwent a modernization refit as most of its contemporaries in those years. The ship sported 29,000 tons and five twin 343mm gun turrets (down to four as one was destroyed). It had excellent armor protection with 12 inches of steel at the belt and 11 inches on the turrets.

The Kirishima was also a World War One warship that used to be classified as a battlecruiser but modernized in the 1930s, like the Iron Duke. It was a 36 600-ton steel behemoth, with eight twin 356mm gun turrets and 11 inches belt armor, with 10 inches for the turrets.

The two dreadnoughts were roughly equal, but what made the difference in the battle were the additional heavy cruisers that the Allies brought to bear on the battle. In one rare occurrence since the start of the war, the Allies were numerically superior to the Japanese, thanks to inadequate strategic fleet positioning from Navy command. The ships that would have been needed for the Coral Sea Battle were used needlessly in the Darwin landings protection thousands of miles away.

Sending the destroyers away with the troopships, Captain Takeshi initiated the fight with his eight powerful guns' full broadside. The 356mm shells raced to their target, the Iron Duke. The first salvo found the range, as the Japanese vessels were well-trained and seasoned veterans of war having a lot of experience with the war in China and several naval scuffles since the war's start. Three shells hit the Iron Duke as it also fired its remaining weapons. Two raked the battleship with a powerful explosion but landed on the thick armor belt protection, so the ship shrugged them off in a fiery blast. The third shot landed on the bow, piercing the deck armor and penetrating below to explode catastrophically. The Duke shook from the blast.

All the while, the shells from the British battlewagon also hit home, with one shell landing on the Kirishima's stern (back), destroying its floatplane launching platform and starting a big fire below deck. The two cruisers gave their best and added two more hits with their 200mm main guns, further damaging the Japanese battleship's superstructure and jamming one of its turrets with a direct impact on the machinery that made it move. In all likelihood, Kirishima was doomed, as it was raked with three ships at relatively close range. But then luck intervened. A minute into the fight, the Japanese battleship's secondary armament (152mm guns) targeted Canberra and hit it with a lucky shot. One of the shells penetrated below deck and hit the ammunition magazine, completely gutting the Australian ship. The resulting explosion blinded the whole battlefield for a few seconds. Debris and ship pieces climbed high in the sky, and a towering pillar of dark smoke rose to the high heavens, only to be pushed back down by the battering rain.

The next Iron Duke salvo did indeed hit Kirishima, but the tough ship again shrugged off the blast with its excellent armor protection. After a mere seven minutes, all three remaining ships (the destroyers were but mere spectators in the struggle, taking potshots at the mighty Japanese ship) were like balls on intense fire.

The heavy downpour helped the sailors on both sides to fight off the raging infernos, but it didn't take long for both captains heading the task forces to start having second thoughts about continuing the battle.

Both captains decided that they'd had enough damage for one day. Iron Duke's casualties were catastrophically high, and four of its turrets were either out of action or close to being. Kirishima had uncontrollable fire below decks, two inoperable gun turrets, and a giant hole amidship that let tons of water gush into the vessel. The San Francisco, not being spared by the fight, also had had enough, with several hits on its structure and a new caution resulting from Canberra's demise.

Almost simultaneously, the two opposing fleets produced smoke screens and moved away from each other. They scored several more hits, but none critical.

The result of the Battle of Milne Bay was a tactical draw. But in the strategic sense, it was an Allied victory since the Japanese invasion troopships had had to turn around and go back to Rabaul. Admiral Inoue's plan had been foiled.

The Iron Duke was sailed under escort to the nearest Australian port (Cairns), where it would be hastily repaired and sent on its way to the eastern coast of Australia to be then moved to the U.S. for major drydock repairs. The San Francisco would remain battle-worthy but would be patched up also in Cairns by a repair ship.

The Kirishima was damaged beyond recognition and limped back to Rabaul, then was hauled to Truk. It was out of action for at least the remainder of the 1942 year, as the Iron Duke was.

Shipping attack
USS Wahoo off Timor Island June 28th, 1942

The enemy ships sailed almost dark, with only lanterns and small lights to show their positions to the rest of the vessels in the convoy. It was difficult for the sub captain to figure out how many ships there were, as the rain battered his lenses, and he had to wipe them off often. He also wore a rubber hat and jacket. The sea was churning, and the wind was strong.

Some of his men milled about on the 76mm deck gun below him. They seemed to struggle to stay afoot, as the gale was powerful, and the weather soaked them even harder than Cloutier. The unreliability of the Mark 14 torpedo to date indeed *"promoted"* the use of the deck gun. Jim was not very confident in his own, as several had been duds. The Wahoo missed a couple of freighters the day before, and they'd narrowly escaped the destroyers that tried to sink them with their depth charges.

Using a deck gun for a submarine was not the ideal option, and in most situations, it was not practical and could be really dangerous. 75mm could not penetrate most armored ships to destroy them. At best, it could damage a destroyer and wreak havoc on a cruiser. Also, a submarine was an easy, un-armored target, so if Wahoo tried to engage a warship on the surface, the outcome would almost be its destruction.

But tonight was the exception. First of all, the japs escorts weren't even destroyers; they were Kaibōkan *("sea defense ship")* that were not as dangerous to submarines. Equipped with a lone 120mm forward gun, Cloutier felt that it could duel with it in the dark and low visibility.

They were very lightly armored, only had a limited amount of depth charges, and were usually manned by raw sailors. At least, that was what the intelligence report had told them before they left Brisbane a few weeks back.

From what he could see (the water impeded his vision), there was one Kaibōkan at the front of the convoy and one at the back. He decided to target the leading one, as it was the closest and had the best angle to attack the Wahoo, while the other would have to sail into position to fire at the sub.

One of his men climbed the ladder back to the submarine hatch to get his order. *"Okay, Simms. Target the lead ship; that's the one with the frontal deck gun." "Yes, sir,"* answered the sailor before going down the ladder and going back to the gun. The men did their thing, loading it with a shell and aiming it. They wouldn't have many shots before the Japs retaliated, so better make it count.

Jim planned to destroy both escorts to take his own time to sink the three fat convoy ships in between them. With one last nod of the head (with tons of water still dripping and drenching him), he gave the go-ahead for his men to fire.

The deck gun barked, and a flash illuminated the sub for an instant. The tracer shell arced in what seemed the blink of an eye to hit the Kaibōkan right on its superstructure. The round exploded spectacularly in the night. The Allied shell hit almost in the middle of the ship and opened a large hole into which seawater gushed in almost instantaneously.

It didn't take long for the ship's forward searchlights to point in Wahoo's direction, but by that time, Cloutier's men fired their second shot, which again raced in an instant to hit the Jap escort on the bow, almost where the gun was. Instead of the characteristic boom of the enemy gun firing, Jim was rewarded with inaction. His men's second shot had either damaged the Kaibōkan gun or killed its handlers. That enemy seemed out of commission, burning, and perhaps sinking, as the sub skipper already perceived a list forward.

All the while, the Wahoo had been moving at its top surface speed (20 knots), and he yelled through the hatch to the men below to steer the ship hard to starboard to change heading. He planned to position the submarine for what must be the other escort ship's rushing attack.

Several minutes later, Cloutier, busy looking to port in the probable direction of the rear escort that was surely trying to come to intercept him, saw a muzzle flash in the water maelstrom. That was the sure sign of the Jap gun firing. A few powerful flares were also launched high in the sky from several of the ships, sort of illuminating the whole battle scene. Visibility was still poor, but some light helped the Japanese sailors to find Wahoo.

What was true for the Imperial Navy ships also was for the Americans. The flare helped them outline their enemy. As the Wahoo's men traversed the turret to face the new enemy, a powerful water geyser erupted about ten meters from the submarine. The enemy Kaibōkan had almost found the range. Jim started to be worried that he may have bitten a little more than he could chew.

He went back and forth, for a few agonizing seconds, from his binoculars to his men handling the gun, hoping that they would hit the enemy before it did.

The 76mm gun finally spat its shell, and it raced toward the enemy's outline but fell short by a few meters. Through the storm, Jim heard his men curse loudly.

The sound he'd dreaded was finally heard. It was the sound of an incoming shell. The enemy shot thundered just above the conning tower and crashed into the churning sea about ten meters too far. Apart from creating another pillar of water, it didn't hit anything. The enemy overshot.

"Hurry up, men!" he yelled, without a chance of being overheard as the wind, battering rain, and the sea bashing on the sub drowned

everything but canon sounds.

And then, the 76mm blasted away once more, and the round zipped by Cloutier's vision to go and explode right on the enemy ship's deck. The blasts scattered like a firework above and through the Kaibōkan, splitting it in two. The things were fragile. And that was that. The Wahoo removed the convoy's last defender in one lucky shot.

He didn't have to order anything for his men as they traversed the gun again, but this time toward one of the poor transports. Jim wondered what they carried. He hoped it was supplies, as it would not be a pretty sight if they were troops transports.

Strategic situation, Australian theater
Landings and overland attacks, June 28 to July 3rd, 1942

If one thing was sure, it was that the Japanese high command came in unprepared for the invasion of Australia. The country was huge, and Marshal Hajime / Prime Minister Tojo would have been wise to listen to Admiral Yamamoto's objections. Australia was as big a theater of war as China but without the road infrastructures. The country was raw and underdeveloped. Only the coastal towns and neighboring lands could be considered modern and supplied with sufficient infrastructure for modern armies. The major coastal cities were also very few and far between. It didn't take long for General Masaharu Homma, the commander-in-chief of the Australian expedition (14th Army), to realize what kind of pickle Japan had stepped into with its ill-advised attack on the Aussies.

It wasn't that it was in immediate danger of being attacked, overwhelmed, or destroyed. It wasn't that the Allies could do something against Japanese pretensions on the west coast. It had to do with the simple fact that the invasion force was isolated and could not do much. After all, the nearest enemy guns were a thousand miles away in Wyndham, and the Japanese would have to figure out *"how to get there"* to fight them.

Within a few days of their arrival in Darwin, the Japanese Imperial Army advanced inland along the western coast toward their first objective, the Wyndham, located 900 kilometers from Darwin. The town possessed a deep-water port and was a little over halfway to the significant city of Broome, another deep-water harbor.

14th Army's logistical situation in Australia would prove an unsolvable problem. Initial plans of an overland advance were rapidly revised, and he sent his recommendations back up the chain of command. He then ordered more landings along the coast to secure the Japanese objectives.

The Imperial Guard Division was entrusted with advancing inland to Wyndham, but it soon faced significant problems. The way south had a series of tracks (dirt) and trails empty of people. The Imperial Army soldiers didn't take a week to realize they weren't in China or the Dutch East Indies anymore. It was a hazardous route that was dusty and hot (the Japs landed in the middle of the dry season). Some sections were effectively impassable sand, while others contained limestone outcrops. While the rough Japanese fighting man was used to the hot and humid jungles of the Asian Southeast, marching through bone-dry land was another matter.

General Homma was the man behind the great Imperial victory in the Philippines and knew how to lead an army. Within a few days of arriving at his new Darwin HQ, he recalled the Imperial Guard Division to the city. He then contacted Admiral Raizo Ishaka of 1st Fleet to set up several landing operations on the west coast, starting with Derby and Brome.

Several regiments of the 64th and the Imperial Guards were thus entrusted with the responsibility, and the operation was set for early July. Only then would the Japanese be able to get something done.

The original planning also included an advance toward the northern coast, but the Army was again faced with the same problem with infrastructures. Landing operations were a little more complex in that area, with a sizeable Allied fleet operating nearby. General Homma decided that he would await the destruction of Admiral Leahy's Allied 2nd Fleet roaming the Coral Sea before he organized any landings toward Burketown and Cairns.

Above the Kokoda track
Ace Pilot Takashi Onishi (23 victories) July 3rd, 1942

Takashi Onishi and his squadron were ordered to transfer to Rabaul, New Britain, by early July. The reasons behind the decision lay in the fact that the Allies did not oppose a lot of resistance in Western Australia and that it was deemed a bit of a waste to have such an elite group of pilots on a secondary front.

But the Japanese ace had already learned something from his battles in Australia and then the Solomon Islands and Port Moresby theater. He finally got to meet more American pilots in combat. Good pilots. Unlike many of his previous opponents, Onishi found the aviators based in Australia consistently competent and aggressive. No wonder, since the Americans had excellent training and, what's more, they were not fighting under the difficult odds their predecessors had been in the Philippines. They had sufficient supplies, sufficient airbase, decent supplies, and better machines. The Curtis P-40 Warhawks and carrier-based F4F Wildcats were entirely different beasts than the old and aging Brewster Buffalos the Japanese air force had met earlier in the year. While not yet the Zero's equal, they still represented a significant threat when driven by a competent flyer.

The squadron was at that moment in time (July 3rd, 1942, engaged in a furious dogfight over the Kokoda trail. Onishi and his comrades had been tasked with clearing out the nest of American planes infesting the sky above General Harukichi Hyakutake and the beleaguered men of the 67th Imperial Division.

A few Zeroes ahead of Takashi decided to make a high-speed pass at two Wildcats, overshooting them with excess momentum. Onishi could not help but groan in anger. It was a common mistake that enemy pilots often exploited. Trying to save his friend, he accelerated just as the Americans turned to fire at the jap fighters and rolled into an effective gunnery pass. He hit one of the F4Fs that immediately streamed smoke and leveled out. It crashed in the jungle below a few seconds later.

Moments later, Onishi flew right at a lone B-25 Mitchell bomber and fired a few bursts at its side, opening it critically and shooting it down. A few of its crew were able to jump out of the plane before it slowly leveled out toward the Coral Sea in a horizontal dive while trailing dark smoke.

Running low on fuel, the Japanese ace gathered his two wingmen (that he'd just saved) and prepared to turn back for Rabaul when he spotted an additional formation of ten B-25 bombers flying low and on approach toward the Japanese ground positions. "Let's get a few of them before we run dry on gas," he said over the radio. His two wingmen acknowledged with the efficient, dull answer of experienced aviators. He picked up altitude to approach the enemy bombers into a rolling dive, one of his preferred tactics.

The American pilots (and gunners, for that matter) had seen Onishi taking down the fighter and the lone Mitchell and so were ready when the trio of Japanese pilots came at them in a steep, perpendicular dive. The sky around the U.S. bombers lit up with machine guns and flak shells in long tracer lines that crisscrossed the Japanese pilot's paths.

Onishi's two comrades were caught in a crossfire, taking several hits. One had his windscreen holed by a .30-caliber round clipped the top of his head, killing the man instantly. His plane went into a tumbling dive and rapidly crashed on one of the towering mountains of the Owen Stanley's range. The second one's zero was riddled with .30 shells and wholly gutted out, trailing dark smoke, while the pilot was hit twice in the legs, with grave injuries that shattered muscles and bones. Stunned and disoriented, the doomed pilot instinctively pulled back on the stick and was lost to sight by friend and foe until he made a complete loop backward and lost consciousness. Most rookie pilots could have guessed the rest of the story: the plane flew until it crashed fierily on the ground in a cataclysmic explosion.

Takashi went into his tumbling and rolling dive, dodging every single shell and machine-gun bullet that was fired his way. At its end, he sent a heavy burst of his canons on one of the B-25s and riddled it on the top of the fuselage, holing the plane in several places. A few seconds after that, the plane just exploded in mid-air.

Being done with his crazy stunt, he leveled his Zero and looked for his comrades, just in time to see the second one crash and explode. Feeling grim, he turned his plane around and headed back for Rabaul in the rest of the squadron's wake. He didn't feel good about the damned bombers unloading their ordinance at the poor sods below and at the fact that he'd lost his two wingmen.

Patrol and practice
Over carrier Yorktown, Near San Diego, July 4th, 1942

Harry Bergman, a U.S. Navy pilot on the USS Yorktown, cruised above the fleet below. The Yorktown, along with a few ships, was sailing in a training exercise just off San Diego Harbor, where the vessels of the U.S. Pacific Fleet were gathered. His job on that day was to patrol above the ships below and eventually land. They were also equipped with bombs to practice some dive-bombing on an old target ship. He looked that way a little as he was awaiting his turn to go and dive toward the old boat. He could see more Dauntless, some clumsier than the others, diving and dropping their bombs. It looked like they were bees buzzing around a nest from his distance. The bombs were duds, so they were only designed to hit and not explode. It was only practice, after all.

Rumor had it that they would soon go into action. The high command was said to be finalizing the details of an operation against Hawaii. Harry believed in the rumors because first, he trained hard every day, and that was a sign that things would soon heat up and fly over the dozens upon dozens of ships that were assembled in San Diego. The Allied fleet was powerful and even had a French battleship complement with the Lorraine and Bretagne.

As he looked at the immensity from his dive-bomber canopy, he wondered what the rest of the war had in store for him. Would he survive the next battle? Harry used to be a land-based fighter pilot and was slowly but surely becoming an excellent dive-bomber flyer.

To date, he didn't know what was better (or worse, for that matter). Fly in a fighter and get into dogfights with the dreaded Japanese Zero aircraft or brave the flak as his SBD Dauntless dove toward the ship to drop his bomb.

Both had their risks. He'd become an SBD pilot by forces of circumstances, as he'd been needed in a fight a while back when the japs attacked San Diego. His flight leader had spotted his talent for the trade, and so he'd been on a dive-bomber ever since.

And he had to admit to himself he liked the plane a lot. He'd read everything he could find on the magnificent machine. Bergman could not wait to have another chance to plunge at an enemy ship. He sometimes imagined himself in a steep dive to send a powerful bomb into one of the infamous Japanese flattops. In these daydreams, he was the hero of the story.

"Bergman," stated the squadron leader over the radio. "It's your turn." "Yes, sir." He rolled his plane left to put it into position for his planned 20,000-foot dive. The SBD responded and angled down toward the practice target.

Liberty Ships and planes
Brisbane, July 5th, 1942

If one thing was sure, in July 1942, the Japanese Imperial forces enjoyed a good measure of air superiority in every theater of the Pacific War. That reality was especially true in the two Australian theaters.

First of all, in Darwin, only a few planes roamed the sky, to the point that the Japanese high command transferred most of its air squadrons to other areas of the Japanese Empire. The second area was in the Coral Sea. Japan enjoyed a quantitative superiority in aircraft carriers, twin-engine bombers, and land-based fighters. The only category where the Allies enjoyed some form of dominance was in the four-engine category (B-17 Flying Fortresses) because the Japanese had none.

In short, the war could not be won by surface ships and soldiers on the ground. The commander in chief of Southwest Pacific Area Command (SPWA), General MacArthur, made that fact clear to the U.S. President. It would be impossible for him to stop the Japanese tide without air assets.

So American industrial production and ingenuity came to his help, with some pressure from Roosevelt himself. The merchant navy was to deliver as many planes as possible through the "milk run," the go-around sea route used by Admiral Leahy's Australian relief fleet (now renamed 2nd Fleet) to deliver planes to the beleaguered Australian front.

Plans to establish a front in Europe were already well underway by mid-1942, even if it didn't look like the Allies would be able to overpower the Axis. The Americans and the British remained confident in final victory, and so they planned for it.

The liberation of the United Kingdom, the campaign in North Africa, plus the urgent needs of Australia and India called for a significant effort in terms of merchant ships to ferry the troops, supplies, and weapons to the frontlines across the world.

The Allies adopted a new class of ships that could be mass-produced. The Liberty ships were a class of cargo ships launched in production in the USA by early 1942. The plan was to mass-produce them on an unprecedented scale in order to be able to fuel any frontlines with the extraordinary industrial output of the American industrial giant.

By June 1942, eighteen American shipyards had contracts in hand to build them, and the first ships were already sailing the seas. They were consequently the logical choice to bring war equipment to Australia.

A convoy of twenty Liberty ships sailed into Brisbane harbor on the 5th of July, and they contained hundreds of boxed aircraft. MacArthur asked for fighters primarily, and he got the excellent and modern Republic P-47 Thunderbolt, Grumman F4F Wildcat (carrier-based fighter), and some Curtiss P-40 Warhawk.

A little over 210 planes were brought by the Liberty ship convoy. They would be dearly needed in the coming months as the desperate Allied situation continued to unfold. MacArthur finally got his fighting chance.

In terms of bombers, more B-17s arrived by flying by themselves, either the long route (South America, Africa, India, and then Australia) or the "milk run" path, by stopping in French Polynesia and other islands that had the airfields to let them land.

With aircraft, the Allies could finally think about doing something different than just surviving the Japanese onslaught.

CHAPTER 3

Yamato Battleship
Oahu, Hawaii, July 6th, 1942

Grand Admiral Yamamoto had a few minutes before he met with his air commander, Minoru Genda, and the commander of the carrier strike force (Kido Butai), Admiral Nagumo. He took a little bit of time to ponder on the strategic situation as a whole. Things were seemingly going well everywhere, but some problems existed and did not bode well.

While the landing and conquest of Darwin in Western Australia had been a complete success, the follow-up advance and conquest were not as easy as they looked on Marshal Hajime's planning maps back in the Dai Honei HQ meeting the month before. Australia was a rugged, underdeveloped country, especially in the western part. The cities were spread thinly along the coastline, and there was not much road infrastructure between them. A sort of road was established from a hodgepodge of dirt tracks and forest trails from Perth to Broome, but it was far from sufficient to support a modern army.

So, the Imperial forces had decided to adapt to the new situation. Instead of advancing overland, they would embark the troops from Darwin and land them at strategic points. The first two landing operations were planned. Their objectives were the cities of Derby and Broome, both possessing deepwater ports that would help further supply the Imperial forces. His radio communication and telegrams with Hajime had also stressed that the Australian expeditionary force needed more troops. The General had reluctantly agreed, detaching two more divisions from the Chinese theater (Kwantung Army) and one additional newly raised unit.

Overall, however, Yamamoto did not think that Japan would succeed in Australia. The place was too large, and the Army forces spread too thin everywhere. If the Army had been able to muster, say, twenty-five seasoned units and the Navy had been able to concentrate the full might of ships on the Australian coast, it could have been done.

But with the mere four divisions already in Darwin and three more coming, he didn't entertain much hope.

At least, the troops there kept MacArthur busy while Yamamoto consolidated his gains elsewhere in the Pacific. He believed he could hold the Americans at bay as long as he remained in control of Hawaii and the main strategic islands with deep harbors like American Samoa or New Caledonia.

The line of thoughts about Australia brought the grand Admiral to the recent defeat at the Battle of the Coral Sea. It was not like the Navy had lost ships or suffered a tactical loss. Yes, battleship Kirishima and carrier Taiyo were damaged, but the latter would be repaired in Truk by the repair ships they had there while the first was back in Japan. But the battle's strategic outcome was that the invasion fleet bound for Port Moresby had to turn around and go back to Rabaul. Yamamoto knew that his Coral Sea and Solomon Islands position would be threatened as long as the Allies held Port Moresby and fielded a powerful fleet. With the vital base, he could also entertain attacks on Australia's northern coast and land the Darwin troops as far as Cairns, further weakening the Aussie's position.

As he was pretty busy with planning his own theater of operation (the war would play itself out in the Hawaiian Islands area after all), he resolved to send some orders (and strong reinforcements) to Admiral Shigeyoshi Inoue to prepare a new operation and to Admiral Ishaka's 1st fleet (based in Timor) to transfer most of its battleships to Inoue's forces in Rabaul.

At least the super-battleship Musashi had just arrived in Truk and would provide much-needed guns to the 2nd fleet that was without battleships for the moment, with Kirishima and Haruna out of action. Yamamoto needed most of Japan's carrier units in Pearl Harbor to guard against the U.S. Pacific Fleet that was certain to come and try to wrest the islands from the Empire's grasp, so he decided that the few light carriers would support Japanese action in the Coral Sea but most notably by the number of battleships spread between 1st and 2nd fleets. He just couldn't spare more.

Completely disregarding the Burmese campaign as too much of a side-show for his mind to waste brain-power on, he moved on to the map in front of him, representing tiny Palmyra, where the Americans had successfully retaken the islands from the small Marine forces he'd put there.

Tactically, they'd scored some good hits on the enemy ships with Shokaku's planes, but the net strategic result was that the small atoll was back into America's hands. Their presence there meant that they would soon finish building the airfield that was already under construction by the Imperial engineers. Once that was a reality and the U.S. Navy dropped planes there, it would be a lot harder to retake and would represent a danger for his flank in Hawaii, but also for the Marshall Islands and Johnson Island, his fallback position if he lost Pearl Harbor.

He put his finger on the map and started to count the number of nautical miles his forces would have to travel in order to send a naval force to the area when a knock on his cabin door was heard. *"Enter."* The two officers he'd been waiting for made their entrance into the room.

Minoru Genda and Admiral Chuichi Nagumo made their respective bowing gestures to salute their superior, and he gave them the same in return. *"Welcome, gentlemen. Thank you for coming to my humble ship for the meeting,"* he added with a friendly smile. Humble was an incredible understatement for what the Yamato super-battleship represented. *"Thank you, admiral,"* responded Nagumo, quickly followed by Genda: *"We are here to serve, Admiral."* Both men were dressed in their full white uniforms as if going on parade. A meeting with the Grand Admiral was always important, and one wanted to look as sharp as possible.

Yamamoto gestured them to the table he was standing over, which sported a map representing the Pacific theater portion that concerned the two men, namely the Hawaiian Islands, the U.S. West Coast, and the series of small islands ringing the area (Midway, Palmyra, Christmas, Johnson, and the Marshalls).

They both removed their military cap, put them under their arms, and approached. *"At ease, gentlemen,"* said Isoroku. The two men sensibly relaxed. The Japanese Imperial Navy was very formal, and it was good to remind the men and officers that they could relax a little once in a while. He needed their minds focused on the problem at hand, not on being formal and distant.

"As our big operation against the U.S. Mainland nears, I would like to discuss the details of the attack, as well as other theater concerns I have, like Palmyra." The Grand Admiral emphasized his words by putting his finger right on the spot, representing the island on the map. The two other men nodded, awaiting what Yamamoto had to say next.

"So, gentlemen, we need to retake the island, for it represents a danger to our strategic position." The Grand Admiral didn't have to do a lot of explaining, as the two men knew their business and understood that having an atoll with an airfield occupied by the enemy represented a significant problem for their strategy of keeping the Americans out of the Pacific entirely. Once they set foot somewhere, they could build up an offensive from there. The U.S. Navy and Marines had executed a surprise landing a couple of weeks before and reclaimed the island from the meager Japanese forces there.

"Admiral, I agree with you. From Palmyra, they can base B-17 bombers and attack us directly in Hawaii. They can also set up a submarine base and have flying boats to help with the recon to detect our fleets." He looked at Isoroku in the eyes. *"It cannot be tolerated."*

Nagumo didn't seem to want to argue the plain facts but more to talk about what his carriers would have to do about it. *"Admiral, with the coming operation against San Diego, we have some time we could use to send a powerful strike force to smash the island's defense. I have all six carriers operational and ready whenever you give the order."* "Thank you, Admiral Nagumo," answered Yamamoto, who walked a few feet to the wall where legendary naval commander Togo's painting was hung. He put his hands behind his back. *"I agree. We can strike in Palmyra and still meet our operational deadline for the attack on the U.S. mainland."*

And with these words, the Grand Admiral walked back to the table, putting his right hand under his chin for concentration. *"Okay, gentlemen. Let's do this."*

The three men talked, planned, and discussed how they would smash the bold Americans who had dared set foot on one of their newly conquered islands.

Meanwhile on Palmyra
Northern Line Islands, July 6th, 1942

The Line Islands were as remote as they got in the Pacific, located south of the Hawaiian Islands. The area used to be controlled by the Japanese through their occupation of Palmyra in the northern part of the archipelago. After a quick and successful attack at the end of June, American forces reclaimed the area with a landing of the 4th Marine Regiment. A naval battle was also fought with substantial losses on the Allied side.

The American forces took control of the atoll and its airfield under construction after a fierce battle with the Sasebo Imperial Marines SNLF half-battalion defending it. The fight had been short but fierce, as there was no cover on the island, apart from some vegetation, and the fighting quickly destroyed that.

Within the atoll's protective lagoon, a Japanese seaplane tender, the Chitose, was also captured by the U.S. Marines once they killed the last Imperial soldier (none of them surrendered).

By July 6th, the Americans had finished working on the airfield that Imperial engineers had started. They'd also re-purposed the Chitose for their own use (so they could use the fling boats for their own recon flights) since they were even able to repair it.

The American Marines looked nervously at the plane on approach, as it was the first time an aircraft would try to land on their makeshift airbase. They'd brought some construction workers with them, but most of the soldiers didn't know anything about airfield construction, so they'd improvised for the most part. They picked up the Jap machines and used them to finish the work. Half of the force also toiled on getting the defenses ready (the Japs had built bunkers and trenches where they could) because everyone was convinced the japs would be back.

The plane that was about to land was a big four-engine B-17 bomber, and according to the news from the higher-ups in the Regiment, it was laden with supplies. Behind the first one, they could see a long line of other Flying Fortresses also approaching Palmyra. The runway was pretty long, as Palmyra had a length of 4.7 kilometers, thus big enough.

They marveled at the size of the B-17 and the nice, droning rumble it made as it approached the dirt of the airfield. It eventually touched the ground, lifting dust in the air. They cheered loudly as it finished its landing and started rolling toward the end of the runway. Apparently also happy at being on the atoll, the pilots and gunners opened their doors and hatches to wave at the Marines.

The big bombers had just enough range to reach Palmyra (5900 kilometers) from San Diego. And so, they arrived in Palmyra to supply the brave men that had the distinction of having brought about the first land victory against the damned Japs in this war. Some had guns, some had more petrol, some ammo, and most importantly, several had food and water, which was in short supply in the tiny place lost in the middle of the Pacific.

Some B-17s would go back, and some would stay on the island, as they would be used for operational purposes and defenses. The U.S. Navy was also planning to drop fighters and shorter-range aircraft with their carriers at some point. But not in the short term, as they were all concentrating on the upcoming battle with the Combined Fleet.

Like the Americans, sailors, pilots, and Marines alike got busy preparing their hard-won atoll for the expected Japanese counterattack, but they remained confident of holding the place if they stayed.

Western Coast of Australia
Japanese landings in Broome and Derby July 10th, 1942

Broome wasn't much of a city of harbor in 1942. It was only a small refueling station for short-ranged ships, and that was about it. It had, however, grown in importance after the Japanese landings in Darwin.

Derby, another small town, had grown in importance during the Japanese conquest campaign in the Dutch East Indies. An airfield was built north of the small city, and its harbor was also useable for warships, so several used the area for refueling.

Both cities got some defenses organized, with the raising of the local militia (about 3000 men) and an Australian Army regiment, making for approximately 6000 defenders for the area. A few coastal gun emplacements were also built in Broome if the Japanese fleet made an appearance.

General MacArthur did not entertain much hope for such a position to hold the Japanese tide. Still, he'd resolved to defend the place with what was available and not let any city or harbor fall to the Japanese unopposed. His rationale was simple. As shown by his bold actions and strategic victories in the Port Moresby areas, the Japanese Empire was over-extending itself. With determined resistance, the Allies could blunt the Nipponese advance.

"The point of the spear is brittle" was one of the famous American General's saying in 1942. By that, he meant that the Japanese military was at the end of a long supply line and thus didn't have everything necessary to win decisively. It was peculiar how it seemingly had the power with the tough divisions, planes, and battleships at the front, but it lacked depth and often didn't have any reinforcements to push for victory. There just wasn't anything after the frontline.

No wonder. The Japanese were attacking everywhere, trying to invade Australia, campaigning in Burma, with half of their army busy in China against the dual forces of the Nationalists and the Communists. Then, they entertained almost a million men to watch the Soviets, notwithstanding all the troops they needed to conquer and hold the immensity of the Pacific. If the Allies mounted a determined resistance in any kind of strength, they had a chance. The Imperial Navy was also in the same predicament, with the Combined Fleet's might in Hawaii to try and hold on to Oahu, and then more ships divided on both of Australia's flanks. According to MacArthur's best intelligence assessments, the Japs didn't even have the oil or the resources to use all their forces at the same time. The Allies only needed to resist everywhere until such time that America's factories built them the military might that would sweep the Nippon forces away.

And thus, MacArthur's theory was tested in Broome and Derby on the 11th of July 1942. The Japs came with their multitudes of ships, with two battleships (the rest had already been ordered to the Coral Sea). The powerful Ise (Derby) and Tosa (Broome) thus shelled both cities, exploding buildings and creating great mayhem across the town's infrastructures. They both dueled for a short while against the insufficient coastal defense guns that were able to hit the dreadnoughts but couldn't penetrate their armored belts and decks.

After several hours of destroying everything in sight with the battleships, the Imperial Army was deemed safe enough to move ahead with their amphibious landings. Hundreds of Daihatsu landing ships surged forward, transporting men from the Imperial Guard Division, the 64th Division, and a half-brigade of Type 95 medium tanks. The small Allied forces defending both cities put up one hell of a fight, and for most of the day on the 11th, Imperial troops were stuck on the beaches. By nightfall, the Japs were finally able to land their tanks, and a night attack was conducted in Broome, pushing the Australian forces back and finally taking hold in the city proper.

In Derby, the Allies resisted the whole night but finally broke after the Japanese air force launched a devastating airstrike against their defensive positions.

Both Australian forces remnants retired to the interior, and the Japanese did not follow them. Their losses were substantial, and they were exhausted.

The Japanese landings in Milne Bay
The Imperial Army attacks, July 11th, 1942

The reason the Japanese found Milne Bay interesting (in strategic terms) was twofold. First, it had roads that led to the southern coast, so its troops could advance from there and then swing northwest toward Port Moresby. Second, landing in Milne Bay was a lot easier, as the Allies would not have time to react. Admiral Inoue's plan, approved enthusiastically by Grand Admiral Yamamoto, was simple. He would sail a powerful battleship task force with troops transports and land an entire division there.

The follow-up to the landing was to build up a supply base and then advance through the mountains and on the southern coast. From there, it was hoped that the advance would be smooth all the way to Port Moresby. The plan also called for some reinforcements (another division) to bolster the attack. But at that time, no more troops were available. So, the Grand Admiral promised Inoue that he would petition Hajime for another Kwantung division. The Admiral still had a few units scattered around (battalion-sized) on D'Entrecasteaux, Woodlark, and Misima islands that he decided to eventually move to Milne Bay if it was necessary. In typical Japanese improvisation, Inoue agreed that he would make it work with a division.

A powerful task force sailed out of Rabaul base on the early morning of the 10th of July. It was powerful because it contained the super-battleship Musashi, but it had few surface units. But the presence of the steel behemoth was deemed sufficient to face the potential Allied reaction.

Admiral Inoue sailed out with the rest of its 2nd Fleet ships, staying near Normanby Island to provide air cover with his three light carriers (Unyo, Ryujo, Zhuiho). He was out of battleships to protect them, so he bunched together everything else available: Heavy cruiser Haguro, ten destroyers, and three light cruisers.

Yamamoto had already ordered Admiral Ihaka's 1st fleet to transfer several heavy units to the 2nd fleet (for example, the battleship Yamashiro and Hyuga). Still, they were not yet available for the Milne Bay operation. So, Musashi would have to do it alone, along with the heavy cruiser Atago, five destroyers, and two light cruisers.

U.S. Navy Intelligence got advance notice of the Japanese operation, thanks to their Magic decoding setup with the OSS and thanks to the many British-Australian listening stations across the area. The Nipponese radio intercepts, duly decoded, were rapidly sent through the chain of command, and it didn't take long for Douglas MacArthur to formulate an answer. He first ordered the Australian 10th Division in Abau, a scratch force of 10,000 men (Americans, British, Australians), to move toward Milne Bay with the utmost speed. He figured they would probably arrive too late to stop the Jap landing but would be in a position to counter-attack.

After seeing what the Imperial Navy sent to protect the landing force, he ordered Admiral Leahy to move with the Allied 2nd fleet to intercept it and destroy the ships there. Unfortunately for the American commander, he was unaware that he was sending the poor Allied sailors to a world of trouble. Musashi was still an unknown entity to the American-British forces. They would soon get to see the super-dreadnought in all its glory. As the OSS reported from their decoded transmissions, it was not "just one battleship."

On July 11th, the Imperial Army forces of the 89th Infantry Division landed without opposition in Milne Bay and quickly overwhelmed the area, immediately setting up defensive positions. The Japanese ships didn't even have to fire a shot, as no enemy was in sight.

However, the 10th Australian Division would soon arrive in the area to challenge their enemies.

Heavy guns duel
Musashi VS Washington July 12th, 1942

Both Allied and Japanese navies were again on a collision course for a duel. A duel that would make a story for the ages. A brave American fleet against a powerful adversary.

Admiral Leahy's 2nd Fleet(the very fleet that had come to Australia's help), which was already sailing near Cairns as a quick-reaction force, immediately headed for Milne Bay (southeastern tip of New Guinea) on the 11th at the first signs of movements from the Imperial Navy. Both MacArthur (the Allied Commander-in-Chief of the Southwest Pacific theater) and the Admiral knew that they were risking it all again and that the fleet had insufficient air cover compared to the enemy. But they did have carriers Ranger and Charger against three Japanese light carriers. Furthermore, several planes had arrived in Australia and were starting to make their way to Port Moresby to bolster the air defense.

Hence, MacArthur ordered all available planes to concentrate either above Leahy's fleet or find the enemy ships, especially the carriers, which were said to cruise between Rabaul and the Louisiade Archipelago near the southeastern tip of New Guinea. They even pressed the B-17s into the battle, even if the planes were not super-efficient against ships. They would still provide excellent air coverage and could search the area extensively to find the Nipponese carriers.

The 2nd fleet entered the mouth of Milne Bay undetected on the early morning of the 12th since it sailed the whole night at full speed in the dark. Musashi also didn't have any radar, scheduled to be installed only in September that year. But at first light, it didn't take long for both sides to be aware of the other. Leahy had split his force in two in order first to intercept the landing force and protect his carriers.

The ships that entered Milne Bay were deemed sufficient to sink the Japanese battleship, and few other surface vessels were reported to be there.

Allied Task Force One contained two battleships, the mighty Washington and New York, flanked by heavy cruisers San Francisco and London, two light cruisers, and five destroyers. They faced the Musashi, heavy cruiser Atago, two light cruisers, and five destroyers.

Musashi was the mightiest battleship afloat in 1942 (along with Yamato). Musashi opened the battle from 20,000 yards away with its unprecedented 460mm guns. On Washington, Admiral Leahy was aware of the Japanese presence at the bottom of Milne Bay (the Japanese ships were bottled in) but could only observe in horror that large explosions soon gushed heavy, towering water by his ships.

"What the hell is that thing firing at us, gentlemen," said the American commander, seemingly awestruck. Some brave deck officer opted for the logical answer: *"Sir. We don't know, Sir."* Leahy seemed uncertain for another second or two but quickly returned to his senses. After all, whatever the caliber of the Japanese guns, hitting anything from that range. Battleships hitting ratio already being well below 4% at optimal ranges; at 20,000 yards, the odds were abysmal. *"All ships ahead. We need to close the range."* It was not the best decision because of the Musashi's firepower, but the U.S. didn't know the Japanese had built another Yamato-type ship yet. A knife fight with such an opponent was beyond Washington's capabilities.

"Also, call for an airstrike and notify MacArthur that we have encountered unexpected resistance and that we need every available help here," finished the admiral, pointing to the officer in charge of the radio room on Washington. *"Yes, sir."*

An air raid on the Japanese landing fleet was planned for about the same time, but it wouldn't hurt for MacArthur and the other local commanders in Port Moresby and Cairns to know that something big and mean was lurking in Milne Bay.

The minutes that trickled by as the Allied ships steamed full speed were the most nerve-racking of Leahy's career, and he'd started to feel like during his encounter with Kirishima earlier in June. The feeling that something big and powerful was closing in on him.

The enemy sent a powerful salvo at a rate of two per minute and, so far, had missed with all their shots. No wonder since the Musashi's crew was pretty raw, and hitting anything from long range was difficult, as said earlier. But that didn't mean they were untrained. Finally, after two straddling shots hit the water on both sides of New York, the super battleship's following broadside struck the U.S. dreadnought with all its fury. Five of its 460mm shells hit the superstructure just above the armor belt and on the conning tower.

The result for the American vessel was nothing short of catastrophic. Two of the shells glanced out and exploded outwardly, creating damage, but more like a spectacular blast than anything critical. They slammed on the deck at an awkward angle and splashed their blast horizontally instead of penetrating inside the ship.

A third shell landed smack in between the forward-most main turret's twin guns and the deck. The heavily protected gun platform splintered in a million pieces scattered on both sides of the ship and peppered the sea all around.

But the heaviest damage to New York was done by the last two shells that followed the two glancing hits a fraction of a second later. They entered the already weakened belt and impaled the battleship like a hot knife through butter, penetrating four decks below the armored exterior. The shells then exploded from the inside of the Texas-class battleship, snapping it like a popping bubble. The great ship opened from the inside and seemed to burst outward as a powerful explosion rocketed it skyward, lifting it momentarily from the water's surface. Fire, debris, and oily black smoke gushed out from the gaping holes, and just like that, New York was completely dead in the water, crippled. The amazing thing was that the ship still floated but was now just a floating hulk on which a great fire burned. Everything went dead on the vessel, and almost half of its crew was either killed, injured, or severely stunned. The bridge was gone, and so were the captain and his deck officers.

As Washington slipped right beside the burning New York, Leahy, open-mouthed, didn't find anything to say or think apart from a vile panic that slowly took part of his inner guts. Yes, they'd boxed the Japanese fleet, and by all standard military logic, they should have made short work of the *"small"* task force of a battleship, heavy cruisers, and a few support ships, but the Americans had badly miscalculated. They'd cornered a rat (and a huge one at that), and the rat lashed out at them for it.

For another half a minute, just the time for the next Musashi salvo to arrive over his ships, he was indecisive about what to do. Then Musashi's broadside straddled Washington with eight of its shells, and the ninth hit the American Battleship on the bow.

The resulting explosion shook Washington to its core, as even the Admiral and his officers were swept off their feet and fell to the ground. The Nipponese 460mm round hit right at the front of the ship and opened it like it had not even been armored. Luckily for Leahy and his men, it had been a partial hit, the shell hitting the water and the ship simultaneously, mitigating the impact. But that hit was enough for the U.S. Admiral. *"Lieutenant Darby!"* he yelled. *"Yes, Sir."* *"Order all destroyers full speed ahead. Every ship is to put up a smokescreen and turn about. We're getting out of here."* "Yes, sir," said an obviously relieved lieutenant. Leahy turned fiercely around toward the radio room officer, who was just tottering back into the main deck, his head covered in blood. The man had hit himself on a bulkhead. *"And where's my airstrike!"* The officer, half-stunned, was still able to stammer an answer. *"Th...e aisrt.....rike is but a mi....nute or so out. They.... Should attack soon."*

Everyone on the ship could feel the sharp turn that Washington was making. Fast maneuvers like that were not usual on big battleships. *"Admiral. Reports from the bow. Water is gushing in at an alarming rate. Chief engineer says you won't be able to keep up that speed for long."* Leahy didn't respond. He kept his eyes on the next enemy salvo.

In the end, that is about thirty minutes later, the American battleships were out of the bay, leaving the troops there to the mercy of the Japanese imperial forces. Musashi didn't pursue Leahy, as it was uncertain of the enemy's presence in the area. Furthermore, the ship was under orders to support the Milne Bay landing and thus stayed in place to shore-bombard the Allied defenses and installations. The Allied destroyers all made it back alive, but not before torpedoing the crippled New York with a few torpedo salvos.

Allied air attack in Milne Bay
Dauntless and B-17s make their attack July 12th, 1942

As it happened, the Americans and the Japanese air force would get above Milne Bay almost simultaneously. But not quite. The American airmen of the 12th bomber squadron (B-17s) and the aircraft carrier Ranger (25 SBD Dauntless) arrived on the scene first.

So, for a critical five minutes, Musashi and its escorts would have to fend for themselves while the aircraft plunged on them. They abandoned all pretenses of firing at the fleeing enemy ships and turned all their might toward the incoming angels of death upon spotting the enemy planes.

The Musashi commenced firing with its special *"Sanshikidan beehive shells,"* supposed to act as a scatter explosion against attacking aircraft. The American planes flew straight through the shells' shrapnel. In short, the intended weapon didn't work. Then, the rest of the ship's AA guns opened up, putting up a wall of lead at the approaching enemy. These guns were soon joined by the ones from Atago, five destroyers, and two light cruisers.

But after so much lead and fire, the American planes continued to blaze down on the Japanese ships. The Japanese curtain of fire was impressive looking, but the effectiveness was not the same.

It was insufficient to stop the Dauntless on their dives. The bombers started their run from the usual 20,000 feet and plunged toward their targets. Several went for the big bastard of a ship they saw at the bottom of the bay. Some others targeted Atago, and finally, a few went for the Light cruisers. On the way, nine were destroyed by Japanese flak, but the remaining sixteen ran the gauntlet and survived long enough to drop their bomb. It made for a spectacular scene from afar, as reported by the Japanese infantrymen in Milne Bay. A swarm of black planes swept down amidst a blossoming array of defensive fire, a multitude of red tracers that rose to the sky trying to shoot them down.

And then the Americans dropped their bombs. Many fell in the water right by Musashi, but two hit right in its deck, igniting major blasts that blinded everyone watching the scene. A large fire cloud enveloped the great battleship for a few seconds and then receded to show an intact Musashi. Scarred, yes, but without major damage.

Two destroyers were unluckier and were destroyed by direct hits, while two bombs straddled Atago but, apart from a few scratches on the paint, were unhindered. Light Cruiser Agano was also destroyed in a maelstrom of fire.

The lookouts on Musashi duly reported the arrival of the Japanese air defenses over the fleet and more Allied aircraft from the south. A great dogfight was about to take place above Milne Bay.

But before any of that happened, the beleaguered Japanese ships and men on the ground would have to endure the B-17 strike that was raining down on them. The big four-engine bombers weren't made specifically to target ships, but its squadron commander figured that since they were boxed in the close bay, it would be like dropping their ordinance at ground targets. So, while their comrades made their dive bomber runs, they put themselves at their optimal 5000 feet altitude and dropped their cargos.

The eighteen B-17s loosed their 4800 pounds of payload, which represented nine bombs each, so a multitude of them was dropped toward the Milne Bay area. Heavy carpet bombing was not a precision weapon, so the 162 bombs scattered in the wind as they fell to the ground. They hit an extensive area on the ground, killing Japanese, trees, and churning water. A few bombs also straddled the Japanese ships, and one of them hit Musashi, which again shrugged off the explosion as nothing more than a nuisance.

And then battle in the air was joined, and the Zeros did their job of protecting their Navy brothers from the big bad Allies. While the airstrike didn't destroy the Imperial Navy ships, it did save Leahy's task force (short of one battleship, of course) that exited the area with all due speed.

The great Milne Bay duel
Takashi Onishi over Milne Bay (27 victories), July 12th, 1942

The Imperial soldiers of the 89th Division cheered and threw their hands in the air, gesturing with their rifles at the empty air as the Zero fighter thundered past them, firing its shells at the Warhawk allied aircraft. Its red tracers arced in a line as if they trailed the P-40 fighter until it connected with its rear tail, shattering it to smithereens.

The stricken pilot lost control of his machine as it rolled over on its side and crashed into neighboring Milne Bay in a splash of water mixed with a blast.

The scene was a mind-blowing spectacle. Above the troops, dozens of planes fought each other, and tracer shells crisscrossed the skies. Just over the water, about a kilometer out, were the Imperial Navy ships, fighting for their lives and pouring all the lead they could at the attacking Allied planes. The explosion created by their anti-aircraft fire formed sort of a wall of smoke and debris in front of the fleet.

And then, of course, bombs were falling amongst the 89th's positions. The Japanese soldiers had just landed; hence, it wasn't like they had had time to build bunkers, so they dug in where they stood in shallow trenches or found holes to hide.

Takashi Onishi, an ace pilot in the Imperial Army air force (at 27 victories on that day in 1942), pulled on his stick to retake some altitude after killing his opponent. His fighter responded by swooping large and up toward the blue immensity of the sky that was the beautiful day of July 12th, 1942.

The air battle was very confusing as both sides fired at each other; the American and Australian pilots also tried to hit ships and troops, while Japanese fighters tried to destroy them. The advantage of numbers was, again, for the Nipponese. Still, this time, it was because Allied air command had sent some of its carrier planes near the Louisiade

Archipelago, where they'd spotted Admiral Inoue's carrier task force. That air battle was for another story, however, as Onishi had not a care in the world what happened elsewhere since he was fighting for his life and the lives of his comrades in the ships and on the ground below him.

He veered his plane into a roll to avoid a burst of fire from a Grumman F4F Wildcat of the light carrier Charger. With a top speed of 318 mph, the Wildcat was outperformed by the faster (331 mph), more maneuverable, and longer-ranged Mitsubishi A6M Zero. But at the same time, the plane's ruggedness compared to the Japanese sometimes helped it win the day as it could take a little beating, something that its enemy couldn't do.

Often, just one shell on a Zero was enough to either cripple it severely or destroy it. The Japanese plane designers had put everything into the engine and armament and nothing into armor. It explained the plane's incredible skill and speed, but the giveaway was that it wasn't very resistant to enemy fire when an Allied pilot was good enough to hit one.

Takeshi continued on his roll to port, spinning wildly. He came back to ground level, zipping past Milne Bay in a flurry of loud engine power, and continued right above the water, about four meters from the calm sea. His plane produced a small wave and spurted some water into the air.

All the while, the allied F4F tried to hit him but only succeeded in straddling him to port and starboard, slashing the sea in great gouts of water with its shells.

Then Onishi put the full gas on his Zero and climbed in a hurry, again dodging a burst from the American tailing him. He pulled hard on his stick and hoped for the best while taking as much altitude as he could. The Grumman fighter behind struggled to catch him, as the Zero was a lighter and faster pane. Onishi thundered with all available speed, directly facing the sun, blinding him partially. But most importantly, it also blinded his enemy, who nonetheless continued on his course, still firing his aircraft shells at Onishi's Zero. Once he reached an altitude of 15 000 feet, the Japanese fighter ace cut his engine and rolled hard to port, straight down.

He only had a few seconds to find the American plane and get his eyes again accustomed to not being straight at the sun. He struggled hard, but he'd always had exceptional eyesight, and he immediately spotted the F4F, as his blurry vision quickly came back. He sped head-on toward his enemy and fired away with everything he had.

He was rewarded with several hits, the Wildcat immediately catching fire, hit in the front engine. The pilot was also instantly killed, several of the Japanese shells hitting and destroying his protective canopy. The plane turned sharply to port, bursting with fire and trailing black smoke.

It crashed into the Milne Bay water in another two seconds, creating a towering pillar of water and fire. "Two for the day!" yelled Onishi to himself alone in his Zero cockpit.

The battle was far from over, and he resolved to find another enemy to kill.

The Battle of Milne Bay Part 1
Aussies vs Japs, July 13th, 1942

The allied counter-offensive had certainly not considered the presence of one of the two most powerful battleships in the world when it was decided to advance to Milne Bay and confront the Japanese.

They'd anticipated a battleship there all right, but the high command plan was relatively straightforward when they sent a superior force to overpower it. Things had not really worked the way Leahy and MacArthur had thought they would.

After furious air battles over Milne Bay for most of the 12th and early morning of the 13th, the allied aircraft, exhausted and depleted, retreated away from the area, leaving the just-arrived soldiers of the 10th Australian Division to face the might of Musashi's 460mm guns on their own.

The Japanese were simply horrified at the prospect of losing Musashi and were mortified by the numerous airstrikes that the Allies had thrown at Milne Bay. But the brave Imperial air force and its Zero multitudes held everything together for the Imperial Navy behemoth. The super-battleship was still hit by several allied bombs and even a torpedo, but it was still bravely afloat.

Most of the damage was superficial, apart from the torpedo hit that reduced its speed. So by 11th AM on the 13th, as the last flight of allied planes left tailed by the Japanese fighters that drove them away, Admiral Inoue cabled the retreat order to Musashi's captain, Toshihira Inoguchi. The big dreadnought had done its job. It sank an enemy battleship and also shot down several planes. But staying in Milne Bay, where it could not maneuver, was asking for trouble.

So, the captain scrambled the ship's engine to leave the bay. Still, as the boat was turning about to escape toward the Coral Sea and safety, several reports were radioed in about the arrival of several enemy ground units near the Japanese Army 89th division's positions. Fighting was erupting between the two forces.

Not long after that, a request from the division commander came in for fire support. Inogushi, while firmly committed to obeying his orders to leave, decided that he would get his gunners to send some parting gifts to the foolish allied soldiers advancing on the 89th's defenses near a small airstrip they'd just occupied.

"Lieutenant Hatamura," said Toshihira. "Yes, sir." "Get gunnery control to fire at the coordinates given by the soldiers on the ground in Milne Bay. It's time to show our enemies that they should not have come here." The deck officer nodded with the usual respectful bow before calling the gunnery officer below deck. Everyone on the battleship was smiling. They knew that they were about to create mayhem for their damned enemies.

The big Japanese vessel fired its first broadside a minute later. The water in front of it rippled, and the blast of its shell vaporized water amidst a large fire cloud. The 460mm ordinances traveled to their destinations in mere milliseconds (they were so close to the shore they could see the soldiers shooting at each other). The explosions they created lifted gigantic mounds of earth high in the sky and obliterated allied soldiers. The craters they made were truly deep and massive.

When Musashi and its escorts had turned entirely away and stopped firing, the allied camp was but ashes, dead and smoking ground. The 10th Division's recon battalion had been utterly obliterated.

The Japanese 89th Division commander then ordered the assault across the small river they'd been defending and sent his men to storm the enemy position. The surviving defenders didn't even put up a fight. They were either out cold or simply surrendered, completely dazed.

The Japanese troops pushed some more toward the shore and started to advance inland toward the trail that crossed the mountains on the south coast of New Guinea. There the rest of the 10th Division awaited them in the relative safety of the interior. The lesson for the Allies was that when Musashi was in the vicinity, it was better to hide.

Extract from General MacArthur's book, Reminiscences, 1964
Holding the tide, July 15th, 1942

The was no helping it. The summer of 1942 was a very dark period for the Allies and the defense of Australia. Our struggle could be divided into two distinct parts. The first one on the Western Coast of the country and the second one on our desperate campaign to hold on to Port Moresby.

The main problem facing us was not an issue of position or combat-effectiveness, nor lack of motivation on the part of the Aussies. We were simply at a disadvantage in terms of ships and planes. On the ground, we could cope, as the Australian was levying more troops, and several U.S. Army and Marines reinforcements were due to arrive by the end of the summer through the *"milk run"* sea route.

The sudden appearance of a second Japanese super-battleship in the theater shocked everyone in high command. The Musashi, as the Japs called the behemoth, had made short work of the aging New York and severely damaged Washington, putting our forces at zero active battleships in the theater, while the enemy had the before-mentioned dreadnoughts and four more (Yamashiro, Ise, Tosa, Hyuga), countless heavy cruisers and support ships.

While a pretty brave and competent officer, Admiral Leahy could simply not cope with that measure of firepower. I resolved on the 15th to discuss this with the Admiral and to agree on avoiding any more surface battles with the Imperial Navy for the time being.

Some reinforcements were, however, announced to Australia. Namely the new battleship Massachusetts, a few cruisers and many destroyers, submarines, and a few light carriers.

Only in the air did we hold our own, with some measure of success over the Owen Stanley Range and in the battle of Milne Bay. We even sunk a light carrier during the battle, which was welcome news.

According to the OSS intercept and message decoding, the Japanese only had two carriers left in the theater, as we did. (We'd sunk Ryujo, and Taiyo was under repairs somewhere out of the immediate area).

But through it all, I was never worried about most of those aspects. Even the Imperial Army's invasion of Western Australia did not really concern me. It was a vast place to invade, and the Japanese could only be effective in taking the coastal towns. Once they were done (even if they took Perth in the south), that was that. They would have to send many more troops to subdue a continent, and these troops were spread thin everywhere else.

The true place I was concerned about was the Coral Sea-Solomon Island-Port Moresby theater. Without a victory in that huge sector, there could be a potential invasion of the heart of Australia (Cairns, Brisbane, Sydney), which would really hurt us. Also, no liberation offensive could be contemplated until we retook New Britain and some of the Solomon Islands. Finally, as long as the damned Japs held the set of islands ringing the Coral Sea and the approaches to Australia, no real reinforcements (or something that I could count on to arrive regularly anyway) would be possible.

In the dark days of the 1942 summer, nothing could be done about such things but defend desperately with everything we had and put a good dose of grit and determination into our efforts.

As the land battle in Milne Bay unfolded by the middle of the day on the 15th, I stayed glued to the radio for reports of the struggle's progress. We needed to win there since, if not, the Japs would be able to burst onto the southern coast and outflank the Australian-American forces fighting in the Owen Stanley Range (Kokoda Track) and Port Moresby.

The third Battle of Palmyra
The Japanese regain the island July 16th, 1942

The powerful Japanese Combined Fleet sortied from Pearl Harbor on the 14th of July with everything that Yamamoto had afloat that could fire in anger. It was finally time for Operation Mi.

The highly complex operation mounted by the Grand Admiral had one primary objective, with a recently added secondary objective. The Imperial Navy's goal was to lure the American fleet out of San Diego and to get into an air and surface battle with the powerful elements of the fleet. The big gun battle that would end it all was what the Japanese hoped to achieve, as their fathers and grandfathers had done in the battle of Tsushima in 1905. The group of ships sortied into three powerful task forces. The central one was composed of Kido Butai (the carriers) and its escorting ships, while the other two were filled to the brim with big gun ships (battleships, heavy cruisers, and the like).

Taskforce 1 was the carrier strike force (Kido Butai), with Akagi, Kaga, Shokaku, Zuikaku, Soryu, and Hiryu, flanked by twenty destroyers, five light cruisers, plus heavy cruisers Myoko.

Taskforce 2 sported the Japanese dreadnoughts battleships supposed to destroy the Yankees, led by Yamato, Nagato, and Hiei. Heavy cruisers Tone and Kinusaga, three light cruisers, and four destroyers also composed the mighty group.

Taskforce 3 was also powerful, with dreadnoughts battleships Kongo, Mutsu, and Fuso flanked my heavy cruisers Maya and Chikuma, plus two light cruisers and three destroyers.

But before they sailed to challenge the U.S. Navy, the men of the Combined Fleet would accomplish their secondary task. They would attack and retake the tiny atoll of Palmyra, which had recently been attacked and invaded by U.S. Marines, led by a small fleet that had boldly sailed into the area.

In order to reclaim the atoll, Grand Admiral Yamamoto brought along the 45th Imperial Regiment along with a detachment of Type 95 tanks since some American armor had been reported by the frantic radio calls from the SNLF Marines who had been defeated by the Americans.

The battle for Palmyra opened with a mighty shore bombardment from Taskforce 2 and Taskforce 3. The six battleships and five heavy cruisers pounded the already battered ground and defenses for a few hours while a coordinated 200-plane strike from Kido-Butai leveled anything in sight.

A few hours later, by 1500 in the afternoon, the first Japanese boots were on the ground, and no resistance was encountered. They advanced inland and again did not encounter enemy soldiers. They pushed through the rest of the atoll and reported that they'd secured Palmyra after a few hours and that no enemy troops were in sight anywhere.

Indeed, the United States, not in the business of leaving troops to die in a futile defense, came to pick up every one of the brave Marines that had conquered Palmyra. It had been a close call, with the last transport ships and destroyers leaving the place with captured Chitose in tow the day before. The Americans had known Yamamoto was coming, as they had intercepted several radio communications and decoded them.

If Yamamoto had been really thorough, he would have found the small task force speeding southward, laden with troops and only escorted by a few destroyers and the former Imperial Navy seaplane tender.

But as it was, the Grand Admiral's design was only to retake the atoll and then move on to the next step of his operation. After receiving the report of the successful reconquest of Palmyra, he ordered all three task forces back on their planned heading for San Diego.

The Battle of Milne Bay Part 2
Aussies vs Japs, July 15th to 18th, 1942

After the Musashi shore bombardment and the subsequent Japanese assault at the feeble allied lines (not all of the 10th Division was at the frontline on the 15th), the 89th Imperial Division swept most of Milne Bay's coastal plain and pushed all the way to the track that led to the low hills ending on the southern coast of New Guinea and their objective, Port Moresby.

On the 16th of July, the Australian-British and American forces of the 10th Division were able to stop them somewhere on the road after the last airfield in the small town of Gurney was stormed by the Imperial troops. The Japanese plan was to walk all around the coastline toward Port Moresby in order to avoid the Owen Stanley Range. They'd also heard of local mountain tracks between Milne Bay and Abau (which was the track the Allies had taken to get to Milne Bay).

The Allies entrenched themselves and came with heavy equipment, like small field guns and the like, while the Japanese forces were traveling light as it had been planned to either have the battleship Musashi supporting them with shore bombardment or else the Imperial Air Force.

But things had not really gone that way. First of all, Musashi had to evacuate Milne Bay because of fear of air attacks and insufficient air coverage (the Navy even lost carrier Ryujo in the operation), and second, the Allies showed up over the theater with unexpected air strength (the reinforcements brought by the Liberty convoy ships were starting to have an impact). This made for a pretty even battle in the sky, sort of negating Japanese air superiority.

So, the situation made for a pure infantry battle, where the defenders (Allies) were in an advantageous position, first because of the area they'd chosen to defend. They were high up in the hills and even in higher elevations, while the Japanese forces were relegated to the Milne Bay coastal plain.

But most important of all, the Aussie had come to battle with more than sufficient supplies of Quinine to fight off the dreaded Malaria sickness that was prevalent in the region. In contrast, the Japs had not brought enough or simply didn't have any.

It didn't take long for many in the 89th Imperial Division to fall sick, and so because of this, the Japanese commander lost over twenty percent of his men, which had to be brought back to the rear.

Both sides sort of fell into a stalemated battle where trench warfare, disease, and lousy weather dominated. By the 18th, the Nipponese commander radioed back to headquarters that he would not be able to advance any further. Some preliminary discussions were held between Admiral Inoue and the Army about sending reinforcements escorted by battleship Musashi and the two other battleships that had just arrived from 1st Fleet (Yamashiro and Hyuga). But in the end, the idea was abandoned because of insufficient air cover.

The problem was worsened a couple of days later when the first much-needed Japanese convoy was sunk at the mouth of Milne Bay by two Dutch-American submarines, causing much hardship and ammo shortages amongst Imperial forces. By the 20th of July, the 10th Division commander sent a message to General MacArthur that he didn't have to worry about Milne Bay for the duration.

Another Japanese offensive plan against Port Moresby had been foiled (for the third time).

Beyond Rangoon
Fighting the Chinese in Toungoo, July 16th, 1942

Private Soldier Ishiro Tanaka was fighting and wondered where he was. Well, he knew they were north of Rangoon after having conquered the city some time ago. He also knew that they were inching toward Lashio to eventually cut the Burma Road, the last overland supply route into China, but that was about it. The fucking officers never told them anything worth a damn, and he hated them all for it.

He was back slugging it out with the hated enemy, the Chinese. To the rugged soldier, they were the only enemy worth fighting against, for they needed to be removed from the face of the earth.

Over the years of fighting in mainland China, he'd learned to hate them so thoroughly that it almost blinded him with fury every time he was ordered to fire a rifle in anger at them.

Blessedly, he'd been again ordered to do so in the battle of Toungoo. He'd given up on getting to face Nationalist forces after being transferred to the Asian Southeast. Still, they'd decided they hadn't had enough of him and the Japanese, for they asked not only to be beaten up in their country but also in Burma!

Tanaka was but a simple soldier with limited information (and he didn't want more), so he didn't know that the reason the Chinese had come to the help of the Allies was because of the threat the Japanese offensive represented to their last lifeline of supply from the external world, the Burma Road.

But little details like these did not and could not bother Ishiro in the least, for he was a fighter, and he fought what they who and where they told him to.

It's just that he was enjoying it more against the Chinese. As he got up to fire his rifle from the makeshift trench he'd hidden into, he had a fleeting thought about Chinese women. It was too bad that they weren't in China proper. Their women were lively. He'd been disappointed by the lack of good-looking women in Rangoon. The Burmese girls were filthy and ugly. Not anywhere near the beauty of a Japanese girl or a Chinese girl. He smiled thinly, and an observer could have been mistaken in thinking that the Japanese soldier did so because he had hit an opponent, but Tanaka had some happy thoughts about his last woman in Rangoon. She had not been really cooperative, just like he wanted them. Ugly but lively. Yes, that was it. He grumbled as he reloaded his rifle, again hidden in his hole.

"Tanaka!" yelled their officer, hitting him with the butt of his samurai saber. *"What the fuck are you doing! It's taking you forever to reload. The fucking Chinese are charging us. Hurry up, man!" "Yes, sir."* Ishiro looked at the officer who was already walking down the line doing the same to the other soldier, admonishing him for slow reloading. His eyes bore down on the samurai-holding man and locked tight on his back, with pure mischief in mind. It was common for Japanese officers to be found with a bullet in their back after a battle; they were really hard on the men. Tanaka resolved that he would shoot the bastard if got the chance.

He stood up again to fire his Arisaka Rifle, aiming at another poor Chinese soldier running toward them. He hit the man in the shoulder, throwing him violently backward. He was sure he didn't kill his enemy, but that didn't matter. He crouched again to reload, and then, as he was just about done, the Chinese charge had reached their position. One of them jumped into the makeshift trench (it was more like a small irrigation trench). Tanaka dropped on his back, aiming at his enemy flying toward him, and fired his weapon, hitting the Nationalist soldier right in the belly, folding the man in two and pushing him back out of the hole as if a giant invisible hand had yanked him back to throw him away.

The rest of the fight was a confused mass of bodies that could barely discern friends from foes in the tight confines of the waterway. Ishiro drew the long knife he picked up in Rangoon from an injured allied Gurka officer he'd found in a street alley. He thrust several times at another soldier's back, piercing the man's lung.

Then, he turned just in time to face a yelling Nationalist trying to hit him with the butt of his rifle. He slashed the knife in a broad stroke and cut his throat. The Chinese fell to the ground in a weird, gurgling sound.

The fierce and confused struggle in the waterway repeated itself across an immense battlefield where the Chinese and Japanese rehearsed another scene of their long, bloody war.

Long after the sun was down and the Chinese in retreat, Tanaka walked the body-littered battlefield and came up to one officer with a bullet in his back. He smiled, thinking of the moment he'd released the bullet and picked up the man's samurai sword. He slung the weapon's sheath across his chest to press the blade against his back. He would not be permitted to keep it, but if he moved fast enough, he could get some good money for it.

CHAPTER 4

Ambush in the Sunda Strait
Wahoo attacks between Java and Sumatra, July 17th, 1942

It was smack on time. As the radioed information sent to the Wahoo had said a few days ago, a major Japanese convoy was about to sail through the Sunda Strait. Skipper Jim Cloutier didn't know how Allied Command had known that the Japs would sail during that specific time frame, but in the end, it didn't matter. As long as he had a nice fat convoy to sink.

One of the main reasons for the Japanese invasion of the Dutch East Indies was that it had several oilfields. The convoy that was in full view of Cloutier's periscope was sailing from Padang on the southern coast of the Island of Sumatra. It had to transit through the Sunda Strait in order to get to the Java Sea and then head for the Japanese refineries in the Home Islands.

The group of ships was advancing in a triple line, with five ships (the oil tankers and a destroyer in the front) in the center and one destroyer on each side. Jim still had his eyes glued to the periscope as he ordered the torpedo operator behind him (American subs in 1942 were tight, and the crew had to work into small confines) to fire. *"Open up with forward tubes one and two, sailor." "Yes, Sir."* And the torpedoes were away.

As he watched their wakes speed toward the enemy ships, creating a slight ripple on the water's surface, he mumbled a silent prayer for the damned defective Mark XIV torpedoes to explode. Hell, it could even miss the boat Wahoo had aimed. The things were faulty weapons, and while Navy command was now acutely aware of the issue, there hadn't been anything done as of yet to correct the problems.

The weapons raced to their target, the second ship in the line, as Wahoo faced the Japanese vessels. And then nothing. He couldn't see the torpedoes' wakes nor any explosion. But the sound operator (the man responsible for listening to sounds in the water to watch for other ships and submarines) was the next one to talk. *"Sir. Two loud metallic clangs noises into the water. The fish have hit the target but failed to explode." "No shit, sailor,"* was Cloutier's answer. *"Fire away with all four remaining forward tubes, and then let's dive. Those destroyers will sure come our way to try and sink us."*

And the wahoo spat its four remaining Mark XIV (the Gato-Class submarine had six forward torpedo tubes) at the now wildly evading enemy ships. As he lowered the periscope, he saw that two of the destroyers were speeding their way. They had maybe ten minutes before the enemy vessels were on top of them. Ten minutes to figure out where to go and how to dodge, for the wahoo could only do nine knots submerged, while any Japanese destroyers could do at least thirty-four.

The best tactic was often just to play dead and dive the boat all the way to the bottom or close to it. "Dive to the bottom," he ordered. "And then cut off all engines."

The submarine slid quietly and slowly to the Sunda Strait's seafloor and came to rest on a muddy patch. The area wasn't reputed deep, so Cloutier decided that it was their best play. At their turtle-crawling speed, they had no chance to evade if they were picked up by sonar, and the shallow depth would give a lot more probability of getting hit by a depth charge.

Then, the all-quiet order was passed along the entire length of the ship. After a moment, they started to hear the Japanese propellers approaching closer and closer. This was the most nerve-wracking moment in submarine operations. The moment when the enemy was almost on top of you, and you didn't know if they would fire depth charges at you.

Another minute and the destroyers were right on top of Wahoo's position. Jim had chosen to drop dead exactly where he'd fired from, hoping that the Japanese captains would figure that he'd tried to move away a little in the ten minutes he'd been given.

The characteristic radar noise was heard, getting nearer and nearer until the propeller's noise started to ebb away a little. Apparently, the enemy had taken the sub skipper's bait and assumed that the Americans had either backed up or moved away. The Japs started to drop depth charges in the ocean, but they were far away from the Wahoo, so they remained unscathed apart from making things shake a little in the vessel.

On the surface, one of the Mark XIV had providentially exploded and gutted an oil tanker, putting it afire. The ship sunk in not even twenty minutes and left a sizeable oily patch on the ocean's surface.

Second Battle of Hawaii Part 1
500 nautical miles east off Oahu, early hours of July 21st to July 22nd

Two powerful task forces were gliding on the calm, mirror-like ocean. Both centered on American aircraft carriers—Task Force One, with the Wasp and Yorktown in the middle. Sailing around them were a multitude of surface ships, amongst others, the battleships South Dakota, California, and Tennessee, just recently patched up for the upcoming battle. Taskforce Two, sailing with Hornet, was ringed with the protection of battleships Maryland, Colorado, and West Virginia. Another smaller task force (French) stayed close to Task Force 2 to protect the carriers, including Bretagne and Lorraine's battleships and three cruisers (Duquesne, Tourville, and Foch).

Admiral Nimitz, named by the Navy's overall commander to head the force and command the Pacific theater, was in Task Force Two. He sailed on his flagship, the battleship Maryland. Admiral Fletcher, one of the commanders of Operation Black Snake in the Atlantic against the Axis in 1941, was heading the 1st task force (on South Dakota). The plan was to surprise and challenge the Imperial Navy, which was also out to raid San Diego (according to the Magic decoding services of the OSS). The enemy was reported to have six carriers and over seven battleships bearing down on the West Coast, along with many smaller ships. Hence, the whole thing was no leisurely stroll in the Pacific, even if the U.S. forces knew their enemy was coming and approximately the direction they were sailing.

The American strategy was centered on the fact that it first needed to retake the unavoidable Pearl Harbor base on Oahu in the Hawaii Islands. Only from there could they seriously contemplate organizing and supplying their fleets to attack the Japanese in the enormous Pacific Ocean. The distance involved in such a war was mind-boggling. It represented so many logistical difficulties that it was just impossible to launch from San Diego, especially since the damned Japs occupied everything else that mattered in the theater, starting with Johnson Island, American Samoa, Palmyra, the Gilbert Islands, the Marshalls, and many more. There simply wasn't any harbor for the Allies to use in the Pacific. Pearl, being 3,200 miles away from the U.S. Mainland, was the great base from which to send forth America's hordes of liberation. From there, they could rebuild the oil facilities, ship repair facilities, planes, and everything needed to fight a modern war in terms of logistics. Then, the American war machine would deploy in earnest and destroy the Japanese Empire. But that line of thought was only wishful thinking in the Summer of 1942. The Imperial Navy reigned supreme, and the Americans reeled from one disaster to the other. They could only react and hope for the best until such time that their shipyards and production facilities started to churn out the units they needed to vanquish Yamamoto and his ships.

Yamamoto knew that the Hawaiian Islands were critical to the outcome of the Pacific War. It was why he'd conquered the place in March 1942 and then got busy cramming it with fighters and soldiers. It was also why the Combined Fleet was based in Pearl Harbor.

There were no specific plans for a return to Hawaii in 1942, but the U.S. Navy's objective was to get the Japanese fleet to sortie, engage it, and *"trim it down a little,"* as per Admiral King's (the U.S. Navy Commander-in-Chief) words. America was not strong enough to simply overwhelm the Japs at that moment in time, so it needed to stay away from any slugging match.

The Magic decryption unit, which had broken the Japanese codes, enabled the U.S. forces to *"read Japan's mail"* and have a good idea of what Yamamoto was planning and where. The Navy had been ready to move when the enemy fleet would sortie. Just such an opportunity had presented itself about a week before with the Combined Fleet's so-called *"Operation Mi,"* a new raid on San Diego.

In preparation for their tactical move, Nimitz and King had decided to completely evacuate Palmyra, as it was the first part of the Japanese plan and the entire Combined Fleet was sailing to the small island to land troops to reclaim it. The island was impossible to defend in strength, and since the entire enemy force planned to sail there before swinging northeast toward San Diego to execute its attack, the whole affair was a foregone conclusion. While the Japanese might have kept their soldiers there if the roles were reversed, America wasn't in the game of sending troops to the slaughter.

For a second raid on San Diego, the Imperial fleet sortied with six carriers, seven battleships, and more than fifty other cruisers, heavy cruisers, and support ships. The Grand Admiral was again making his play for the mainland and the main U.S. Navy base on the West Coast, but this time with everything available on hand.

Yamamoto was a great strategist and a great leader, but nothing could be straightforward with him. Japanese naval doctrine was based on the battle of annihilation, or decisive battle (the Kentai Kessen Doctrine), to win the war. The Nipponese admiral believed in this doctrine, as he had been a student (like all of his contemporary fleet officers) of the incredible 1905 victory of the Battle of Tsushima, where the then Japanese fleet had wholly destroyed the extensive Russian Baltic Fleet and thus won the war against Tsarist Russia in a single day.

The victory, led by none other than the legendary Admiral Togo, had launched Japan on the world scene and confirmed its status as a world power. The 1942 commander-in-chief of the Japanese Navy wanted to emulate his illustrious predecessor. To achieve this, he prepared a second raid on San Diego. Its objective was to draw the U.S. Navy out to Sea. With an intricate sequence of complicated maneuvers and layered task forces, Japan would catch, fight, and ultimately destroy the Americans. Thus, the Japanese Navy was very obvious about it and wanted their Yankee enemy to sortie to face them. Quite frankly, the Americans would not have needed to have any code-breaking advance notice of the attack since Yamamoto's strategy was to be direct and draw the Americans out to destroy them in one giant battle. The Grand Admiral was all too aware of America's prodigious industrial potential and wanted to destroy the U.S. vessels while he still had some form of numerical and qualitative advantage.

In Tokyo, both Marshal Hajime and Prime Minister Tojo believed that a significant victory at sea would bring Washington to the negotiating table. Yamamoto also agreed. While the three men had argued considerably about the Empire's wish to invade Australia and Burma/India, they agreed that something needed to be done about the U.S. fleet.

And so, the most powerful naval force of the day was out at sea and hunting. Little did it know that the USA knew about all the details and that it could become the hunted.

The central task force of six top-of-the-line carriers would be in the lead, with an extensive screening force of almost thirty ships, including destroyers, the best anti-aircraft cruisers, and two fast battleships, the Hiei and the Kongo. There would be two more large task forces on the *"flanks,"* north and south, where most of the big gun battleships would be located. Yamamoto banked on the American, being drawn in by Admiral Nagumo's carrier strike force to try and destroy it.

Once the enemy moved too deep toward Kido Butai (another name for Japan's leading carrier task force), the Grand Admiral would fork his flanking fleets north and south and close the jaws on the unsuspecting U.S. Navy. He then hoped that he would be able to bring his big guns to bear and destroy the enemy. A close-in knife fight would be won by the Japanese as they had the most battleships and other big gunships.

Japanese naval intelligence believed that out of the five known U.S. main fleet carriers, three were in the Pacific. The others elsewhere in the World because the U.S. Navy had obligations in the European theater against Nazi Germany and Fascist Italy.

Japan had a significant advantage in numbers over the USA regarding aeronaval capability. Yamamoto hoped that the fleet would find and destroy the American flattops. Finally, in true dreadnought battle tradition, he also predicted that the U.S. Navy would try to use its battleships and other surface units to finish the rest of Japan's surface units. The hoped-for Tsushima-type battle would occur somewhere near the American coast. The Imperial Navy, with its numerical superiority, would win the day and send the enemy to the bottom, thus confirming Japan's supremacy at sea and bringing the U.S. President to the negotiating table.

Finally, most Nipponese submarines in the area were positioned near the U.S. Coast and in a great arc facing the Hawaiian Islands about 400 miles out. The submarine screen would thus advance together with the rest of the Navy on its course for San Diego.

As it was, even if the Americans knew the Japs were at sea, they still had a battle to fight and win. Their knowledge of where the Japs were didn't change the fact that they were outnumbered in every ship category, most notably in aircraft carriers.

From Rabaul to Lae
Takashi Onishi in Lae on the New Guinean coast, July 1942

He'd hoped for something better. Well, it had looked better than Rabaul. The major Japanese base might have been a necessary military installation for the Empire; it was not a pleasant place to live in. The city, formerly the administrative center of the Australian-mandated territory of New Britain, had been destroyed by a major volcanic eruption in 1937.

The harbor had still been workable, so the Japanese had decided to use it for their own devices and took over the area. But it was still heavily covered with volcanic ashes, and the ground shook every now and then from the volcano that was still spurting smoke and rocks. Some lava also fell down its side. To Onishi, it was like hell. The airbase they'd been in was not much better, as the runway was dark with volcanic ash, and their accommodation, an old and worn-down hangar, was dirty and had a sulfur odor like the rest of the god-forsaken place.

Understandably, Onishi and his squadron's mates were consequently happy when they received the orders to transfer to the Lae airfield on the northern coast of New Guinea. Finally, they would be rid of the stinking place!

Flying over the small, non-descript airfield, he'd first been reasonably optimistic about the look of the place. Just maybe, for once, the Army would think of their pilot's comforts, for the Empire wasn't known for the best accommodations for its fighting men. The country lacked the resources to take care of its troops properly, as its logistical arm (not the most prestigious of assignment in the Imperial forces) struggled to keep up with the exponential expansion of Japan's border and the unimaginable distances it had to travel to get the supplies to the men.

And then he'd landed on one of the most worn-down airfields of his career, and there had started the disappointment. The runway was short as Lae was hemmed between mountains and sea, so it wasn't even entirely level. It went down in a gentle slope from the low hills all the way to the sea. It was also a short airfield, only long enough for nimble zeroes to take off. Anything heavier could not be stationed at the airport.

The place didn't have a control tower and only had an old, bullet-riddled hangar to house the planes (the Allied frequently raided Lae from Port Moresby). As Onishi discovered, pilot accommodation hadn't been much better than Rabaul. The foul sulfur smell was indeed gone, replaced by the humid, pest-infested, and mosquitos-thick hospitality of the New Guinean jungle. Malaria was also very present, but luckily, they had some Quinine to get treated when they caught the damned disease.

Takashi hated the place, but he had to give it to high command. They were a lot closer to the action and had shortened their flight time to Port Moresby and the Coral Sea in a considerable manner by being posted in Lae. Within a few hours (two at most), they would be over the Australian base and back by lunch if they flew out right after breakfast at 8 in the morning.

Not that it was something to look forward to, as Japanese rations were not a lot of a hell better than what their logistical arms could provide. Steamed rice and some canned meat or fish when they were lucky.

Second Battle of Hawaii Part 2
400 nautical miles east of Hawaii, July 21st to July 22nd

Naval battles were often decided by the side that detected the other first. In the age of battleships and gunnery, it had been an advantage, but nothing that the other fleet could not overcome, as once the first salvos were fired, they could usually fire back if they had the same class of ships. But during the Second World War, where carriers ruled the waves, it was a matter of who detected the other first.

In this case, fate balanced in favor of the Combined Fleet. It wasn't because the Americans had known the Japs would sail to attack the mainland that they knew exactly where to find them in the immensity of the Pacific Ocean. The Imperial Navy spotted the enemy fleet (cruiser Reno) first because of their excellent long-range submarines sent as a screening force before the rest of their comrades. The information was quickly radioed back 400 miles west, where Kido Butai sailed. Admiral Nagumo, the commander of the task force of six carriers, immediately sent orders for the search operations to begin. The submarines had not spotted any capital ships (battleships or aircraft carriers) yet.

With planes searching in an arc covering the western sea they were facing, the Americans had not yet found anything, most of the Japanese fleet being out of range. At midday, carrier Shokaku, Zuikaku, and Akagi were ordered to scramble their planes for a strike on the ships that had been spotted by the submarines. One of the most forward, the American Task Force One, comprised two cruisers of the Atlanta class (San Diego and Reno) and five destroyers. The carrier planes reached their destination and found their targets by about 14h00. 150 planes descended on the ships. The American ships blazed with their flak at the sky full of Japanese. The area above the small U.S. Navy task force was quickly filled with flak tracers and hundreds upon hundreds of the resulting flak explosions.

It was no easy feat to hit a plane in flight as they dove at full speed toward a ship or else try to destroy one as it lined up to launch its torpedo, and the success rate tended to be relatively low. Nonetheless, the gunners from cruiser San Diego, one of the most modern in the fleet, were able to down five Aichi D3A dive bombers. Two exploded in mid-air since they were hit directly, and the other three trailed smoke and either crashed or limped back to their carriers (none would make it back that day). The Reno did its part by downing one, and the destroyers collectively hit theirs as well.

Amidst the chaos, two Japanese submarines also approached and launched their torpedoes at the enemy. After the Japanese planes ran the flak gauntlet, they loosed their ordinance while the subs did the same. The weapons raced to their intended target, and many hit home. The two cruisers and the five destroyers dodged madly and avoided several of the enemy weapons, but in the end, the volume of fire got the better of them, and they were hit by several torpedoes.

When the Japanese strike force headed for home, three destroyers were sunk, one cruiser (Reno) was listing heavily to port, and San Diego sported a large fire amidship. All U.S. vessels were hit, but the Japanese did not hit anything critical.

A few hours later, planes from Akagi returned and finished the job, sinking the two stricken cruisers that were easy to spot with their large plumes of dark smoke that gave their presence away as far as ten kilometers out. The ships didn't even put up a serious fight; most of their flak guns were either silenced or their handlers dead or busy trying to save their boat. The Nipponese pilots planted their torpedoes in the sinking vessels just for good measure and turned back toward their carriers.

The Japanese strike force headed home in a victorious mood.

Second Battle of Hawaii Part 3
The airstrike on the American Task Force, July 21st

The Atlanta class cruisers were impressive ships and sported very potent anti-aircraft defenses against Japanese air assets. The American vessels packed a lot of punch for such small vessels, and Minoru Genda got to appreciate their full fury as one of his two wingmen, Lieutenant Honda was blown out of the sky with a direct hit as they were lining up to drop their torpedo in the water. The air commander's plane shook from the blast and even received some shrapnel, but the damage was superficial.

The fire coming out of the twin cruisers, bunched up together with the destroyers to concentrate their effectiveness, was truly unique, and Minoru wondered if the Americans had the same armament on each of their ships. He dreaded to find out what type of weaponry the same design could do if mounted on a battleship.

While he was counting down the seconds in order to drop his torpedo, he wondered why Japan had not done the same to its ship. To a man like Genda, the threat of carrier-based planes was now too obvious to ignore. The war would be won by planes, not big guns dreadnoughts. He hoped the Imperial Navy would beef up the anti-aircraft defenses on its own ships.

He shook his head to focus himself once more, deciding it was pointless to ponder on things he had no control over, and more importantly, he had better things to do than worry about what might be or what might have been. He had ships to sink. He pushed the release button to drop his *"fish"* into the water and banked hard right, pulling the plane's lever toward him to raise his altitude as fast and as sharply as possible. American anti-aircraft tracer shells followed him all the way but missed, the blazing rounds arcing away in the sky. He also sent his Nakajima B5N dive-bomber into a roll to avoid the enemy flak better. Being unpredictable was an excellent way to survive.

As he climbed back to a decent altitude, he tried to see if any enemy planes were coming to their beleaguered friends in the ships. He didn't see any, which was good, but at the same time meant that the enemy carriers were not in the vicinity.

He watched several of his airmen take their turn diving toward the madly dodging ships below. After another ten minutes, all of them had expanded their ammunition, so he ordered everyone back to the carriers.

A few hours later, he was back over the ship and rehearsed the same moves with his men. This time they were less numerous, as the boats were partially destroyed already, and anyway, there didn't seem to be any carriers in the general area around the stricken task force. The end result of that battle was that they sunk both Allied cruisers with ease, as their flak guns had not even fired, their handler either dead or busy elsewhere.

As he flew back for the second time toward Akagi and refueled, he hoped that his next strike mission would be against carriers.

Over the Owen Stanley Range and into Port Moresby
Airstrike, July 22nd, 1942

The Japanese pilots flew from Lae and then directed their planes south toward Buna, where they joined up with the twenty bombers force that would be under their care for the coming strike on Port Moresby.

Takeshi Onishi spotted the incoming twin-engine aircraft that came from Rabaul, and for a moment, he felt terrible for the pilots driving them. Rabaul was such a shit-hole that he thought Lae was a paradise compared to it.

They rapidly approached the Mitsubishi G4M flight. Their squadron commander waggled his wings to signal the lead bomber to follow and bunch up in formation for defense. The tactic was simple. The slow aircraft would all fly close to each other, trying to get an overlapping field of fire with their machine gunners.

As he again gave a long look toward the sleek-looking twin-engine bomber, he hoped that they wouldn't lose too many of them. From earlier attacks on the Australian base, he'd figured that the attrition rate for the aircraft was about 20%, which was pretty high. He wasn't paid to think, but he just felt that it wasn't good odds.

After an hour of flying in a straight line toward the southern coast of New Guinea, they finally came up to the Owen Stanley Mountain range, towering at 15,000 feet. The mountains were gigantic but did not have any snow, given their latitude. Instead, they were covered in thick jungle, making for an impressive wall of greenery. They flew just over the rocky summits, and their view gave way to the beautiful blue immensity of the Coral Sea and its turquoise, vibrant color. If Takashi hadn't been at war and going to kill some Allies, he would have been impressed. But as it was, he was trying to focus on their approach to Port Moresby.

They planned to dive down at full speed from the moment they flew across the mountains at an angle that would get them directly over the Australian base. They knew they would be detected but didn't want to give their enemies any chance of doing something about it.

They'd tried the logical way of doing it. Flying above the town, the Zeros exchanged fire in dogfights, and some G4M's were shot down. Takashi had proposed his idea to the captain, who had decided they would try it. In this plan, the two plane types would use their incredible speed and nimbleness to dive down at full speed, launch their bombs, and strafe at random (the Zeros didn't have bombs, so they would just blaze away with their 20mm canons).

Then they would climb back again at full throttle and turn back over the mountains and back to base. In this way, they hoped they would keep casualties down to a minimum. The only drawback was that they wouldn't aim at anything, just random bombing.

It wasn't something that the high command would have approved of, but the captain was tired of seeing men die and had had some friends over in Rabaul, so he contacted the bomber flight commander the day before they flew to Port Moresby to propose the plan. The man had wholeheartedly agreed. And their gentleman's agreement was that they wouldn't say a word about it, only that their mission was a success.

The Japanese airstrike swooped down menacingly at the town while Allied fighters scrambled in the sky to battle their enemy as usual. But this time, the Japs behaved differently, and the Allied pilots didn't realize what they were doing until it was too late. They took too much altitude, so they overflew the Nipponese pilots while diving.

Onishi and his mates blazed away at anything that chanced itself in front of its targeting sight randomly. The G4M's did the same and dropped their bombs at random "over the city" as they felt like. Then the Japs lifted in unison as high and as fast as possible, turning back toward the mountains.

They even dodged the entirety of the enemy interception force as the Allied fighters tried to compensate for the Japanese dive and followed, so by the time they were almost down at Port Moresby's level, the Axis pilots were already climbing high and at full speed.

The whole squadron flew unscathed over the Owen Stanley's without even a scratch on their paint jobs. They all flew home in great spirits. It wasn't every day that they could boast a successful raid without one death.

Second Battle of Hawaii Part 4
400 nautical miles east of Hawaii, July 21st to July 22nd

The Japanese Navy had sort of been lucky to spot the Allied fleet before its own was detected, but ultimately, it was not great since they'd only found cruisers. They sunk them all right, but that success alone would not win the battle. They needed to find the carriers. But their enemy's proverbial luck was even better than theirs.

The pilots of U.S. carrier Yorktown struck gold. With a well-timed, if lucky, recon flight, they spotted two of the enormous Japanese flattops, the Kaga and Akagi, amongst a large grouping of ships. Soon after that the torpedo bombers from Yorktown launched themselves at the Japanese naval task force, reaching the area they were located at about 1700, under a slowly setting sun. They dove hard and fast but were intercepted by the robust combat air patrol (CAP) of over forty Japanese zero planes. After ten minutes of furious air battles, flak fire, and destroyed American planes, five torpedoes were in the water, all going in the direction of Kaga, who got hit by one of them.

Only ten U.S. pilots made it home to their home ship, but the torpedo had hit Kaga hard on the port side, and the great ship developed a slight list and a raging fire that blocked all aircraft landings for the rest of the operation. At 1800, Admiral Nagumo ordered Kaga to head for Hawaii, escorted by battleship Hiei and several destroyers. The ship started to limp slowly back to the Islands. The Imperial Navy could simply not lose a main fleet carrier as it would not be replaced in a long time, so the Japs didn't take any chance and retired the wounded beast, protected by several escorts, including ten destroyers.

At the end of the day on the 21st, no other fleet detection was made, and the fleets continued to sail toward each other, with the Japanese angling sharply north to try to lose the American spotters while Fletcher and Nimitz continued in a straight charge. The Americans were pretty happy about their first real encounter with the Imperial Navy.

While they lost two excellent heavy cruisers and three destroyers, Nimitz's pilots had hit a Japanese carrier without getting a dent on their own flattops' paint jobs. The American commander banked on another successful day on the 22nd. Nimitz was an aggressive commander who believed in attack, so he continued to charge ahead.

Admiral Fletcher, commanding the other task force near his superior, also agreed to push the attack. The naval odds were still heavily leaning in Japanese favor, but the U.S. Navy had hit an enemy carrier so far, and the Japs had not even attacked either one of Yorktown, Hornet, and Wasp.

As dusk and then night fell on the brave sailors, they resolved to push the attack as hard as they could the very next day and hope for the best. Such was the American way of war. Go for broke and try to win. Japanese mentality was a little different when it came time to consider losing – or saving – a capital ship.

The Imperial Navy had nice and powerful ships, but not many more to replace them if they were lost. Japanese shipbuilding capabilities were well below the American one and Grand Admiral Yamamoto, along with the rest of the Nipponese naval commanders, were acutely aware that capital ship losses were to be avoided at all costs.

Second Battle of Hawaii Part 5
Decision, July 21st-22nd

While the numerically inferior Americans were determined to continue the battle the next day, the Japanese camp viewed the situation differently. Yamamoto had a different set of objectives and felt like he had more to lose by getting stubborn. From his point of view, the surprise he'd sought was gone. It also seemed that the Americans were not behaving as he'd anticipated and only engaged with their carriers (that remained to be detected).

He found it highly unsettling that the U.S. Navy was at sea and apparently in force. Furthermore, it was obvious they'd been out even before he set out of Hawaii. The reports from Nagumo were talking about a large airstrike that came from at least two, probably even three carriers, judging by the number of planes that attacked the Akagi and Kaga. That meant the military intelligence claiming they only had two carriers in the Pacific was wrong.

Furthermore, the enemy seemed to have known where the Imperial Navy would be. If that was the case and they knew the grand Admiral's plan somehow... It was pointless to try and surprise them with his pincer move attack. After all, the best way to win a battle was to be in control, and the Japanese mastermind didn't think he was the one dictating events.

Having studied in America, he knew that Japan could not win a war of attrition against the giant U.S. industrial powerhouse. And while he found himself willing to continue to attack and maybe lose another carrier or two to destroy the U.S. fleet, he quickly pondered the risks against the potential gains.

The raid on San Diego would not happen, and he would be engaged in a full-scale carrier battle if he continued to push aggressively. The Americans were at sea and in force, but their main battle fleet had not yet been detected. Did they even have their battleships in the area?

The Imperial Navy already had one seriously damaged carrier (Kaga), and they still didn't know where the American flattops were. It would be a hazardous situation if the enemy was again able to strike Kido Butai before they were found.

By dusk, he was wavering on the continuation of the fight, and when night fell, he gave in and ordered the fleet to turn west and return to the safety of the Hawaiian Islands. After all, he held the strategic upper hand with Pearl Harbor. As long as he controlled it, the U.S. Navy would have to come his way, which would be predictable. Hence, he had some form of luxury in awaiting the Americans that would have to face his carriers and the multitude of planes that Japan was busy transporting to Oahu and the other Islands in the chain. By the next time the Americans attacked, he hoped it would be in a place of his choosing.

He'd also shown the U.S. Navy the futility of trying to take islands around Pearl Harbor (Palmyra) as he could quickly retake it. Thus, while he may not have been able to execute his *"battle of annihilation"* strategy, he was confident that he would be able to do so eventually, either by another operation like *"MI"* or another one where the Americans attacked the Hawaiian Islands, and he engaged them his carrier plus his land-based aircraft.

Japanese Losses	American Losses
CV Kaga, torpedo hit, damaged.	CA Reno - sunk
	CA San Diego -sunk
	3 DDD sunk

U.S Fleet
Bridge of the Battleship Maryland, July 22nd, 1942

At dawn the very next day, Admiral Nimitz was looking at the glorious view before him from the bridge of his flagship, the battleship Maryland. The ship wasn't the most powerful in the American arsenal, but the Admiral rather liked it for some reason. The ship, originally built as a fleet flagship, came along with a large admiral of the fleet cabin, which helped Nimitz to like it. He also often said to anyone who asked that the ship was his lucky charm.

However, it wasn't just for luck or comfort. It was a well-protected and well-armed ship that could sail at 21 knots. Nimitz had wondered if he would get to see his favored battleship in action at the battle that unfolded the day before, but it seemed that it wouldn't be the case now.

The recon mission reported that the U.S. Navy faced an empty sea in the early morning hours. The few radio intercepts seemed to suggest that the enemy had vacated the area during the night.

He contemplated following the Japs to Hawaii for a moment, as they were still reasonably close to the U.S. Mainland. But he thought about the extreme risks he would take for his fleet. The islands were reportedly full of land-based planes, and there was always the possibility that the whole affair was a feint and that Yamamoto would turn around again and attack. He just didn't know and wouldn't for a while since the Magic decoding services from the OSS weren't instantaneous. Their reports and analysis would take days to get to Nimitz's desk, and the battle would be over by then.

He contacted Fletcher to let him know of his decision and ordered the fleet to go back to San Diego. They'd lost some cruisers but seriously damaged an enemy carrier, so it wasn't a bad day.

.

The Battle of Lashio
Conquering the Burma Road, July 22nd to 29th, 1942

The Burma Road was a critical supply route for the Allies. It linked Lashio, in eastern Burma, with Kunming, in Yunnan province, China. The road snaked upward to China for 717 miles long and was constructed from 1937 to 1939. While not an ideal highway to bring in supplies, the Chinese Nationalist government was forced to do so after the Japanese occupation of the country's coast.

It was an incredible achievement. With over twenty thousand workers and an impressive budget, it was built over a terrain that was all but impassable. But the Chinese and the Allies made it work, fueled by their desperation to get or send supplies. The finished product was a tight, confined, often cliff-edging road across the high mountains and challenging countryside. But it worked.

Since the Chinese army kept a staggering total of forty Imperial Army divisions busy fighting them in China proper, the Japanese high command understandably sought to cut the link between their enemies and the outside world. General Hisaichi Terauchi's 15th Army was thus tasked with conquering northern Burma and the city of Lashio in particular.

Ishiro Tanaka, a soldier in the elite 18th Imperial Division, advanced cautiously behind the Type 94 tank's protection, rifle leveled and at the ready. The enemy bullets were ricocheting on the tank's armored hull, and while he felt somewhat safe, it wasn't unheard of to receive a stray bullet after it hit the tank, so he advanced while crouching low. It didn't make one difference in the world, but it gave him the impression that he did something about the situation. He was followed and flanked by his mates from the squad and many others from the Division.

As he advanced, he tried not to look too much at the ground as the unit advanced over a ground littered with dead Chinese soldiers. The

Type 94 tanks rolled over the bodies quite easily, but the result wasn't pretty for the defunct. Once the track had mashed them up, they were nothing more than mangled flesh. Even a man like Ishiro, who had seen it all, found it difficult not to retch and throw up like several of the men did (especially the new, raw recruits who had arrived from the Home Islands).

The 15th Army's campaign was going well. After their victory in Toungoo, General Terauchi ordered them to pursue the retreating Allies, and they pushed them hard for the last week. Still, then the Anglo-Chinese had decided to make their final stand at the city of Lashio, at someplace that was the beginning of the so-called "Burma Road." Their new officer, a fellow named Yamagashi Togun, had not told them a lot about the place nor why the Imperial Army wanted the city. In typical and arrogant Japanese officer fashion, he told them what they needed to know; their victory in Lashio would cut the Chinese supplies and help their brothers in China proper.

Tanaka had accepted the info for what it was. Besides, he'd fought in China and knew how difficult the conditions were. He was happy to hurt the damned Nationalists so the rest of the Army in China could finish them and come help in the Pacific.

He looked at Togun's back for a moment as the fellow was in front of him, closest to the tank (for maximum protection). Tanaka had not decided yet what to do with him. He resolved to wait for a little, as anyway, if he killed this one, the Army would just send another.

Inwardly, he smiled. He was proud of having killed three officers so far in his career. It wasn't something anyone talked about in the unit, but everyone knew that the officers had been killed by one of their own. It was sort of a common practice in the Imperial Army, so nothing was considered amiss.

Suddenly, a giant blast rocked the ground and showered them with dirt. Togun called for them to continue to advance. Their orders were to take the small wooden ridge just on the left of the town of Lashio by the railway. Once taken, it would unhinge the whole Allied line. That was why they'd been supplied with the tanks; otherwise, the brass would have just ordered them to charge without a care for the casualties.

Then, more explosions started to swamp their position. The Allies had launched a powerful artillery attack on their section of the line. Ishiro's world rocked and shook as he was thrown off his feet by a nearby shell that landed on a Type 94, opening it like a tin can and igniting a catastrophic explosion that engulfed no less than 25 Imperial soldiers (none that was close by would survive the blast).

He was hurled in the air by the powerful blast and landed flat on his back, saved from severe injury by his backpack and the large golden flag he'd looted back in a town near Rangoon. It took him some time to get back to his senses. After about a few additional minutes, he finally understood where he was and what was happening.

He'd been rocketed away from most of the danger area, as the shells were still falling and exploding amongst his comrades. He could see at least four of the tanks wholly gutted and dozens of Japanese soldiers dead or with ghastly injuries.

The explosions fell in succession, blasting the earth and sending dirt, men, and tank parts in the air in towering pillars of debris. Tanaka saw his new officer, Togun, saber in the air, urging the men forward through it all. At least the damned man was brave.

That convinced him to pick himself up and run the shelling gauntlet. He couldn't find his own rifle, so he took one from the many dead soldiers lying around everywhere. As he ran, he fell two more times, as the ground shook so much from the shelling that it was difficult to keep his balance.

All semblance of order was gone from the unit, and it was everyone for himself as they ran toward the Chinese position. The ridge they were defending was a slight rise in the otherwise level ground, so most Imperial soldiers arrived on top of it, panting. But Ishiro didn't notice it, as adrenaline was flooding his veins, and the craziness of battle engulfed his rational mind.

The Japanese soldiers jumped the Chinese position, and a furious hand-to-hand battle ensued. It was a struggle born out of both sides' epic hate for the other and the bitterness of their conflict, devastating China and neighboring nations since 1937.

Tanaka trusted with his bayonet-tipped rifle and pierced a few enemy soldiers before he got his own grazing injury on the left shoulder from an enemy bullet, knocking him out cold as he fell and hit his head on a rock.

His battle was done, but his comrades continued it and finished the Chinese. No prisoners were taken, as was the usual way of doing things between the two belligerents.

The town of Lashio would end up falling a few days later to the 15th Army, effectively cutting the Burma Road and all supplies to China. Ishiro was all fine after a day in the field hospital. The wound to his shoulder was superficial, and he only got a big bruise on the head. He was thus back on duty the very next day.

Back in Pearl
Yamamoto visits wounded Kaga, July 25th, 1942

The Grand Admiral looked at Kaga's damaged port side with great interest. The Japanese leader was inspecting the carrier from a motorboat while several workers got busy repairing the ship in the Pearl Harbor area.

The Kaga would need to go into one of the recently repaired (and cleared of debris) dry dock spaces in the harbor. The damage would be too difficult to repair since part of it was below the waterline, so the workers needed a dry space to work in.

The enemy torpedo had hit Kaga hard on the port side, opening a significant gash in the armor and igniting a great fire that almost destroyed it. A lot of water had also poured into the ship. Proof of that was the many pumps installed around the vessel, exiting the water off and dropping it in the harbor. From afar, it almost looked like a gigantic fountain. Yamamoto had been interested in inspecting the result of the American torpedo hit. According to the preliminary naval engineers' report, Kaga owed its survival because it had a thicker than the standard protection for a carrier. The ship started as a battlecruiser but converted to a carrier following Japan's signing of the Washington Naval Treaty. So, its armor was much stronger than a purpose-built carrier like Shokaku, for example.

From Yamamoto's standpoint, it looked impossible that the ship didn't sink. "Incredible that the ship didn't go under," said Chuichi Nagumo, the commander of the carrier strike force, who was inspecting along with the Grand Admiral. "Indeed," answered Isoroku. "And to think that the Kaga had been hit by two more torpedoes that didn't explode. We were fortunate." "The American incompetence with their weapon is striking, Sir," added Lieutenant Garimachi, the officer in charge of the motorboat that stood beside the two naval commanders. Yamamoto didn't reply but thought the man was right.

The Imperial Navy was indeed lucky that the U.S. forces had faulty torpedoes. Stories abounded across the Pacific theater on the fact that the U.S. Navy scored several direct hits without the weapons exploding. The Grand Admiral wondered how many ships could have been lost. *"The real question, lieutenant,"* continued the Japanese strategist, *"Is when the Americans will correct their weapons. Because believe me, they will, and when they do, the Imperial Navy has better be ready."* "Indeed, sir," said the motorboat officer, bowing in respect but with a tone that suggested that he highly doubted it. Isoroku knew that the man didn't believe the Americans could correct their torpedoes. Like many of his comrades, he was infected by the *"victory disease,"* born out of the incredible success the Imperial Navy had had so far. He decided that it was pointless to try and correct the youngling. He would eventually learn.

"Admiral Nagumo," he instead continued, *"when do you think that the Kaga will be battle-worthy again?"* *"Admiral, my engineers say that it will be out for probably a month, perhaps even more. It will depend on their inspection once the ship is dry and once they can better assess the damage."* Yamamoto nodded silently, with a worried look on his face. They needed every ship in their defense of the Hawaiian Islands, and Kaga would be sorely missed. For a moment, he thought about recalling the two surviving light carriers from Inoue's 2nd fleet in Rabaul but rapidly relented. The force was already struggling as it was and had recently lost a carrier, the small Ryujo. It wouldn't do to strip the admiral of his only naval air force if he wanted to get some results in the Coral Sea.

As he listened to one of the other officers describing the damage and what they would do to repair it, his mind wandered, thinking about the overall situation and his worries. He pondered how the Americans had guessed right about his attack in Palmyra and the West Coast. Maybe something was amiss there. Or else they'd just been lucky? After all, it was only normal for the Japanese to retake the tiny atoll in the Line Islands and attack the U.S. Mainland. He discounted his worries as mere coincidence.

"*Admiral,*" Nagumo said, yanking Isoroku out of his daydreaming. "*When do you expect the enemy to come and attack us again? Do you think we should mount another operation against the mainland?*" The old naval commander betrayed his usual worry about losing one of his precious fleet carriers. He'd almost been proved right with Kaga's predicament.

Yamamoto thought a little before answering because, at that very moment, he didn't have any idea what course Japan should take. He still wanted to trigger his desired "*battle of annihilation*" but wasn't sure the Americans would bite. Perhaps he would need to attack the mainland to get them to exit their San Diego lair. Maybe he should also consider something entirely different, like raiding the giant Boeing aircraft factories near Seattle. That kind of operation was within the scope of the Japanese range now that they had Pearl Harbor. "*I am not certain yet, Admiral. What do you think?*" Surprised by the lack of a firm answer on the course to follow, Nagumo sort of baffled a response. "*I.... think we should use the strength that we have gathered to keep our fleet safe in Oahu and await the unavoidable American assault from there.*" Of course, thought the Grand Admiral. "*Well, maybe should be better off to do as you say, or else we should continue to poke the bear and see how it reacts...*" answered Isoroku. Nagumo, not happy about the second part of the answer, only bowed respectfully to signal his acceptance without showing too much of his displeasure.

The more Yamamoto thought about it, the better it sounded. Maybe the damned U.S. Navy was well holed up in San Diego, but he wondered what kind of reaction he could trigger with an attack on Seattle...

White House
Oval Office, July 25th, 1942

"You would think that the Japs understand that we've broken their naval codes by now, don't they, Admiral?" Roosevelt tapped on his desk in the Oval Office. He was meeting with the commander-in-chief of the U.S. Navy, Admiral King. *"That's just it, Mr. President. We don't think they have. They have continued to behave like nothing is amiss, and we've decoded several messages on troop movements and other tidbits like convoy routes and schedules, and all have panned out to be true."* The Americans were having a field day with the Japanese supply routes in the Dutch East Indies, even with the small number of submarines they had in the theater. According to the Admiral, the enemy didn't seem to be very good at escorting their merchant's vessels. At least not on par with what the Allies were doing in the Atlantic. It was almost as if the Japs didn't care.

"I've read the final reports on the battle's outcome, Ernest. Not very good that we lost all those ships." *"True, Mr. President. But at the same time, we have badly damaged a main fleet carrier. We believe that we hit Kaga and that it will need serious drydock work to be operational again."* The Admiral paused to shuffle through his paperwork. *"We think that the enemy doesn't have enough capacity to operate major repairs on their capital ships. At least not of the type needed to repair the Kaga's damage. They will need to bring things and men from Japan."* The Japs were doing just that, according to another report Roosevelt had read, but it didn't matter; it still meant that they were minus one carrier in the meantime. *"Is there any way we can use this to our advantage, like attack now that they are less than one flattop, or else try to destroy Kaga while it is in drydocks?"* *"Well,"* answered King with his usual rough mood (he seemed exasperated by the President's question). *"I do not think it is the right idea. The Japs are numerically superior to our forces, and the many planes and airfields they have installed around the Islands compound the problem in the sense that, according to our estimate, it doubles or even triples the number of planes they can send against our fleet if we*

get too close to any of the islands." "I see," grumbled Roosevelt as an answer. King continued. *"However, we can use the incredible advantage we have concerning the broken codes to wait for the Japs to sortie again and attack them at sea when they are far enough away from the Hawaiian Islands."* The President already knew that it was a good option for the U.S. Navy. But it was not an option he liked. His wish was to retake Oahu as soon as possible and take the war to Japan as fast as possible. But the United States was the victim of their inaction before the war. While the Japanese, Italian, and Germans armed themselves to the teeth, the country had been busy with civilian problems and wanted to stay out of the developing war. In the end, all of the isolationism in the world didn't change the fact that the war came to America's doorstep anyway.

"Very well, Admiral," he said, relenting. *"When do you expect Yamamoto to sortie again?"* *"Well, Mr. President, we estimate that he will stay in port for a little bit of time. Not because he doesn't have the strength but because we believe that the Japs don't have the fuel for another big operation. They must bring the stuff from Japan. Well, even more complicated than that. They first have to get the oil in the Dutch East Indies, transport it to their Home Islands, and then refine it to reship it again toward all the theaters they fight in."* The Admiral paused for breath. *"Yamamoto has enough to operate around the Islands and defend them but not necessarily enough for another grand-style operation like the one he just mounted. Perhaps a few weeks in the future, but not before."*

"Thank you, Admiral." Roosevelt had another meeting coming up. *"Keep me apprised of the situation, and please get me those production estimates I asked you for tomorrow's get-together."* *"Yes, Mr. President,"* answered King, standing up, picking up his paperwork, and leaving the Oval Office through the side door that a secretary had just opened.

"Are you ready for your next appointment, Mr. President," said the lady. *"Yes, Helena. Just bring him in."*

The man who entered the room was the United States Vice President, Harry Truman. The meeting between the two men was about internal problems and some senators they needed to bring back into line. *"Harry,"* said Roosevelt, standing up with all the difficulty in the world (he could barely walk). *"Mr. President,"* answered the other man with a smile. They shook hands wholeheartedly. *"Sit down, my friend, let's deal with this little problem of ours...."*

Truk Atoll, Carolina Islands
The Japanese maintenance and repair problem, July 22nd, 1942

Repair ship Akashi was one impressive Japanese ship. Converted from an old Great War battleship, it had giant cranes, tons of armor plates, and all the necessary items to repair ships during a campaign.

By June 1942, it had been tasked to repair the Haruna directly within the protected atoll confines. The battleship had received extensive damage from earlier battles in the Coral Sea. It had thus been ordered to Truk base to get repaired by the Akashi.

The repairs on the dreadnought had gone along well for the whole month of July, and it only had been slowed down by the need to get spare parts from the Japanese Home Islands. But in the end, it was all good, and the work resumed on the 15th of July.

The 22nd of July was ending, and as the sun set down over the horizon, Haruna was declared operational. The battleship was patched up but not pristine new, as in order to do that, the Navy would have needed to transfer it to Japan proper.

Akashi then started work on the Taiyo; another ship damaged in the heavy Coral Sea fighting. The carrier had a gutted flight deck and a destroyed plane elevator, which were easily repairable. So, the engineer declared that the carrier should be fit for duty within a reasonable time frame (sometime in August).

The men and sailors of the repair ship would have a lot of work ahead of them as more and more Japanese ships would arrive damaged at the atoll base. Sometimes, the crippled vessels would have to be towed to the Home Islands, and other times there wouldn't be parts for them. The Empire was a hodgepodge of factories and competing interests between the Army and Navy, and often, the ships could not be repaired properly because there just weren't enough resources.

The main type of unrepairable damage due to lack of specialized parts was the guns. It wasn't like the repair ship or Truk Base had a warehouse of 356mm guns waiting just in case a battleship lost one.

Another area where Japan could have done a lot better was replacement parts for its smaller machines, like planes and the like. The Nipponese industry provided new weapons at a pretty decent rate but was not able to supply the parts to keep them running. Hence after five months of campaigning in the Pacific, the Imperial forces started to experience the same type of problems as their equally unplanning allies in Germany that were faced with a gigantic part shortage problem after a few months of campaigning in the Soviet Union.

Japan was all shining and glory at the front, but everything behind that kept the fuel in the war machine was not so amazing. The country banked, like Hitler's Germany, for a short war. In July 1942, the Japanese planners didn't think too much of the burgeoning problems with parts and supplies, but it would eventually come back to bite them as the conflict dragged on.

CHAPTER 5

Southwest Pacific Area Command (SWPA)
MacArthur in Brisbane, July 27th, 1942

"We will finally be able to do something about the damned Japs in Broome and Derby, Richard," said General Douglas MacArthur in one rare display of enthusiasm. The man was usually calm and composed. But the prospect of a counter-attack on the Western Coast of Australia energized the old commander.

Richard Sutherland, the General's chief of staff since the dark days of the Philippines campaign and the dreadful Bataan siege, wholeheartedly agreed. *"Indeed, sir." "So, the newly arrived 5th Marine Brigade and the 12th Armored should be in position in Perth soon?"* MacArthur asked while he stood in front of the map pinned on the Brisbane SWPA's HQ wall. Only he and Sutherland were in the room, which was furnished with several chairs, a movie machine (the General liked to watch newsreel and anything that portrayed the war up close), and, of course, the usual table where a ton of maps were laid down.

The overall southwest theater commander was happy about attacking the Japs in the west, but if it had been his choice, he would have done nothing to attack them. They were already pretty bogged down in the Australian outback immensity.

But while MacArthur was a fighting General and, as such, commander overall Allied forces in the theater, he did have to consider the political aspect. And in this case, it was just that. The Australian Prime Minister, John Curtin, had been applying a lot of pressure on the General to do something about Japan's occupation of the country's Western Coast.

One could hardly blame the man, as reports came in daily talking of the harsh Japanese occupation, atrocities, war crimes, and attacks on the civilian population. Imperial military administration did not have the kindest of reputation. Strategically, the enemy presence in and around Darwin didn't pose a threat, but the Aussies could not accept the way the Imperial soldiers conducted themselves on the civilians under their yoke. After all, the General could hardly go against the wishes of Australia.

Important reinforcement had arrived in Brisbane on the 17th of July. American troops that had been wrested by MacArthur's influence over President Roosevelt, for General Marshall had earmarked them for the fight in Europe.

The SWPA commander had hoped to turn the tide against the Japanese in Port Moresby and New Guinea with these forces but had sort of been arm-wrestled into sending them to the beleaguered West Coast.

The Australians, in general, and the citizens in the threatened sectors, in particular, entertained genuine fears of the Japanese invading more towns and even conquering the major city of Perth. While MacArthur and Sutherland had concluded the possibility as highly improbable, it was not seen in the same light in civilian circles.

After several meetings with Curtin and even a letter from Roosevelt that decided to side with the Australian Prime Minister, the general relented and ordered the troops sent to Perth. The soldiers and tanks didn't even land in the harbor and instead sailed for the West Coast right away.

Now, the troops had finally landed and got organized for the advance northward. It had been decided to go on land because of the looming presence of the mighty 1st Fleet, which could sink the feeble naval elements that the Navy and RAN (Royal Australian Navy) could field in the area.

While the Japs could not entertain advancing through hostile country, the Americans could look at the possibility since the Aussies were friendly to them and would organize the supply as they ground on northward toward the two occupied cities of Broome and Derby.

MacArthur's plan was straightforward in its execution. Advance on the main *"roads"* toward the objective towns and attack them. According to the OSS and army intelligence, the enemy had never encountered any kind of serious armored formation. The 4th Armored Division, entirely composed of the new and powerful Sherman Tanks, would come as a nasty surprise to the Imperial Army and even to their puny Type 95 lightly armored tanks.

To cover the advance and attack against the unavoidable Japanese response on the sea and in the air, the general also committed most of the air reinforcements he received throughout July. Over 300 planes of all types would thus be available for the operation.

It would take some time for the troops to get in position to attack the Japanese Army, but time was something that MacArthur felt the Allies had on their side.

Battle of Cape Rodney and Moresby attack, Part 1
The Japanese fleet advance on Port Moresby July 28th, 1942

So far, the campaign for the Japanese conquest of Port Moresby had been unsuccessful. Both Japanese land attacks were stalled. The first one, via the Kokoda track, had been bogged down for weeks by the end of July. The Australian 1st Division and a couple of Marine Battalions had pushed the Japanese offensive back into the depth of the Owen Stanley Range and created another stalemate from which the Imperial Army didn't seem to be able to break.

After some startling initial success with the strength of Musashi's guns (and the sinking of a U.S. battleship), the second offensive in the Milne Bay area was also stalled amidst supply difficulties, malaria problems, and a vigorous defense from the Australian's 10th Division (with mixed British and Americans forces). The 89th Imperial Division occupying Milne Bay was thus forced on the defensive.

By the 24th of July, as the failure was confirmed on both fronts, Admiral Shiyegoshi Inoue received new orders from Combined Fleet HQ in Hawaii. Yamamoto, eager for some kind of victory after his lukewarm performance during Operation MI, instructed Inoue to force the passage into the Coral Sea with his reinforced fleet and bombard Port Moresby with his guns.

High command also sent two new regiments (directly from China) with good-quality weapons and lots of experience to reinforce General Harukichi Hyakutake in the Kokoda track. Some heavy artillery was also sent down and landed in Buna on the northern New Guinean coast in order to bolster the attack. Inoue was finally instructed to put top priority on the Kokoda track supply. Reading between the lines, this last order meant that he needed to pour all the supplies there and let the other forces wither on the vine. The 89th Division in Milne Bay was already suffering for lack of everything, but their predicament didn't seem to compute in the resource-starved Japanese reality. Finally, a few additional G4M bomber squadrons arrived on the 27th and 28th of July from their long voyage that had started in Manchuria, as the Army there continued to be bled white for the ever-growing needs of the Pacific War.

2nd Fleet was to sail to Port Moresby and obliterate the base with its battleship guns. Air cover would be, supposedly, taken care of by the two small carriers and the planes from Rabaul and Lae.

At least Admiral Inoue had the firepower to make it work after the transfers of battleships Hyuga and Yamashiro to his command, plus heavy cruisers Furataka and Nachi. Haruna was declared operational again after lengthy repairs in Truk by the Akashi fleet repair ship. It arrived in Rabaul Harbor on the 25th, two days before the operation against Port Moresby launched. Finally, Musashi closed the order of battle for the powerful Nipponese fleet. Two carriers (Unyo and Zhuiho) would provide air cover for Inoue's ships. Twelve light cruisers and just a little over twenty destroyers flanked the powerful task force with a screen of auxiliary vessels.

On the other side of the chessboard, the Allies (General MacArthur and Admiral Leahy) were notified of Japanese intentions through their code-breaking information but wondered what to do about it. It was one thing to know where the enemy was and would be. It was another to try and prevent him from doing so.

Code-breaking information wasn't an exact science. Even with messages as clear as day, the Japs used codes within codes and used numbers or designations for targets and coordinates. So, this meant that a lot of guesswork was involved. The information that both Allied commanders received was that the enemy had plans to enter the Coral Sea in force, and there could only be one reason: an attack on Port Moresby.

The Allied 2nd Fleet was pretty roughed up from the intense battles of the last few weeks. It would be able to field one battleship against Japan's five. Leahy also estimated that they would be outnumbered in heavy and light cruisers and, of course, in destroyers. If the Imperial Navy brought landing troops with it, there wouldn't be much to put in its way.

Both commanders exchanged telegrams as they were not in the same location and agreed on not trying to initiate a surface battle with the Japanese, instead only seeking an air engagement. The estimates were a lot better, with two carriers on each side. Ranger and Charger both had sufficient air strength to go up head-to-head against the two light Jap flattops. In addition, the Allies were receiving planes on almost a weekly basis, enabling MacArthur to field several fighter squadrons that could be based in Cairns and Port Moresby proper. Both Allied commanders thus hoped that their airpower could make the Jap turn back.

Admiral Inoue's powerful fleet sailed out of Rabaul on the 27th of July and stopped in Buna to land the ordered supplies. The Army also started to step up its airstrikes on Port Moresby from Lae and Rabaul.

By the end of the 28th (as night fell on the beautiful Coral Sea), the Japanese 2nd Fleet rounded the eastern tip of New Guinea and made good speed near the southern coastline toward Port Moresby. The Nipponese Admiral was expecting to be in the gun range of the Allied base by midday on the 29th.

Its Allied counterpart, Leahy's 2nd Fleet, stayed close to Cairns on the Australian Northern Coast, where it planned to launch its planes. The stage was set for another battle in the Coral Sea.

The Japanese strategic situation
State of Imperial forces, July 1942

The Imperial forces had landed in Australia and large regions in the western part of the country by July 1942. The Imperial flag floated in faraway places like northwestern Burma and American Samoa. The Allies could not do much about it as their forces had been severely limited in terms of defenses from Australia to India to the Pacific Islands.

By the end of July, a picture started to emerge. As was the same in the Pacific Islands like the Fijis, Samoa, or the Line Islands, Japanese expansion had reached its high tide in Australia and Burma.

The Imperial forces could no longer advance in the great leaps and bounds they'd done only a few months earlier. The main culprit was the supply situation and the simple fact that Japan defied logic with its successes. If one considered its capabilities as an industrial nation at war, it had already done the impossible.

Everywhere, the offensive had either considerably slowed or ground to a halt. Significant battles still happened in Burma, but it was because the Imperial Army had the momentum and was still relatively close to its supply base. Ground troops needed less energy to keep operational compared to a mix of planes, ships, transports, and ground soldiers.

By the time it finished its Southeast Asia conquest, Japan would have needed to prioritize and choose where to put its maximum effort. Instead, it decided to attack everywhere and do everything, which amounted to a major problem in the making.

The Imperial forces entertained five ongoing major efforts. The first was the oldest. The war with China gobbled up almost 40% of the Imperial Army, with forty divisions warring with Nationalist and Communist forces. It was also (unfortunately for the Empire) the front that the Army prioritized and competed for resources that would have been needed against the more dangerous American enemy.

Then, there was the Burmese offensive aimed at India. Its totally unrealistic objectives (conquer Burma, invade China from the south, and then conquer India) were born out of the ease the Japanese forces had advanced so far in the war. For Army Command (Hajime) and Japan's Prime Minister (Tojo), it seemed that they would win wherever they sent their troops. The only problem was that the Allies were bound to regroup at one point and put enough force to bear on the advancing Nipponese troops to stop them. After all, the 15th Army only had five divisions for the whole theater. Still gearing up for war, India had enormous potential in terms of the number of divisions it could field.

The third significant effort was in the Coral Sea. There was a large fleet, over five divisions, tons of planes, airfields in various states of construction (Solomon, New Caledonia, Fijis), and a relentless campaign to storm Port Moresby. While the Japanese were bound to succeed in doing so, they were expanding resources that they would have needed elsewhere for other vital objectives. The real question was this: Once Port Moresby was conquered, then what? Would Japan really open a new front that it could not sustain in Northern Australia?

The fourth was the landings in Western Australia. They'd met with success right off the bat with the occupation of the crucial city of Darwin. The town was the perfect base from which to conquer the Aussies. But the Japanese offensive had been stalled right from the start by a lack of proper supply and, most importantly, by the ruggedness of the Australian terrain and the distance the Imperial Army had to travel to get to the next objective.

Something had been done about that, and other landings had been executed, giving Japanese forces control over two other important cities, Broome and Derby. But ever since then, Japan's capability to project its bayonets further had faltered. The troops received barely enough food, gas, and other war necessities to remain in place. It was currently unthinkable to advance southward toward Perth, even with a landing.

Again, just five divisions controlled a vast land area, and only the Allied inability to field troops in good numbers kept the Japanese might in place.

And the last effort was the most important, and the one Japan should have paid the most attention to. The Pacific and the myriad of islands it controlled, starting with Pearl Harbor. By the end of 1942, Grand Admiral Yamamoto continued to call in every available resource (oil, planes, soldiers, food, spare parts, ships...) he could get his hands on, to the detriment of the Coral Sea campaign and the reinforcements of far-flung islands like Samoa, New Caledonia, and the Fijis. The dreadful combo of distance from the Home Islands and the size of the Combined Fleet busy operating against the American Mainland stressed the Japanese supply capability to its maximum limit. For example, a ship like Yamato consumed oil at the same rate as twenty destroyers and a few heavy cruisers during an operation. While not yet in a situation where shortage would be commonplace in the Hawaiian Islands, the writing was on the wall for the Imperial forces in Oahu; time was not on their side.

On an intellectual level, men like Hajime (Army commander in chief), Shigetaro Shimada (Navy Minister), and General Tojo (Prime Minister) understood that Japan's resources were stretched many times beyond what was sustainable. But they remained steadfast in their belief, born out of the almost impossible successes they'd enjoyed so far, that Japan and its fighting spirit would win it all in the end.

If the Empire had had some time ahead, their thinking would have made sense. After all, the Imperial forces had captured an incredible number of resources and could, in all likelihood, multiply Japanese industrial capability tenfold. But those things took time and couldn't be done in times of war.

For all his faults during the war, only Yamamoto understood Japan's predicament and saw the wall it was about to hit. The Grand Admiral did try to stress the matter to the other Imperial leaders, but they did not listen.

So, what Japan was left with was the best compromise between expansion and consolidation. It remained to be seen if and when the American industrial giant would be able to break the Imperial hold on the Pacific and the rest of Asia. If Yamamoto could hold in Hawaii, maybe he would win enough time for the Rising Sun to get strong enough.

Battle of Cape Rodney and Moresby attack, Part 2
The Allied attack and the Japs reach their objective, July 29th, 1942

As another glorious morning broke on the 29th of July 1942 in the beautiful blue immensity of the Coral Sea, the Japanese 2nd Fleet was shown in all its might. There were five battleships, two carriers, five heavy cruisers, and many escort ships. The great host sailed somewhat close to the New Guinean southern coast and bombed everything that had the folly of being close to it. The smart ones moved to the interior as news of the great battle fleet approached. Unfortunately for the towns along the coastline, they couldn't move.

Cape Rodney was such a place. It wasn't a major military installation because only a few squads occupied the town and operated a couple of old naval defense guns. What the Japanese fleet unleashed on the place was totally unrelated to its importance or its threat level. Standing orders from Yamamoto were strikingly simple: obliterate everything along the southern coast and leave nothing to the enemy. In this way, the Grand Admiral wanted to choke the Allied out of the Port Moresby area.

The guns of the dreadnoughts and their heavy cruisers brothers dropped hell on the small town and obliterated pretty much anything that was standing. Admiral Inoue, looking with his binoculars at his ships pounding the non-descript place, grunted in satisfaction and was about to issue the next set of orders. The fleet was to continue sailing toward Port Moresby.

But suddenly, alarm sirens blared all across the ship, and the admiral even saw a few flashes from the flak guns that sent tracers in a climbing arc. And then, a few seconds later, every Japanese ship opened up in the sky in a grand display of fireworks, tracers, and explosions. The Admiral also felt his ship starting to fire, as Musashi (the super-battleship was his flagship for the operation) fired everything it had at the oncoming enemy planes. Inoue moved to the port side to watch for the incoming Allied aircraft. He saw several growing dark specs about five kilometers out.

Flak explosions were peppering the airstrike, and it seemed that the Japanese guns would obliterate them. But Inoue knew better. It was hard as hell to hit a plane moving to attack a ship. Above the incoming dive bombers, a layer of planes was also busy dogfighting, he estimated at perhaps 20,000 feet. He could see a couple of fighters spiraling down in flames toward the sea and the crisscrossing ordinance that each side fired at the other.

The Allies had brought a lot of fighters. About double the number that Inoue had, explaining the complete lack of interception on the incoming aircraft that wanted to send their bombs and torpedoes at the fleet's ships.

Some of the fighters from the Lae and Rabaul groups were expected shortly to fly cover as it was still early in the morning, but for the moment, the 2nd Fleet would have to fend off the attack with its meager thirty-five Zeroes and flak guns.

The Admiral kept focused on the incoming bombers as their approach was almost over. Every half a minute or so, he was rewarded by one of them exploding in mid-air or else hit by a flak explosion, so it crashed into the sea. The anti-aircraft fire got more and more concentrated as the enemy approached. Some attacked almost at sea level since they had torpedoes. Others were diving from high over the fleet, ready to release their deadly cargos.

"Torpedoes in the water!" yelled one of the deck officers, getting the news from one of his men outside. *"Dive bombers on approach!"* yelled another officer, also in contact with the outside lookouts. The Admiral looked up and saw several of the enemy aircraft plunging toward his ships. As it was impossible to see from the deck (the ceiling was not transparent, after all), he had no idea if Musashi had been targeted. He remained confident in the ship's capability to weather the bombs like it did in Milne Bay.

Then, all across the fleet, towering geysers of water rose in the air as the bombs started falling. Unfortunately, some smoke and ship explosions also happened since several Allied weapons found their marks.

Even Musashi shook from a bomb that landed on its superstructure. It felt like a great sledgehammer slammed the battleship, knocking everyone standing that wasn't holding to something on the ground.

The enemy torpedoes also did their damage, even if several continued to be defective. Three destroyers were hit, plus the Furataka and the Haruna. The resulting blast opened gaping holes in the ship's sides. The small destroyers did not survive, while the other two boats remained afloat but with substantial damage.

The air attack eventually ended, and the Allied strike left a fleet afire and smoking, with a sea littered with debris. The final tally was Musashi lightly damaged, Haruna with port-side torpedo damage and reduced speed, heavy cruisers Atago and Furataka seriously damaged (mangled turret and gaping hole on the port side), battleship Hyuga with a gutted main gun turret, and finally, four destroyers and three light cruisers destroyed.

The result was definitely not exciting, but Inoue resolved to continue onward toward his mission. Most of his capital ships were undamaged, including his carriers (that sailed twenty-five kilometers further east of the main gun task force so they had not been attacked by the Allies). The Admiral's operational objectives could still be reached.

An hour later, the Lae and Rabaul fighter groups finally arrived over Inoue's fleet to protect it, so for the rest of the way to Port Moresby, it remained unmolested by the enemy.

Objective Chongqing
15th Army plans to invade China from the South July 1942

In July 1942, the Japanese Army captured Burma after an impressive blitzkrieg campaign that saw them advance from Thailand to Rangoon and then the northwestern parts of the country. They closed the Burma supply road with the battle of Lashio and immediately prepared to attack west Yunnan. Their successful campaign opened a new front from which they could attack the Nationalists.

The Southern Expeditionary Army Group (15th Army), commanded by Lieutenant General Shojiro Lida, was expected to fight along the Burma Road, conquer Yunnan, and threaten Chongqing, the capital of Chiang Kai-Shek's Chinese government. The army was composed of the 57th, 33rd, and 71st divisions, along with the 18th Division and two armored brigades (Type 94 tanks). Some considerations were also discussed on bringing in more reinforcements. However, the dismal supply situation forced the Army command to relinquish the idea and instead rely on putting pressure on the Chinese in a different fashion (by using its forty divisions fighting in China proper in an all-out offensive at the same time as the Yunnan attack).

The campaign was set to start in the first two weeks of August 1942; whenever the supplies needed to operate, it reached the divisions at the frontline. Army command would coordinate it with a major offensive in Central China to overwhelm the Nationalist forces. The Indian offensive was thus postponed by a few months to take advantage of the new situation that arose from the Burma Road conquest and the opening of a southern Flank against their arch-enemy.

Private soldier Ishiro Tanaka was thus stationed, by the end of the 2nd of August, along the Nu River as the rest of the 18th Imperial Division. Their movement in southern China had not been as hard as had been anticipated by divisional command, and the men were somewhat happy. The real problem was more about the supply situation. Like the rest of his comrades, he was hungry and in an eternal search for more ammunition. But at that moment, on the evening of the 2nd, Tanaka harbored a thin smile and some happy thoughts. As he walked to the other squad's position (as ordered by his officer), he found a dead comrade, probably shot by a Chinese sniper. The man had fallen into a small ditch with bushes that partially covered his body. Tanaka had spotted the man only by sheer chance. The Imperial positions were still being organized, and their defensive cover was sketchy at best. Lieutenant Togun had sent Ishiro to check on the men down the line and see if their trench had been completed. The 18th was setting up shop along the Nu River, where the new frontline between China and Japan was taking shape (until such time that the Imperial forces launched their planned offensive).

The Nu River, also known as the Salween River, flowed through the three countries of China, Burma, and Thailand for a distance of around 2,400 kilometers before draining into the Andaman Sea at the Gulf of Martaban. The area around the body of water was lush with vegetation, and the river itself was a stretch of half a kilometer wide broken, rocky, and marshy ground- perfect for a frontline.

The dead Japanese soldier had a nice little bundle of rice on him (that Ishiro wolfed down in an instant) and a brand-new Arisaka Rifle. Tanaka decided that the man must have been a new recruit. It was funny how these raw soldiers died in droves, seemingly on the first few days after arriving at the frontlines. He picked up the weapon and inspected it.

The Arisaka rifle was designed by Colonel Arisaka Nariakira at the turn of the 20th century. The man's contribution to the Imperial cause earned him a promotion to lieutenant general and baron's title from Emperor Meiji in 1907. It was well-deserved since the weapon endured for a long time. In fact, it fought along with the Imperial Army until 1945.

The one in Tanaka's hand was the paratrooper version, prompting him to give another look at the dead man at his feet. Upon his additional body examination, he found a couple of packs of cigarettes and an ammunition pouch, which came very handy for the bullet-starved soldier he was. He was happy since he would be able to exchange the smoke for some food or more ammo. Being done with his new search, he gave his attention back to the weapon in his hands.

The Arisaka rifle was used everywhere in the Imperial Japanese Army and the Imperial Japanese Navy. Ishiro had heard rumors that the paratrooper version was a lot better than the normal Army ones, so he was delighted with his find.

The rifle Tanaka had found harbored the imperial ownership seal, a 16-petal chrysanthemum known as the Chrysanthemum Flower Seal stamped upon the top of the receiver. It was in perfect condition, so Tanaka picked up his own rifle (slung around his shoulder) and dropped it on the ground, removing the ammo in it.

Being done with his chance search and very satisfied with his new weapon, he wondered when he would be able to fire it in anger, as testing right now was out of the question. First, he just didn't have enough bullets to spare for that, and then there were standing orders to husband ammunition because of the supply shortages.

The naval attack on Port Moresby
The Imperial Navy shore-bombards, July 29th, 1942

The big guns finally reached their optimal range to shell the Australian base by the end of the afternoon on the same day (29th). A couple more Allied airstrikes were repulsed in the meantime, with more damage to the fleet (torpedo hits on Yamashiro, one light cruiser, and a destroyer sunk).

As he looked at the big guns of his dreadnoughts exploding in all their fury, shrouding in smoke and fire, Admiral Inoue reached two unwavering conclusions.

First, he would be able to gut the Allied base and shell it to oblivion. So, his mission's objective would be reached, and it would help the land offensive that General Hyuatake was about to launch on the Kokoda track.

But it also was obvious that no more Japanese fleet would venture like this in the Coral Sea between Australia and New Guinea. The burgeoning Allied airpower was getting too dense to contemplate such a scenario without major carrier reinforcements, which Inoue knew would never be available. At least not before Yamamoto was done with defending Hawaii.

Musashi finally sent its powerful broadside toward Port Moresby. The super battleship slightly recoiled to port as it could just not stand idle from that powerful a blast. The sea in front of the fired guns rippled for a thousand meters, and the resulting firestorm created by the 460mm shells shrouded everyone's vision on the ship for several seconds.

Like those from the other Japanese ships, the shells traveled to Port Moresby's harbor, airfield, and any other target that the Imperial Navy could see in milliseconds since the 2nd fleet was firing from short-range.

In minutes, the dozens upon dozens of catastrophic explosions rocked the town and started to obliterate the harbor. The ships still there (a couple of old destroyers and three minesweepers) were disintegrated by the Japanese battleships' mighty rush of pure power. The harbor installations (cranes, docks, hangars) were also transformed into a maelstrom of fire, molten metal, and broken concrete.

There were four coastal batteries protecting Port Moresby: Basilisk Battery (Idlers Bay), Gemo Island Battery, Paga Hill Battery, and Bootless Bay Battery. They all got silenced rapidly by the more powerful Axis guns, but not before they took their toll on the Japanese by sinking a destroyer (that was already damaged by one of the airstrikes) and scorching the armored sides of several of the battleships.

Paga Hill was one of the strongest positions, and it dueled for a while against the mighty Nipponese guns. Its canons could fire a 100-pound shell of Lyddite (HE), armor-piercing at a distance of 18,000 yards.

It attracted the super battleship's attention after hitting Musashi a few times on its armor belt. The gun emplacement was soon destroyed by a powerful broadside that exploded it spectacularly. The whole area (the guns were located on a hill overlooking the harbor and the city) rose in the air as if a volcanic explosion had lifted it from the ground it was anchored on.

The basilisk battery was the second of the four-gun defense battery, and it didn't last very long. It was well armored like a battleship turret, and its gun had a decent caliber (5-inch) but not strong enough to do more than scratch the Jap ship's paint. A couple of well-aimed salvos from Yamashiro destroyed it as it tried to duel with one of the light cruisers.

Bootless Bay, the third gun defending the harbor, was located at an angle from Paga Hill and was supposed to cover its flank if ships sped into the port and approached from Paga's blindside. It was a 6-inch battery. It lasted longer because the big battleships busied themselves with other targets. It gave a good account of itself before being silenced by a few well-placed shots from the heavy cruiser Nachi.

The fourth and final gun emplacement was located on Gemo Island, and it stood right in front of Fairfax Harbor's entrance. It was a well-armored 360-degree angle twin 6-pounders. It was well protected by a concrete glacis and could fire at an angle on the Japanese ships, being higher in elevation. The gun handlers scored several good hits on already damaged Yamashiro before the battleship Hyuga took it as a target. Within twenty minutes of a few 356mm broadsides, the whole defensive fortification was gutted and exploded in a spectacular, starlike fashion, spreading its debris across the island and into the water, reminiscent of a champagne bottle opening (a big one). No gun could survive the igniting of its ammunition magazines.

After they were done with the defenses, the ships concentrated their fire on the airfield installations. By the time the shells stopped falling in that area, the runway was a lunar landscape, and the hangars were balls of raging infernos. The base (if it would still be called that when the Japs left) would not be able to organize any sort of flying operations before a major construction and repair effort was made.

The harbor installations were much the same. The entrance was blocked, and everything was destroyed, so it couldn't be used by supply ships nor to embark or disembark.

As the renewed Japanese offensive on the Kokoda Track was about to hit the Allies in all its fury, their Port Moresby supply base was destroyed. The brave men of the 1st Australian Division and the Marine forces were stranded with no short-term hope of resupply or reinforcements.

Powerful enemies must be out-fought and out-produced
The awakened industrial giant

Extract of Roosevelt's January 1941 address to the Congress and the American people – <u>a year and a half before the Pacific War.</u>

(...)

"Powerful enemies must be out-fought and out-produced," President Franklin Roosevelt roared in front of Congress in his address to the nation. Most of his fellow citizens were also listening over the radio waves. All of America was gearing up for war. "It is not enough to turn out just a few more planes, a few more tanks, a few more guns, a few more ships than what can be turned out by our enemies," he said. "We must out-produce them overwhelmingly so that there can be no question of our ability to provide a crushing superiority of equipment in any theatre of the gathering world war."

Roosevelt paused for a fleeting instant, thoughts and images going lightning fast in his mind. Two years earlier, America's military preparedness was not that of a nation expecting to go to war. In 1939, the United States Army had ranked thirty-ninth in the World, possessing a cavalry force of fifty thousand and using horses to pull the artillery. From 39 to the end of 1940, the President did what he could to coax a reluctant nation to focus its economic might on military preparedness. Isolationist sentiments were running strong in America, and Roosevelt had started despairing that his countrymen would ever wake up to the growing danger. Then the British Islands fell, and the SS Ipswich massacre had happened. Nazi troops killed helpless prisoners of war, and "luckily," photographs were taken and, by chance, made their way to the media, creating an outrage of epic proportion. Then, there was the sinking of an American ship by a U-boat. Of course, America had been aggressively patrolling the seas and, in a sense, was provoking the Germans, but no matter; it also pushed public opinion toward war. And then there was the threat of Imperial Japan.

"I have a dream for America," he said with a grave voice, continuing his address. "We are already the biggest economy in the World, but we need to be even bigger," he put his hands on the desk in front of him, looking at every congressman he could lay his eyes upon. "We need to bury the Axis in steel and power." At that, most people in the room stood up and applauded.

"Here are my goals for America's factories: 60,000 aircraft in 1942 and 125,000 in 1943; 120,000 tanks in the same period; and 55,000 anti-aircraft guns. We will also build a navy the likes of which the world has never seen so that never again democracies can be threatened by the forces of fascism or any other countries wanting to wage wars of conquest."

The room exploded again in applause. America would become the arsenal of the democracies, Roosevelt silently vowed to himself. He would make sure of it. From all across the USA, countless factories, which produced tons upon tons of goods for the civilian economy, would gear up toward tank, plane engine, and war parts production. (...)

Because of Roosevelt's impetus and the prodigious American capability to produce at a frenetic pace, production figures had already started to ramp up in a big way by the summer of 1942. It was a good thing since the USA was by then at war with Japan and losing badly at that. But ever since the famous American President's speech, the industrial giant had awakened. They geared up from the great cities of the east to the Pacific coast. From the great factories of the steel belt, they geared up. From the great hinterland vastness, they geared up. Places like Detroit, so well-known for their prodigious capability to produce cars, switched to making tanks. The dozens upon dozens of large shipyards, usually building merchant ships, switched to warship production. The Axis powers didn't know it yet, but they'd already lost the war.

The only saving grace for Japan at that time was that America wasn't yet able, in 1942, to project its power because it couldn't deploy it properly without the Hawaiian Islands. It also faced severe shipping difficulties with war materiel to Australia via the arduous "milk run" sea route or sending any kind of reinforcement through the Indian Ocean. At that early stage of the Pacific War, the Allied problem was logistics not available firepower.

The only area that Japan still dominated was in the naval category. Not because the U.S. Navy was many times smaller than the Combined Fleet. It had more to do with the fact that America was busy fighting a two-front war and that priority was given to the struggle in Europe.

Also, Japan had a head start rearming militarily in the 1930s after the global depression. It invaded weaker China and other parts of Asia and faced very little resistance. In general terms, it gave the Japanese leader an unrealistic view of their country's capabilities against the American industrial giant.

In the summer of 1942, the USA was not strong enough to challenge the Combined Fleet one-on-one, but things would soon change. Japan would not get any main fleet carrier for another two years (the Taiho and the Shinano were at least two years away from completion) and get a paltry two light carriers by the end of 1942 and another two in 1943.

During the same period (1942), the U.S. Navy would receive one main fleet carrier (the Essex) and three light carriers. By the end of 1943, another three main fleet carriers would join the fray (Yorktown 2, Lexington 2, Bunker Hill), along with a staggering eleven light carriers.

In the battleship category, the Japanese would not produce another one for the rest of the war, while the US would get, just for 1942-1943 alone, five new ones (Mississippi, Idaho, Indiana, Massachusetts, Alabama). Several more were planned for 1944 and 1945, including the American's own super-battleship project, the 70,000 tons Montana.

While the Japanese would not believe that the production discrepancy was so large, they understood, on an intellectual level, that it was a lot smaller than the Americans. In short, they couldn't lose any capital ship because it couldn't be replaced. The US, in contrast, could absorb some losses.

Yamamoto was right to be worried.

Extract from General MacArthur's book, Reminiscences, 1964
The catastrophic Port Moresby situation, August 1st, 1942

By the end of July, I received the disastrous news of the complete destruction of Port Moresby as a base. While we'd made the Japs pay a hefty toll for sailing to the New Guinean southern shores, it had not been enough to save the harbor and the airfield supporting the Australian 1st division plus the Marine brigade bravely defending against the enemy in the Kokoda Track and the area in general.

The state of affairs was very different from what I envisioned it was supposed to be at that time. Instead of my forces being on the offensive and trying to reach New Guinea's northern coast, they continuously upped the ante and seemed intent on taking the base for itself. The amount of force it brought to bear was so powerful that there was nothing else we could do but reel back in disarray. If it fell, then the whole of the Northern Australian coast would be exposed.

The picture was not all dismal, however. Seeing the results of the Japanese landings on the West Coast (Darwin, Derby, Broome), I did not believe that the enemy had the logistical capabilities to overwhelm our defenses in Australia simply because they would need more men and supplies than they had available. The Imperial Navy was equipped with many ships, and we couldn't oppose it in a head-to-head confrontation, but ships did not conquer land. Nevertheless, the Australians did not want any more Japs on their land, as the news from their harsh occupation trickled down eastward.

Hazardous logistic risks had to be taken in making decisions for planning and launching operations. These risks had to be taken if the war was to be pursued aggressively and if the Allies were to seize the initiative and hold it. Even with the successful Japanese destruction of Port Moresby, I resolved that we would also double down like the Japs and put every effort into trying to hold the place.

On August 1st, I met with Admiral Leahy and the commander of the

RAN (Royal Australian Navy) to discuss a new blockade-running operation with all the ships we had left. The troops holding the Kokoda position would not be able to do so without supplies, and I resolved to get it to them. The situation was a little better than the last time we reinforced Port Moresby, with a lot more planes to cover our vessels.

The Port Moresby airfield facilities also needed to be rebuilt, as supplies could also be flown from the air, and fighters needed to be based close to the action. Cairns and the other northern Australian airfields were too far away. So, the fleet that would try and land reinforcements to Port Moresby would contain all the engineers and construction equipment we could cram in there, along with a new regiment of Marines that had just arrived in Brisbane on the 23rd. The Australians also contributed with a couple of newly raised battalions.

Little did we know that the Japanese were not done with their surge to take Port Moresby. A few days after the final plans for the 2nd fleet to cross the Coral Sea to resupply our base, a renewed enemy offensive was launched in the Owen Stanley Range (Kokoda).

The Japanese advance on the Northern Australian coast
Shores of the Arafura Sea 300km from Darwin, August 2nd, 1942

The Japanese forces bivouacked along the Arafura Sea on the northern Australian coastline. It was the beginning of August, and the bewildered Imperial soldiers only found deserted Aboriginal villages, dry ground, and a hostile countryside along their 185-mile march since they'd left Darwin. The troop supply levels were abysmal, and their morale had reached the same level. Their "offensive" from Darwin had been gruesome, and they'd lost many soldiers along the way.

The Imperial Navy did not venture into these parts, as air cover was insufficient. In contrast, the Allied air presence was getting heavier by the day, and several submarines roamed the Arafura Sea, waiting for fat Japanese convoy ships. So, most of the supply was sent overland, not reaching the troops for weeks.

Northern Australia, east of Darwin, was undeveloped Aboriginal land. It was a wild, untamed country. Stretches of dusty trails, deserts, dry ground, scarce water, and patches of *"forested ground"* were legion, but not a road in sight. Just empty, untamed countryside. It was depressing.

The division had lost over 25% of its fighting power just marching eastward. Not even one battle had been fought. In fact, not one Allied soldier or white people had been seen. Only the dark-faced locals that fled at first sight of anything Japanese. As he looked at the heat-undulating horizon, General Kajome Kanato, commander of the 55th Imperial Division, had had enough. "Tell the officers that we're going back to Darwin first thing tomorrow." "Yes, sir. "The captains, gathered for the occasion by the General, all harbored an immense sense of relief.

The Imperial Army was getting nowhere in the Australian immensity. The 55th's mission had been to reach the Gulf of Carpentaria and eventually cross Queensland to attack Cairns, but Kanato now saw that it was utterly impossible to do it on land. Anyway, he'd been highly skeptical from the start, as attacking the major Australian town with just a raw division would not do the trick. Only the typical unrealistic mind of Army command in Tokyo could draw such plans.

Without orders from Army command and no news from any kind of supply overland convoys from Darwin, his men would soon starve if nothing were done about it. The main problem was not just the supplies. It was also that there was nothing to conquer, nothing to plunder. Nothing at all.

The captains, bowing their acceptance of the order, turned about and walked out of their general field tent. Kanato looked out to sea. The view was magnificent. The blue immensity of the Arafura Sea was sprawled in front of him, but he just could not enjoy it. The god-forsaken patch of country that was Northern Australia was simply not suited for any type of modern campaigning. And besides, there was nothing of interest to get here.

He gathered his stuff and ordered the men to pack up the field HQ. For better or for worse, he was turning back toward Darwin. Kajome walked out, setting his scabbard and his Samurai officer sword on his hip, while a few soldiers, already working on the tent's ropes, bowed as he walked by them. Finally, the 55th was going home.

Strategic view of Japanese production and reinforcements
The paper tiger

"Paper tiger" is a literal English translation of the Chinese phrase zhilaohu. The term refers to something or someone that claims or appears to be powerful or threatening but is actually ineffectual and unable to withstand challenge.

The term was well-suited for the Japanese Empire in World War Two. However, Japan wasn't a *"paper tiger"* in the sense the word usually conjures up. It had a formidable navy with competent airmen and was undoubtedly a major power. But Japan's armed forces were woefully unprepared for the task they were set to do, subduing the world's most populous nation and simultaneously waging war with two superpowers.

Japan's economy was barely larger than Italy's despite having nearly twice the population. The Empire of the Rising Sun certainly had plenty of tanks, planes, and ships. However, it still was one of the poorest of the major powers, just barely above the USSR, a country that had to drag itself out of agrarian backwardness while contending with a war of conquest.

Japan could have had only one strong Army, Navy, or Air Force. Instead, it tried to develop the three at the same time. The Japanese focused on just a few key areas to compete, namely fighter aircraft and capital ships (carriers and battleships). The gap with the Western Powers still remained huge, and once the initial Allied inferiority was over(created by their paltry spending on military expenses), the game was up for Japan. When Japan wasn't focusing, the disparity got downright laughable. The British built over ten times as many tanks as the Japanese and the Americans twenty times. Japanese tanks were typically comparable to the lighter tanks of their enemies, incapable of facing even a Sherman, which in turn had all the difficulty in the world against German armor.

Britain and the USA each built more than fifteen times as many artillery pieces. Japanese infantry was likewise poorly equipped and certainly incorrectly supplied. Their equipment was typically recognized as being the worst of all the major powers, on par with what it should have been for the First World War. Part of this had to do with geography; the Pacific War was conducted over immense distances. Often, Japanese troops were intentionally undersupplied so that they could move quickly over rough terrain to surprise their enemies. This strategy paid dividends early on, but it floundered severely when faced with fully equipped and supported Allied forces.

But the most prominent factor was simply a lack of a consequent Japanese industry for what the country's leader set it to do. While the shipbuilding industry could churn out a couple of fleet carriers every two years, the Americans would build ten in a year.

Even if they wanted to, they couldn't supply even a fraction of their troops as well as the Americans could. Japan was never up to the task of subduing Asia, and they really should have known, considering how it had fought for over four years in China, one of the world's poorest and most troubled nations, with no victory in sight.

The finality of the matter was that it could indeed fight and very well at that. It just couldn't keep up with its enemy's production and organization levels.

In the end, Imperial Japan gave the Allies a great run for their money, and for a long while during the euphoric months of 1942 and 1943, it seemed that they could win.

Renewed battle on the Kokoda Track
Japan double down on the attack, 3rd to 6th August 1942

General Harukichi Hyakutake gave the final go-ahead for the general attack. Most of his men had already roused up from their miserable, muddy trenches; the artillery boomed and sent arcing shells after arcing shells over the enemy. The moment had finally come. He'd thought that his war was over and that he would have to die in one of those glorious banzai charges while losing at the hands of the enemy. But it seemed that he'd been given a new lease on life and another chance at success. According to what he heard, Grand Admiral Yamamoto had pushed the idea of a renewed offensive through the Kokoda Track to Army command after the failure of the Milne Bay landings. The operation was a joint coordinated action by both arms of the Japanese Imperial forces.

A few hours earlier, several powerful G4M bomber attacks had been launched at the Allied position facing his own. He also hit the Allies with the new artillery brought up with significant effort from the northern coast through the terrible jungle of the track. Over fifty heavy guns, shipped direct from the Philippines (leftovers from the Bataan Siege), were painstakingly lifted up the towering mountains against all odds: malaria, mud, rain, and enemy air raids.

By the end of July, his forces (the 67th Division) had been reinforced by two elite regiments from the Kwantung Army and fully replenished in supplies. The General was astounded by the sudden plentifulness of his deliveries. Guns, food, ammunition, fresh, experienced elite soldiers. He figured that other Imperial soldiers somewhere would go hungry and without support for a while because he'd never seen anything like it in his career.

His orders from Imperial High Command were simple. His force was to open the way to Port Moresby. This time, he would be significantly helped by the new troops, heavy air bombing, and, most importantly, the destruction of the Port Moresby base by Admiral Inoue's 2nd

Fleet.

The Imperial Navy had utterly demolished the harbor, airfield, and anything standing. They'd paid a hefty price in ships for the success, but it opened a new opportunity for Hyakutake's forces.

The General excited his bunker, perched on a small hill (dug into the rock itself) with a pair of binoculars in hand. Looking at the frontline, he could already see his men pushing hard toward the Allied trenches. The brave Japanese soldiers forced their way through a hail of bullets and explosions. They died in droves but pushed the enemy back several meters; the fight seemed inconclusive for another half hour, in which both sides attacked and counter-attacked.

But finally, the Imperial forces prevailed, and the enemy retreated further down the track, probably to a new defensive position. Japanese intelligence spoke of low Allied morale and great supply difficulties since the destruction of Port Moresby a few days ago. For once, the Japanese forces had what they needed to overpower their opponents.

The renewed battle for the Kokoda Track was fought bitterly for the next three days, the Allies reeling backward evermore. The Australian Americans were simply overwhelmed, hungry, and out of ammo. For a moment, it seemed that they would surrender and that the Port Moresby position would fall.

The 67th Division pushed its way all the way across the Owen Stanley Range, losing an untold number of men along with the two new regiments, but by the 6th of August, they were in sight of the southern coast and finally over the dreaded mountains.

At that moment, Admiral Leahy's 2nd Fleet again arrived just in time to rescue the poor soldiers that were about to break.

2nd Fleet to the rescue
Admiral Leahy saves the day, August 6th, 1942

Admiral Leahy sailed out of Cairns with great worry for his fleet and the convoy ships it was protecting. The 2nd Allied fleet was on a mission to save the desperate situation in Port Moresby after the devastating Japanese naval attack a week before. The battleships had pounded the harbor, defenses, and airfields to such an extent that the city was now a pile of rubble. No more ships could dock and unload their supplies, no air operations could be undertaken, and every building in sight had been leveled.

The Admiral's objective was simple. Land supplies for the beleaguered defenders, but most importantly, land the engineers, workers, and equipment that would be used to repair the harbor and rebuild a semblance of an airfield. Without these, Port Moresby would fall.

The problem was confounded by the seemingly unstoppable Japanese offensive launched in the Kokoda Track. The enemy had done the impossible and brought up guns and more troops up the rugged terrain. They'd also increased their air presence and aerial bombing campaign, both on the forces defending the track and Port Moresby. The offensive had started on the 3rd of August, and the beaten-up Allied troops of the 1st Australian Division and the Marine Brigade retreated backward. They were now busily entrenching themselves in the small coastal plain around Port Moresby and in the broken, rugged rubble of the town itself. The military situation was beyond desperate. The men were hungry, almost out of ammunition, and had lost all their supporting logistics with Port Moresby's destruction.

The small town used to have a good harbor, now smashed, as Leahy could see with a quick inspection from offshore. Its entrance was blocked by a minesweeper, sunk on the spot by Japanese gunfire as it had tried to escape. The docks were now pockmarked and mostly sunk into the water, as part of it had been made of wood, metal, and concrete. The Admiral could clearly spot where the big enemy shells had impacted, as gigantic craters littered the whole facility area. A bit on the left, maybe a kilometer offshore, he took note of the destroyed airfield if it could still be called that. From his point of view, the place now looked like a lunar landscape that countless meteors had hit.

In the distance, he could see the towering Owen Stanley Range, which wasn't far from the coastline, at about twenty kilometers from the town. Explosions and small arms fire could be perceived from where the fleet was as the Japanese pursued the retreating Allied forces. Leahy figured that the enemy was probably still 18 kilometers out of Port Moresby as the Australian 1st Division fought a bitter fighting retreat. He decided that the damned Japs would get a little of what he could give them: lead. *"Officer,"* he started, not even turning while giving his order. *"Order heavy cruisers San Francisco and London to open fire."* *"Yes, sir. What about us?"* said the same and now eager officer. Leahy had a quick look at his ship's (the Washington) mangled bow damage, a leftover of its deadly encounter with battleship Musashi. *"Fire as well."*

The fleet started to fire as they were ready, and the Admiral saw clouds of fire and grey smoke envelop their guns as their shells arced high toward their targets. The naval rifles fired high and intentionally far, as they didn't want to hit any Allied soldiers, so the shells landed almost at the foot of the mountains, hitting the Kokoda Track gap. He was satisfied to see blossoming mounds of earth and rock from that distance with their resulting explosions. The whole area lit up in fire as they'd just opened a gate into hell itself. *"Order all the ships to continue firing for another 10 minutes."* *"Aye, Sir."*

As the shelling continued, filling the ambient air with the loud noises of the powerful naval guns, he looked again at the destroyed Port Moresby. The Japs had not been able to destroy the Island at the mouth of the harbor and Bogirohodobi Point, approximately 1.5 miles (2400m) to the east. But they'd smashed every standing building and silenced every gun that dared challenge them.

Before the Japanese attack, approximately 500 European civilians lived in the town, plus about 2000 natives, who had their village built over the water some small distance from the center of Port Moresby. They lived apart from the white residents, but that simple fact had not saved them from Japanese wrath. Their floating city, situated between Tuaguba Hill and Ela Hill on the eastern shore of the harbor, was now a smoldering pile of still-smoking embers. Nothing was left of the feeble wooden construction. He tried to imagine the terrible suffering these people had endured during the Imperial Navy attack.

Damn. Everything was gone. Residential buildings, offices, government offices, branch offices, radio stations, the electric power plant, church, school, European and native hospitals, even the ice plant, bank, hotels... Nothing was left. He had not yet received any reports of the number of dead, but he was sure it was extremely high.

At least the fleet had not been bothered by any Japanese naval task force. Inexplicably, the enemy had not shown itself to attack Leahy's ships. The Allied Admiral didn't know, but the Imperial Navy command had already decided to stop sailing on the southern coast until Port Moresby was taken so they could have sufficient air assets to cover their vessels. In their attack, the Nipponese had lost eight ships, and several of their heavier units were severely damaged (two heavy cruisers were being towed to Japan for major drydock repairs). Battleships Haruna, Yamashiro, and Hyuga had already been ordered back to Truk to be worked over by the repair ship Akashi.

The Japanese approach was a little different from the Allied one. Leahy had sailed with its damaged ships, regardless of their status. If they floated and could fight in any way, he brought them, for such was the emergency. Port Moresby could not fall.

He looked one more time as his battlewagons poured one shell after the other at the far-away Japanese forces and imagined the maelstrom the poor sods had to face. Given what they'd done to the city, he didn't really feel bad for them. *"Commence landing* operations."

The 2nd fleet landings were executed like an amphibious assault, as everything needed to be landed on the shore and beach (Ela Beach) near the city. It was far from efficient, but that was the Allies' only option at the moment. Priority was given to supplies for the beleaguered troops, but soon, the workers would land along with the construction equipment.

At least the beach right beside Port Moresby had been spared any destruction, as the Japs didn't attack sand with no defense. The Allied amphibious landing ships got to shore quickly, and everything was disembarked rapidly. Time was of the essence, and the fleet wouldn't be able to keep the enemy at bay for long.

Somewhere on the southern Coast of Sumatra
150 miles off Padang, August 6th, 1942

"And that's that, boys," yelled Cloutier enthusiastically. Everyone on the bridge cheered loudly. The fat merchant convoy ship was sinking after they'd hit it with their fourth Mark IV torpedo (the first three ones had not exploded).

They still had shitty weapons, but the Japs were beyond incompetent in terms of merchant shipping protection. It was almost like they weren't interested in escorting their ships. Jim had heard once in a Perth tavern that the Japanese were all about honor and glory. He figured that, maybe, the task was below the brave sailors of the Rising Sun. He didn't know or care; as long as he could kill ships without dying in the process, he was okay with the whole concept.

"Helm," he started to the sailor at the submarine wheel. *"Yes, Sir?"* *"Stay underwater for the next sixty minutes, and then we'll re-assess. If nothing on the periscope, we'll surface."* The submarine skipper wasn't really nervous, as the merchant's vessel didn't have any escorting ship so that no one could throw depth charges at him. But you never knew if the boat was able to raise someone on the radio.

Cloutier retired to his cabin for a cup of coffee and some course potting for his next hunting area for the next hour. He was thinking of going down the coast toward the coastal town of Bengkulu. The city was not as active as Padang, but at the same time, it entertained less risk. The Wahoo had sunk three ships in the last ten days, and it was time to move on to greener pastures.

Bengkulu wasn't known for having oil tankers, as the town didn't have an oilfield nearby, but it had several rubber plantations. He figured he could catch a couple of fat convoys full of the thing. He was almost done making his calculations for his next set of orders when the internal radio blared the *"Captain to the bridge."* An hour had gone by in the blink of an eye. He walked the short distance to his post.

"Anything, lieutenant?" His first officer was busy looking through the periscope. *"No, Sir. We can surface anytime."* He gave the nod to the sailors, and the sub bubbled up. It was always good for morale to have the crew get some fresh air. Life in a sub was not easy, and the atmosphere was always stale and stinky. Opening the hatch to get some fresh ones in was never bad for morale. Besides, he always tried to get each of his men a five-minute break on the conning tower to bathe in the sun and breathe something clean for a change.

Sometime later, the first few men were up and about on the surface, probably enjoying themselves, when an ominous sound was heard through the opened hatch—the sound of an airplane. The five sailors near the conning tower started to yell in panic and slid down the ladder. *"Enemy plane!"* shouted one of them. And then it was too late.

The Japanese Zero, called in the area by the merchant vessel's SOS call as it sank, saw the submarine surface and took its time on its approach, dropping out of the sun and like a hawk when it was ready. The men on the outside of the sub never saw it coming. While a Japanese fighter was not a real threat to the Wahoo (it couldn't sink it with its 20mm shells), a good strafing nonetheless could kill the sailors outside. And it did. The Jap pilot's burst shredded three men as they ran back to the hatch (they'd been standing by the deck gun). They were killed instantly.

"Close the hatch and dive!" was Cloutier's order, regardless of if a man still stood outside. He didn't know if more planes were in the vicinity or what it was. From his perspective, it could have been a bomber for all he knew. The hatch was closed in a hurry, but no living man was left outside, as the first two had been able to get in before the lid was closed shut.

The wahoo then dove, but not before getting another volley of the Zero's weapons, making loud clanging noises on the vessel's hull. As they all sunk to the bottom, everyone was silent. They'd just lost some excellent comrades and friends.

"Go south at the following coordinates once we are at depth, and stay submerged," was all that Cloutier said, handing out a piece of paper before going back to his cabin. Everyone on the boat was silent for a long while, thinking of how close they almost died and the people they had just lost.

The Siege of Port Moresby
Japan double down on the attack, August 7th, 1942

General Harukichi Hyakutake surveyed the damage to his forces as he walked the shattered grounds just at the exit of the Owen Stanley Range. The Allied fleet had pounded the area to fine dust for hours on end before a few airstrikes from Lae and Rabaul chased them off.

He marveled at the firepower that had been poured into the space his men had emerged from. He tried to imagine how horrible it must have been for them. After the Allied fleet's departure, the General had been able to deploy his men properly in and around the town. He'd first tried a direct assault on the morning of the 7th, but the enemy proved to be yet too strong for an attack of this type.

In order to dislodge them from the rubble that was now Port Moresby, he decided to wait for his heavy artillery to be brought from the track. He didn't know how long it would take, but he figured he had some time. The enemy naval guns were gone and would, in all likelihood, not be back for fear of heavy air attacks.

He still received a pretty steady stream of suitable supplies, so he was confident he could ride the Allies out. After all, what could they do? Aerial recon had reported that the harbor was destroyed and that the Allies landed their desperately needed supplies on Ela Beach just beside the town. That route was also not available as he'd positioned his men near it, so anything coming back that way would be under the fire of his men. No, the enemy was hauled up in the shattered pile of rubble and debris that was now Port Moresby.

The Imperial forces were arrayed in a semi-circle around the town and busy digging their trench. The weather and general conditions in the plain on the south coast were a lot better, so Hyakutake knew that all would be well.

On the other side of the coin, the Allies were busily trying to get organized. Their situation was close to desperate, but it had improved somewhat with the 2nd Fleet's operation, which landed supplies and bombarded the Japanese as they pursued them in their retreat. Admiral Leahy had saved the Allied soldiers.

They had enough food and ammo for at least ten days. That was how much time they had before they ran into problems again. The military engineers that landed with the supplies were flanked by every civil one that could be found near Cairns. They'd also brought plenty of hands like dock workers and general construction guys.

Top priority was given to protect these men as they worked around the clock and under Japanese fire to get the harbor operational again.

It was hoped that the Allied fleet would again make an appearance to bombard the enemy, but at the moment, it was sort of unlikely since the Japanese air presence was quite heavy, and a mighty dogfight was fought for the skies above the town. Both sides were battling each other to a draw for the moment, and one fleet or the other would appear once air superiority was achieved.

For his part in the operation, Admiral Leahy was praised to high heavens by General MacArthur but, at the same time, had paid dearly for his success. Three more destroyers and two light cruisers had been sunk, while his last four undamaged cruisers (San Francisco, London, Canberra, and Australia) all received several hits. They could sail back toward Cairns, but not one of the Allied 2nd Fleet's ships was unscathed.

While the Japanese had decided not to risk their previous ships until such time that they mastered the sky in the Coral Sea, the Allies were not in a position to do any more fighting for the time being. It would still have to run supplies into Port Moresby if and when the harbor was repaired, but the American Admiral had his own plans about that.

CHAPTER 6

A new U.S. mainland raid
Pearl Harbor, August 7th, 1942

Admiral Isoroku Yamamoto looked out the Yamato's bridge viewport toward the Pacific Ocean's blue immensity. Twelve days after the 2nd battle of Hawaii, he led another sortie with the Combined Fleet toward the American Mainland. He would have left sooner, but the oil shipments had taken their own time to get to Oahu, and a few tankers had also been torpedoed by the troublesome American submarines.

The Grand Admiral's last operation had been a failure. He had not been able to snare the U.S. Navy into the intricate trap he'd set. Instead, the enemy had come forward and attacked his carrier force. He still wondered about how the Yankees had been able to anticipate his move.

The price he'd paid for his missed attack was a heavily damaged Kaga, still in port in Pearl. Hell, it had even been put into drydocks to repair the torpedo damage below the waterline.

He was not the type of man to dwell on the past too much. The objective stayed the same. Stay in Hawaii and keep the Pacific door shut for the American forces. As long as he held the island and the harbor, The Empire stood a chance to keep the powerful Allies at bay.

In order to succeed in the long term, he needed to trim down the enemy's naval forces. At that moment in time, in 1942, Japan entertained some form of superiority in numbers and quality, but Yamamoto knew that it would be a pipe dream to only rely on that and wait for the onslaught in Hawaii.

So, he needed to slide out of his lair and challenge the US while it was still inferior in numbers, giving the Imperial Navy the best chance of success. Isoroku portrayed himself as a good poker player. When you have a good hand, you play it. And that was precisely what he planned to do.

His last two ventures against the San Diego base had been met with abject failures. It was a combination of the facts that the U.S. Navy was concentrated there and that the enemy expected Japan to attack it.

He'd consequently decided to change the recipe a little. He would execute an operation against Seattle in the north. His objectives were twofold. First, raiding the giant Boeing factories would not be bad for the damn place that produced the B-17 flying fortresses, and wrecking them would be to Japan's advantage.

The second objective pertained to his overall one; destroy the U.S. Navy at sea. With a raid so far from California, he hoped that the Allied admirals would sail out of San Diego and try to intercept him. He planned for the fleet to be split in two and would try to cut the Yankees from retreating with a sizeable, big gun fleet.

He hoped that once his strike was a success in Seattle, the U.S. Navy would come and challenge the Kido Butai carriers. Yamamoto would keep a fleet on the southwest of Nagumo's strike force and would thus attack the Allies while they were busy against the carriers that struck Seattle.

The fleet he was sailing out of Peal with was another gigantic group, close to 750,000 tons of steel and might. First and foremost, the carrier fleet of Kido Butai was composed of main fleet carriers Akagi (Nagumo's flagship), Shokaku, Zuikaku, Hiryu, Soryu, and the small light carrier Hosho. In all, 315 embarked planes would be part of the operation.

Then followed the mightiest surface fleet ever to roam the sea. Leading it was the super-battleship Yamato (Yamamoto's flagship), followed by Nagato, Hiei, Kongo, Mutsu, and Fuso, all-powerful dreadnoughts in their own rights. More big guns flanked them with heavy cruisers Tone, Myoko, Chikuma, Maya, and Kinusaga. Ten light cruisers and twenty-seven destroyers also escorted the fleet. Most of those auxiliary ships protected the carriers.

The Grand Admiral sailed resolute toward his northern objective, wondering if he was up to the task of beating the United States. From the moment he'd planned the surprise attack on Oahu, he'd known that Japan was asking him a tall order. But he'd resolved he would try as best he could.

The war was not going so bad to date. Of course, the conflict was still young (only six months old, after all), but the Imperial flag floated from Burma to Samoa and Hawaii to Darwin. However, as he'd expected, problems were starting to arise with all these far-flung fronts. The supply situation was not improving. In fact, he was beginning to get worried about his own oil consumption while operating so far from Japan. If he'd had the oil, he would have sailed at least ten days prior but had had to wait for the merchant fleet to deliver it. He'd also received reports from other fronts where difficult choices had to be made.

The Port Moresby offensive, prioritized in terms of supplies, created problems in other parts of the Coral Sea and the Solomon Islands. Simply said, some soldiers went hungry, and gasoline was scarce in many airfields supposed to be ready for an Allied attack.

The Australian west coast adventure was not doing so well either. It was utterly bogged down in rugged terrain and a lack of necessities like food and fuel.

However, he had to admit that he was pleasantly surprised by the stunning victory in Burma. While he didn't know where the Army was going with this, at least they were winning. According to what he'd heard, they were now poised to attack China from the south. He hoped that the new plan would break the Nationalist Chinese's backs, for the forty divisions stuck there fighting (and the humongous amount of supplies they consumed) could come in handy in the real struggle against the Western Allies in the Pacific.

"Admiral." Said one of the deck officers, walking by him and bowing respectfully. *"Yes,"* answered the still-daydreaming Yamamoto. *"The fleet reports ready to sail out. Admiral Nagumo wishes you Godspeed, and he hopes to see you soon near Seattle." "Thank you, officer,"* answered Isoroku.

His plan involved a split of his forces into two big task forces. He would sail east toward San Diego, along with the small carrier Hosho for protection, and try to rouse up the Americans, while Nagumo would sail northeast at full speed and raid Seattle.

His own battleship fleet would sail for a moment toward San Diego and then fork north on the third night and sail full speed far away from San Diego. He hoped to get the U.S. Navy out of its lair and exposed with that simple maneuver. Once done with Seattle, Nagumo's carriers would come back down, and then Yamamoto would turn around and face the Americans. Both pincer jaws would then destroy the Yankees once and for all.

Codebreaking fails
San Diego, U.S. Mainland, August 6-7th, 1942

The breaking of the Japanese JN-25 naval code was one of America's most outstanding strategic achievements during World War II. It enabled the U.S. Admiral to know what and where the Japs would be in many instances.

But it was not failure-proof, for it wasn't an exact science. Even if the American codebreakers at the OSS could read what Japan said over the radio waves, it didn't mean that they could read their mind. A lot of the information's interpretations came along with a lot of guesswork.

For example, the Japanese could plan an operation, and the U.S. could be aware of it, but it wasn't a foolproof way to succeed. Even if the Americans knew exactly what they talked about and planned in a broad sort of way, Japanese operational planners were not stupid enough to actually give the real names of their objectives, nor necessarily the direction where their fleets were going.

In some cases, they did, like in the Coral Sea a few weeks earlier, where the Allies had known which ship and where they were going. Sometimes, they didn't, like when Leahy encountered (and was surprised) by Musashi in Milne Bay. The Allies had known that there would be battleships in the Japanese operation. They just couldn't figure out that it would be one of the two mightiest dreadnoughts ever constructed.

In the case of the newest Combined Fleet sortie, it was one of those times where they guessed wrong. They knew from the intercepts that the entirety of the Jap fleet was to sortie, and they also knew that it planned to attack the mainland. They also figured that the enemy's objective was not San Diego. But never in their lengthy assessment did they think that Yamamoto was targeting Seattle.

The place was so far from Hawaii that it didn't register to them that the Nipponese would dare do this. With their conclusions, they played right into Yamamoto's hands.

They decided that Los Angeles and its harbor were the targets. Since they figured by now that the Japs were trying to lure them out to sea to slug it out with them, they obliged, but as in the operation over ten days prior, they sailed due west toward the Hawaiian Islands to meet with the enemy. Nimitz, at some point, planned on turning his ships back toward the mainland, where he wanted to use the added numbers of land-based planes to close the gap in carrier planes (Japan enjoyed a good superiority in them because they had five carriers to the U.S. three).

There would indeed be a battle, but it would not be the Americans dictating where it would be fought for the first time in a while.

Dogfight over Port Moresby
Over the blue Coral Sea, August 7th, 1942

Japanese ace pilot Takashi Onishi thundered just a few meters above the blue water of the Coral Sea, spreading droplets and vapor on both sides of his Zeros. It almost looked like the aircraft was a vessel as it flew so low that a ship-like wake followed it.

He rolled his fighter sharply left, taking a bit of altitude in order to dodge the spray of 20mm shells from the F4F Wildcat firing at it. The American ordinance pierced the water harmlessly, missing Onishi by several meters.

Onishi's plane was almost sideways after its roll, so its left wing was barely above the water, maybe a few inches. The fighter seemed to hold on to the ocean for a moment, tracing a new, thinner wake than before, spreading droplets and vapor as it accelerated.

The Zero's velocity enabled Onishi to climb faster through the raging dogfight that was taking place above Port Moresby's area. In the air, planes crisscrossed the blue sky, shooting at each other and filling the ambient area with red tracers. On the ground, much the same, as two lines of trenches shot their ammo at each other in a glorious maelstrom of guns, rifles, and machine guns.

Axis and Allies alike were battling heavily to win the mastery of the sky, for once achieved, it would mean victory. The Japanese would be able to sail their fleet in safety and bombard the beleaguered town defenders to oblivion with their battleship guns. The same was true for the Allies. If they secured the air, they would also ship supplies and reinforcements to the base.

Bullets were still zipping past Takashi's plane as he rolled and rolled to avoid them and try to be as unpredictable as possible to his enemy. He looked at his altimeter and decided that he would make his move at 21,000 feet.

He pushed the Zero's throttle to the maximum, making the fighter shake and groan in pain. The Allied pilot struggled to catch him, as he was slower.

When the Japanese ace reached its targeted altitude, he cut his engine's power, soon breaking the Zero to a dead stop, and he swung the fighter around in a bold stroke. His maneuver not only surprised the rookie pilot it also brought him face to face with it. Onishi sent a burst of his 20mm canons toward the F4F. The shells hit the enemy plane on the canopy and the engine. It destroyed the propeller/engine that exploded instantly on impact, and the canopy hit killed the pilot.

Onishi restarted his engine, and as his propeller started to turn again, he leveled his plane while watching the wildcat shatter into a million pieces toward the ocean.

One more victory.

The Japanese attack on Seattle
The strike on the Boeing factories, August 11th, 1942

Nagumo sent the radio signal back to Yamamoto in the Combined Fleet. His planes were fueled up, and several were already circling above his carriers, awaiting their brothers to fly to the Boeing factories. A few minutes later, the go-ahead signal was sent back by Yamato. It was the moment that the Kido Butai Admiral dreaded. He did not want to risk his ships and planes toward such a faraway factory. He would have stayed in Oahu if it had been up to him.

He turned around and gave the head nod to the radio officer who would send the order to Genda in his Zero fighter. It was time to go toward the American Mainland.

At least so far, they had not spotted one Allied ship or any aircraft. Nagumo hoped, for a fleeting moment, that it was finally the moment he'd hoped; the Japanese replayed another surprise attack like the one in Pearl Harbor last March.

As he watched the plane fly away toward the eastern horizon, he silently wished them luck. Above in the sky at 20,000 feet, Minoru Genda, the flight leader for the strike, signaled everyone to close upon him and the other leaders. They still had a long hour-and-a-half flight time.

Boeing was the big player in American industrial output during the war, representing nearly 28 percent of America's total aircraft production in 1942 and throughout the war. The planes it produced (B-17s, B-24s, B-25s, and B29s) were (or would be) amongst the best in the Allied arsenal. As part of the cooperative effort taking shape in the USA, the company also leased its plane designs to other companies like Ford, North American, Douglas, etc.

Before the war, Boeing was a prominent manufacturer of commercial aircraft with its *"Boeing Plant 2"* (also known as Air Force Plant 17). It was built in 1936 by The Boeing Company in King County, Washington, in the United States. It was located between the Duwamish River and Boeing Field, east of the 16th Avenue Southbridge, facing East Marginal Way South. The factory was an intricate part of Seattle itself, and tons of the residents either worked there or as part of its suppliers' ecosystem.

It produced over 145 B-17 bombers monthly (and soon would also be making the B-29s), a number that would have wholly stunned the Japanese if they'd known. By comparison, the best Japanese factory barely produced twin-engine bombers at a rate of 30 per month.

To hide the factory from possible aerial attack, the U.S. Army Corps of Engineers built houses of plywood and fabric and installed fake streets to camouflage the roof. The idea was to blend the facility into the surrounding neighborhood across the river. Unfortunately for the Americans, several Japanese spies duly reported the factory's location in early 1941 (before the war and Japanese-American internments), so Yamamoto simply assumed it was still there and directed Genda to bomb the area.

While the American Navy command was totally blinded by Yamamoto's clever move of attacking where no one expected him, it wasn't like the United States had not taken care of its coastal defenses.

As a result of the fall of the Hawaiian Islands, the necessity of guarding American coastlines became urgent on the Pacific Coast. The threat was further demonstrated when the Japanese struck San Diego in the early summer-late spring of 1942.

Hence, over seventy radar station sites were rapidly proposed and organized. By the beginning of July 1942, a total of 65 were operational, and one of them was ready just in time for the surprise Japanese strike on the Boeing 2 Factory in Seattle.

The Klamath station, as it was called (station B-71), was installed in Redwood Park near Seattle and disguised as a non-descript farm. The complex included a power building, operations building, a privy, and anti-aircraft guns. So, it didn't take long for the operators to detect the large flight of Japanese planes and figure out that there were no scheduled flights that day, nor did the mysterious aircraft respond to any of their requests for identification. The urgent information (the enemy planes were but mere minutes from Seattle at that point) was relayed to the major airfield in charge of Seattle's defense, the large Boeing Field. Several squadrons of P-40 Warhawks were stationed there, and they scrambled upon the raising of the alarm.

Fifteen minutes into getting the alarm, the sixty or so fighters were in the air and speeding to meet up with the many dark specs closing in on Seattle that had appeared over their horizon's views.

The Japanese airstrike was a little over 240 planes, Nagumo having kept the rest as fighters to fly over the fleet in defense if American carriers lurked in the area and decided to launch a strike at Kido Butai. Of these 240, 80 were Zero fighters and manned by the absolute best and most skilled pilots of the Imperial Navy. In August 1942, most were still alive and well and could wreak havoc on anything that was not as experienced as them, which was often during the early days of the war.

Seattle was a key area to defend for the United States, but it wasn't where the best pilots were maintained, as a Japanese attack was judged highly unlikely. And so it was that the Allied pilots were severely outnumbered AND outmatched in skills.

The two large aircraft formations clashed just a little before Seattle Harbor, and a furious dogfight ensued. With the substantial number of planes attacking Seattle, the Japs quickly broke thru the insufficient Warhawk fighter screens and thundered above the Boeing 2 plant to drop their ordinance. The flak, also important but not heavy enough to stop an airstrike of that size, fired away, blasting a few Val bombers out of the sky but not in enough quantities to avoid the disaster that was about to befall the Boeing Factory.

The bombs started to fall in their dozens, and the industrial plant was so big that the experienced Nipponese pilots could hardly miss. Explosions blossomed across the factory and, unfortunately also on the city as it was awfully close to Seattle, sort of part of it as the town had spread over the years.

The blast rocked the ground, exploded roofs, and shattered windows in a maelstrom of fire and dust. Raging fires soon ignited as more bombs fell. It didn't take long for a big part of the large factory to be engulfed in flames. Many workers died in the initial blast and even more in the resulting fires.

Genda and his brothers shot down over forty-five of the Warhawks in the skies while losing fifteen of their numbers. The rest of the American fighters had to retreat to base, all being damaged. The Japanese airstrike left Seattle a mere twenty minutes after it arrived, but those twenty minutes had been sufficient to shatter one of America's most extensive industrial facilities.

Genda turned (looking back) toward Seattle one last time before speeding back to Akagi and reporting his success. The city he flew away from was engulfed in a massive, towering column of dark and grey smoke.

Bridge of Battleship Maryland
400 Miles off Los Angeles, August 11th, 1942

"Repeat that, sailor," was all that Nimitz could usher out of his mouth in a barely perceptible voice. The radio operator, unsure now if he wanted to repeat it seeing his Admiral's ashen face, hesitated for a second. *"I.... Report from San Diego, Sir. A large Japanese airstrike has just been executed on the Boeing Factory in Seattle. Major damage reported."* *"Well, ill be damned."* The American Admiral didn't know what else to say. The freaking Japs had pulled a fast one on him. Just as he'd thought, he had things under control with that codebreaking of theirs at the OSS. *"Get me some damage assessments or something more, sailor,"* Nimitz added before turning to Admiral Fletcher, his newly minted chief of staff. *"Frank, tell me this isn't happening."* *"I'm afraid it is, Admiral,"* responded the man who and recently been commanding Nimitz 2nd Taskforce before Admiral *"Bull"* Halsey retook command (he had been in the hospital for a few months).

"Admiral." It was the radio operator. The man seemed to have received more information. *"Over fifty fighters lost, and the Boeing Factory is on fire, damage assessment to be confirmed; fires are engulfing the facility."* *"How many did they get,"* asked the commander. *"Between twenty and thirty Jap aircraft, Admiral."*

Nimitz was not the sort of man to go down on the mat and stay there. He always rose to the challenge, like an invincible boxer asking for more punch and wanting to give some. *"Frank. We need to find those damn Japs and make them pay. If they struck Seattle, it means they are far away from their base and that they'll have to come back at it at one point. There isn't any option to do otherwise. I want to get them."* *"Yes, Admiral,"* answered Fletcher in his clear voice. *"I'll get some course-plotting and options for you within the hour."*

At that, Nimitz walked the distance from the bridge to his cabin to think for a moment while his chief of staff worked over where the fleet would sail to try and intercept the enemy. The fucking Japs had done it. They'd caught him with his pants down. King would be furious. The President would be furious. Hell, he was beyond furious.

He was dead tired of the Imperial Navy dictating the pace of the war. He resolved to intercept Yamamoto on his way back, and if that didn't do the trick of sinking all the Nipponese ships, he would have a go at Pearl Harbor at the earliest possible time.

He wondered if he could also try to catch the enemy admiral wrong-footed. The inklings of an idea started to form in his mind. The Japanese commander expected Nimitz to dumbly come at him like a bullfighter and attack Hawaii.

So now he knew what he would do. He would attack Hawaii, and then he would surprise that supposed Grand Admiral strategic mastermind of theirs where he didn't expect it...

Somewhere in the Pacific, vastness
The fleet sails to battle on August 13th, 1942

Sun-Tze, the military sage of ancient China, wrote in the eleventh chapter of his immortal analect:

(...) The skillful tactician may be likened to the shuai-jan. Now the shuai-jan is a snake that is found in the Chang Mountains. Strike its head, and its tail will attack you; strike at its tail, and you will be attacked by its head; strike at its middle, and you will be attacked by its head and tail both. (...)

In August 1942, Admiral Yamamoto's Combined Fleet was deployed for the first time in a manner of the Shuai-Jan. Its head was the Nagumo task force (Kido Butai). The body and the tail were the Grand Admiral's battleship squadrons and other powerful surface ships.

The American had raced north for the last two days, spotted by a few Japanese submarines to intercept Nagumo's fleet, which was also detected and shadowed by Allied long-range Catalina planes. Yamamoto's plan unfolded as he'd envisioned it. The carriers and their escorts were due north, midway between Seattle and Hawaii.

The Japanese dreadnoughts and their smaller but mighty brothers were located 500 miles south, sailing eastward to intercept the Yankee forces on the flank and initiate the battle that the Imperial mastermind sought: the battle of annihilation was at hand for the Rising Sun.

The Grand Admiral planned that by the time Nimitz and Nagumo were ready to launch their carriers, the Nipponese surface force would be near gun range. The recon report on the enemy battleship strength told of a number of dreadnoughts superior in number to the Imperial Navy: American battleships South Dakota, California, Maryland, Colorado, Georgia, and West Virginia, with the addition of two French ones (a strategic surprise to the Japanese): The Lorraine and the

Bretagne, freshly arrived from the Atlantic fleet.

The American Admiral, knowing that the Japanese big guns lurked in the area, decided that it was time for a confrontation and that he would also seek it. After all, his report talked of only six Nipponese dreadnoughts to his eight. He had fewer carriers, but he believed he would not have better odds if the Japs stayed holed up in Hawaii.

In all, the fight that loomed large somewhere in the Pacific between Hawaii and the US Mainland would be one of the most extensive to date in 1942.

THE TWO OPPOSING FLEETS:

JAPAN			
In Pearl Harbor - combined fleet Grand Admiral Yamamoto			
CVL Hosho	BB Yamato	Ca Tone	10 light cruisers
CVL Chiyoda	BB Nagato		
CV Akagi	BB Hiei	CA Myoko	27 Destroyers
CV Shokaku	BB Kongo	CA Chikuma	
CV Zuikaku	BB Mutsu	CA Maya	
CV Hiryu	BC Amagi	CA Kinusaga	
CV Soryu			

ALLIES			
U.S. Pacific Fleet San Diego, Admiral Chester Nimitz			
CV Wasp	BB South Dakota	CA Atlanta	10 Light cruisers
CV Yorktown	BB California	CA San Juan	19 Destroyers
CV Hornet	BB Maryland	CA Juneau	
CVL Long Island	BB Colorado	CA Vincennes	
CVL Bogue	BB West Virginia	CA Wichita	
	BB Georgia		
Free French Fleet San Diego - French Vice-Admiral Émile Muselier			
BB Bretagne	CA Duquesne		
BB Lorraine	CA Tourville		
	CA Foch		

Extract of Tameichi Hara's book Teikoku Kaigun no Saigo
1967
Inglorious escorting, August 5-14th, 1942

After we got back from the successful Port Moresby operation, where the battlefleet destroyed the Allied base, we were ordered back to Truk as escort for a few transport ships that were eventually to sail to Japan with other destroyers waiting for them there.

We would have just left them to their own devices in normal circumstances as they were perfectly capable of sailing to the Carolina Islands base by themselves. But the Allied submarine threat, which was growing ever more troublesome, forced Navy command to make sure the ships were escorted by anti-submarine ships.

Once we arrived at the beautiful atoll, we stayed there for a blessed five days. The place was paradise on earth, and the war had not reached it yet (American bombers were out of range and had other fish to fry at that time).

On the 9th of August, we were again tasked to escort a few oil tankers bound for Rabaul. I remember the state of mind of the crew during the execution of this task. Merchant vessel escorting duties were not the most glamorous job in the Imperial Navy. In fact, it was considered one of the lowest and never tended to attract much attention.

Only after the Allies forced high command to address the problem did some escorts start to protect the unarmored civilian transports. But even then, and throughout the whole war, Japan never truly got any good at protecting its merchant ships. Our stupid honor code caused us to want to fight, not escort and drop depth charges at submarines. Every Imperial sailor dreamed of its own Tsushima and the glory of it all.

In short, Japan didn't believe in logistics. Instead, we all believed in one crucial lesson of Sun Tzu's *"The Art of War"*:

(....) Hence, a wise general makes a point of foraging on the enemy. One cartload of the enemy's provisions is equivalent to twenty of one's own, and likewise, a single picul of his provender is equivalent to twenty from one's own store. (...)

After all, the Empire had trudged along with this maxim for the entire length of its history up to that point. It worked for Sun Tzu, and it worked for Japan because it was split up into many small warring states, for which military rations could be found literally anywhere.

Consequently, when we made war in China and Korea, we did the same thing and pillaged the populace. In a battlefield where it wasn't available, like at Khalkhin Gol against the Russians in 1939 in Manchuria, the Imperial Army got clobbered. So, of course, when the war started, we allocated destroyers to escort our precious battleships, not merchant vessels. The idea at first didn't even appear to our brave and smart military strategists.

They didn't know submarine stealth was made for attacking shipping lanes. Hell, even our antisubmarine capabilities relied on the fact that submarines were loud (while Allied submarines made sure they stayed silent and were designed as such). So, we never could really fight the kind of antisubmarine warfare that would have been required to shield our merchant shipping, which would have given the country a slight chance against an industrial giant like the United States. Instead, we grumbled every time we had to do it, and our commanders never gave it the attention it so desperately deserved. Only after the war did we understand the extent of the disaster for the Imperial forces and how bad we performed at it.

In addition, the general belief in Navy command was that Americans could not use submarines. One must wonder why this brilliant idea was hatched in the command circles. Well, we can thank Satou Kenryo, Director of the Military Affairs Bureau and one of Tojo's stooges. He considered himself the foremost expert on the USA because he had been a military attaché to the United States, and he decided that:

(...) *"American soldiers are unpatriotic. They chew gum, go to dances, watch movies, and can't even march in a straight line."* (...)

His view pervaded the Japanese military because nobody else had the credentials to provide an opposing viewpoint, and doing so would have put them under suspicion of treason anyway - how could anyone exaggerate the competence of Japan's enemies?

With the next step in this logic, we indeed went out of our way to come to a stupid conclusion. Apparently, if the Americans couldn't endure the hardships of marching in a straight line, how could they manage the hellish conditions of living and fighting in a submarine?

Our brave and intelligent leaders certainly didn't believe that was possible, and thus, we expended little effort on antisubmarine warfare. As we simple sailors were limited to our own little scope of the war, we never truly learned of the extent of the problem until it was over.

The Yunnan offensive
18th Imperial Division on the Nu River, August 15th, 1942

The new border between Chinese and Japanese forces, the Nu River, was a sizeable rocky expanse bordered by lush, forested areas that both sides used to dig their defenses. The river rested in the middle of a wide riverbed because it flooded often. Several small trees and bushes dotted the otherwise boulder-rich landscape. The river itself wasn't too deep as many fording areas were available to cross it on foot.

Ishiro had been told by one of the sergeants that sometimes the river bulged to great size because of the monsoon season. That was why the trenches on both sides were far removed from the river itself, for there was always the risk of sudden flooding.

The Japanese forces, exhausted from their campaign in Burma and the conquest of the Burma Road, had settled into positional warfare for the last few weeks. The concept was fine with Tanaka, as supply had finally caught up with them. The campaign in Northwestern Burma to cut the supply road to China (Burma Road) had been long and arduous, so he didn't mind a little positional warfare.

He'd heard rumors of an offensive toward Chungking and had seen the trickle of reinforcements that gave fuel to those rumors. According to a couple of guys in the squad, they'd overheard Lieutenant Togun talk to another officer about the attack that would be launched soon. But Ishiro wasn't so certain. The Army lacked the bare necessities, and, frankly, they didn't eat enough and only had maybe one good battle's worth of ammo. After that...

So, he decided that the attack would only be when they were fully resupplied. The following day, Togun and the yelling sergeants roused him up, like the rest of his comrades. *"Get your gear and suit up. We're going across the river."* Tanaka and his comrades thought this was the stupidest of decisions, as the 18th was far from combat-ready. Well, it could fight; it just remained to be seen for how long and how well.

As artillery shells started to whistle above their heads, to go crash down in great blasts and booming sounds toward the Chinese lines, he gathered up his gear and his new paratrooper Arisaka rifle. That brought up a thin smile since he really liked it and decided that at least he would be able to try it. He started walking from their squad's makeshift bunker to the trench line overlooking the river. Their *"bunker"* was a protection they'd build for themselves, accumulating boulders on top of each other and installing a makeshift roof with the trees they cut down from the area. They added a nice large tarp, making the thing waterproof. At least it protected them from the rain that came almost every day. The damned monsoon season was in full swing, and it seemed that the sky was like a pierced bucket. Water literally poured on their heads several times a day and every night. Everyone in the 18th was wet and miserable. So, their little *"bunker"* was perfect; at least they could get away from most of the damned humidity for a few hours between their duties and whenever the officers and sergeant weren't watching them.

They'd been told that they were lucky, as usually, the monsoon started in June, but the 1942 summer had seen it arrive in late July. Tanaka wondered how in hell they would be able to fight properly in this weather while hungry and with scant ammunition. He guessed that, as usual, it wasn't the officer's problem. It would be up to the soldiers to find a solution. He grumbled his whole way toward the trench, like all his comrades. They were all in a foul mood.

In the grand scheme of things, the 18th Division and their grumblings were only part of the Imperial Army's Grand plan to attack its Chinese enemies. Not necessarily a lot was expected from the soldiers on the Nu River apart from focusing the Nationalist's attention and resources while another big offensive was launched in China proper. The conquest of the Burma Road and the entry into West Yunnan province would threaten Chongqing, Chiang Kai-Shek's capital, while the real offensive with dozens of divisions would be launched in central China.

Ishiro finally arrived at the trench and saw the opposing side, which was blossoming with blasting mounds of earth and debris. The Nationalists were getting a hell of a beating from the Imperial artillery. Some of the machine-gun nests also fired at the Chinese, proof being the hail of tracer bullets landing toward the trench on the other side. The officers waited a few more minutes, busy herding their charging *"cattle"* to the frontline, rousing them up, and slapping a few into obedience.

As they were about to charge, the clouded sky, which had been menacingly proposing rain again, decided that it was a good time to drop it on the miserable Japanese soldiers. It started to pour heavily. And then it poured so hard that it was hard for Ishiro to see on the other side, so thick was the falling rain.

The whistle was heard across the line, and everyone stepped up over the trench. The river was passable, but Tanaka, along with several of the men, looked nervously to the west, where the river flow came from. The damned Nu normally bulged rapidly when it rained. "Banzaiiiii" was the guttural sound they all made, charging and running into the knee-deep water. Bullets buzzed about Ishiro as several of his comrades on each side of him fell to Chinese fire. There was no time to help the wounded or fallen, and he, for a moment, felt a little bad about the injured who would just drown in the water, but it couldn't be helped. They needed to cross the thing as soon as possible, for the Nationalists were murdering them with their withering fire.

After a couple of minutes, Tanaka and the rest of the men, exhausted and panting, arrived at the base of the Chinese defensive trench. The officers pushed them on, and Togun slapped Tanaka with the flat of his sword to urge him onward. The officer's gesture brought a malicious look to the soldier's face. The lieutenant didn't know it, but he was already dead. Over the last few days, he had been on Ishiro's case and had even tried to confiscate his new Arisaka. Only the timely intervention of a sergeant who was afraid of what Ishiro could do (there were rumors around the unit about his tendencies to shoot in the back...) saved his rifle from Togun's clutches.

Tanaka would have been ready to forget the whole affair, but now that the damned officer humiliated him, he resolved to find his usual solution to that type of problem.

And then he forgot about it for a while as the Japanese soldiers were in the trench and fighting in close quarters with their hated enemies. The fight lasted for a moment, but Nipponese fury won the day, and the Chinese forces in that sector were obliterated, the rest of the Nationalist unit retreating northeastward.

Long after the battle, while the 18th Imperial Division was pursuing the fleeing remnants of the Chinese forces defending along the Nu River, one lone, dead officer was found with a bullet in the back. The orderlies picking up the dead body didn't even glance a second time at it. They were simple Burmese farmers pressed into service by the hated Japanese. So, they didn't have any opinion about how the stupid man died. They had so many dead to pick up and burn that it was simple-run-of-the-mill for them.

The Naval Battle of the Pacific Part 1
Carrier strikes and gun duels, August 15th, 1942

The 32-ton elevator catapulted in the air and disappeared in its own column of smoke and fire. The blast rocked the Long Island's crew off their feet, stunning most of them. The first bomb had slashed through the 3-inch armor like a knife in hot butter and exploded below deck in a cataclysmic eruption of fire and death.

The light carrier had just been returned to duty after its near-destruction at the battle of Palmyra earlier in the war. It appeared that it would again need some love if it survived the current ordeal.

Several of the men on the deck were atomized by the wall of fire that rolled across it, the explosion having started where four torpedo bombers and seven fighters had been ready to fly away, full of gasoline and ammunition. Hit by another Japanese bomb, they only fueled the blast.

On deck, the anti-aircraft officer had been busy blazing at the incoming Japanese planes when the explosive blast created a flash of light — and several of the flak crews and guns were gone.

Below deck, men died in droves as fires spread everywhere, and the entire carrier became an inferno. Long Island started to list hard to starboard, its radar gone, the bridge destroyed. The Captain was still alive but pretty banged up, while most of his bridge officers were dead or incapacitated.

The light carrier presented a terrifying sight to the rest of the American Task Force. They stared in horror at the carrier covered in smoke and flame. The men saw the Jap aircraft that had bombed Long Island whiz over their heads. Then, more explosions rocked the carrier as bombs and rockets exploded in all directions.

All across the American carrier task force, the scene repeated itself many times over. After a furious dogfight over the ship, the devastating Japanese airstrike swooped down on the Americans. Admiral Nagumo's spotting plane had detected Admiral Halsey's ships before he did. The old Japanese admiral had then launched a powerful strike of 175 fighters, dive-bombers, and torpedo bombers. The planes from the five main carriers (Akagi, Soryu, Hiryu, Shokaku, Zuikaku) and the two smaller light carriers (Hosho and Chiyoda) had lifted off the Nipponese decks. They flew toward their enemy to smash them to oblivion.

In all, the Imperial Navy plane's attack did not even last twenty minutes. By the time the Nipponese pilots turned back toward their carriers, they'd crippled Long Island, lodged a bomb on the other smaller carrier, the Bogue (wrecking its deck for flight operations), and lodged a total of six torpedoes into Wasp (1), Yorktown (2), Vincennes (1) and Juneau (2).

While the two large carriers now sported heavy damage and powerful fires, flight operation could still be attempted, and damage control teams worked hard to get things under control, so an hour after the strike. The Bogue and the Long Island were different, as they couldn't take the kind of punishment that their big brother could.

The two cruisers that furiously fired their anti-aircraft ordinance at the Japanese planes didn't fare any better than the two light carriers, as both were seriously hit and would sink before the battle was over.

"Damn Japs," Halsey grumbled as he surveyed the catastrophic damage on his beloved fleet from his vantage point on Hornet. *"Good thing that our planes had already launched, Admiral,"* said Arthur Westmoreland, his chief of staff. *"And also, not bad that we didn't get hit,"* finished Halsey. *"I want a full report on damage assessment within the hour."* *"Yes, sir."*

The Battle of the Pacific, as it would come to be called later in history books, was triggered by the Combined Fleet's raid on the Boeing factories in Seattle a few days before. Alerted, Nimitz had immediately sailed his fleet on an intercept course. Since Yamamoto sailed back toward Pearl Harbor, It had been relatively easy for the U.S. Navy to cut across the Japanese path, triggering the battle.

The U.S. Admiral was under order to engage the Japanese regardless of the odds because President Roosevelt was raving mad about the attack on the mainland and on the Boeing factories. The first fired shots at the carriers and promised the remainder of the fight to be epic.

Following the attack on their carriers, American aircraft approached the Japanese fleet about an hour later. Several of the pilots already knew that they wouldn't have a carrier to go back to. Fueled by their rage, they sped toward the large Japanese fleet, facing the large combat air patrol hovering over the Imperial Navy carriers.

When they got to 1,300 feet, they launched their bombs. The enraged Zeros shot down some of the American planes. The 100-plus planes raid had plunged right at the main Japanese carrier strength. They died in troves, destroyed by flak, ace Jap pilots, or simple lousy maneuvering. But they did unload their ordinance.

Most Japanese flattops were consequently hit. Some received glancing blasts, like Akagi and Soryu, but others were more seriously hit. The decks of Zuikaku (1 bomb on the flight deck) and Shokaku (2 bombs, bow, and conning tower) were ripped apart by powerful explosions.

Hosho, one of the world's oldest and first-ever aircraft carriers, was hit by both a bomb and torpedoes that exploded about a minute apart. The ship was rapidly engulfed in a powerful fire vortex and secondary blasts.

The same story repeated itself on the small Chiyoda, another light carrier that had recently arrived in Pearl Harbor. Unfortunately for its sailor, it arrived just in time to be sunk. No less than three bombs blasted the decks and penetrated deep within the ship's bowels. The resulting explosion, which was nothing short of catastrophic, made the ship open like an expanding ball of steel, followed by a blinding flash. The ship was gone a few seconds later, replaced by a large patch of smoke on the ocean.

A few minutes after the enemy left to go back to their carriers, Akagi's deck was a maelstrom of activity. Everyone buzzed about their duties. One man seemed idle and immobile—a sea of calm in an ocean of activity. Nagumo, looking at the damage with his binoculars. He was somewhat relieved. He would probably lose the two light carriers that seemed to have been severely hit, but his main carriers seemed okay. He, however, shot nervous glances at the Shokaku and Zuikaku, even if the reports so far talked of manageable damage.

The damage was a lot more severe on the American side, and Halsey had already received the order to retreat at best speed south. Admiral Nimitz, about to engage the Japanese surface fleet about 110 miles from his position, learned of the disastrous Japanese strike result with his typical cold-headed mind.

He would use the battleships to cover the fledging carrier force in its retreat. The American surface ships thus sailed to battle. Still, the Admiral's orders were to stay at long range, so the fleet took a south-easterly heading that would make sure the Japanese would eventually catch up but would never get to medium or short-range if the U.S. Navy maneuvered the right way.

Yamamoto, for his part, received news from both strikes almost at the same time due to communication issues. The distances involved were tremendous, and radio transmissions were unreliable. Both carrier fleets were wounded, and it seemed that Nagumo had for once been able to inflict more hurt than he received.

Furthermore, the Allied fleet was still within a possible interception scenario range. Like a good poker player, the Grand Admiral decided that he had a good hand and that it was time to up the ante. *"Order the battle fleet full ahead."* And at that, Yamamoto crossed his arms behind his back and walked to his cabin to think. *"Call me when the situation changes." "Yes, Admiral."*

Shot down
Somewhere in the Pacific Ocean, August 15th, 1942

There was noise aplenty and all around him—explosions after explosions. Ace pilot Harry Bergman watched the exciting American attack while hiding under a floating piece of his torpedo plane. He'd been shot down earlier.

As he floated, he cheered loudly (no one could hear him anyway) at his brothers fighting for their lives over him. He was also amazed by the amount of flak ordinance that the Japanese fired in the sky. From a sea-level perspective, it looked a lot heavier than in the air because of altitude. The anti-aircraft rounds all seemed to explode in the same general area from the ground.

Bergman was covered in black oil, and he had a small gash on his forefront (when his plane hit the water since he never bailed out). His SBD had been strafed from above by a Zero fighter as Harry was making his approach toward what seemed the biggest of all enemy carriers (he didn't know, but he'd aimed at Akagi). The enemy pilot had skilfully approached under the guide of the blinding Pacific sun and attacked from their topside. His 20mm shell burst exploded the gunner's canopy, and ripped apart the plane's wings so that it had not been possible to fly the thing level. One of the shells had also narrowly missed Bergman behind his back. While he was unscathed, it wasn't possible to say the same for his parachute (on which he was sitting). A shell had burst through the canopy and landed smack between his legs. Luckily for him, it had not exploded and went right through the plane's fuselage at the bottom. But it had ripped the chute apart.

So, Harry had to get the Dauntless to land on the water. He'd eased it as much as the leftover controls permitted him to and then touched the sea, bringing the plane to a dead stop and yanking him on the control panel. He almost lost consciousness but had been sharp enough to extricate himself from his partially sinking SBD. After a minute, the plane was half-sunken but didn't seem to want to drop anymore. He figured that some air bubbles kept the aircraft afloat.

An F4F Wildcat thundered a few meters above his position, closely followed by a Japanese Zero that was firing a continuous burst of fire that exploded harmlessly on each side of the American plane as it tried to dodge frantically. It maneuvered smartly amongst the small water geysers created by the Nipponese pilot but didn't get hit.

After a few seconds of moving left and right in an unpredictable manner, the U.S. pilot looped backward in a risky move (he was very close to sea level, after all) and climbed sharply before turning on itself and firing at the Jap Zero, that could only watch in stunned horror as the American ordinance hit it. The enemy fighter exploded, and its still flaming/expanding remains hit the water in a great splash.

Bergman cheered loudly and tried to signal to the pilot that he was there, hoping that the U.S. Navy ships would eventually come to his potion to rescue him.

The furious battle eventually ebbed, and the Japanese ships sailed full speed ahead in a south-westerly direction, leaving Harry alone in the water. He was miraculously alive and well. It took the better part of two days before a Navy destroyer blessedly found him and picked him up. The ace pilot had seen him after killing the Jap Zero and reported his position when he landed back in Yorktown.

The Naval battle of the Pacific part 2
Dreadnought's duel, August 15th, 1942

By the end of the afternoon, both surface fleets got within range of the other. Of course, the mega Yamato guns (460mm) were able to fire first as they had a superior range to all U.S. battlewagons by at least fifteen kilometers.

The super-battleship also had just been fitted with the first operational Imperial Navy radar, and the thing, while crude, came in handy for Admiral Yamamoto's range finding and to direct the rest of the ships.

So, the first shells landed amongst Nimitz's ships, and while exploding in great fury and making for impressive pillars of water that splashed on the American decks, no hits were scored. The range was extreme, and at that distance, it was more than just a little difficult to hit a moving battleship, let alone one that knew you were shooting at it, hence that dodged frantically.

By the end of the afternoon, both sides were sufficiently in range to open up with all their fury. A great gush of fire and smoke poured out of the mighty guns on the battle fleets as they shot their anger at the other.

The first hit of the day belonged to battleship South Dakota that straddled the Nagato with several shells, hitting the Japanese dreadnought's superstructures. The ship became a raging ball of fire for a moment but sailed out of it relatively unscathed as its armor shrugged off the blasts. The distance affected hit probability at that distance (12,000 yards). It also affected the blast's power, as, by the time the big naval ordinance flew all the way to the target, it lost a lot of velocity.

And then, after that, both sides fine-tuned their gunnery and started to hit the other more regularly. The second to score was Yamato. The big warship had been firing for a while; thus its gunners finally hit because of the volume of fire and the inescapable logic of probabilities. Three of their mega shells blasted at the rear of the old World War One (pre-dreadnought) battleship Georgia. The three hits, producing a blinding light and powerful shockwave, completely gutted the vessel's engine room and its conning tower. In one broadside, the Japanese super-ship had killed a ship. Georgia was dead in the water, with electrical failure and a destroyed engine.

Nimitz was, by that time, pretty busy directing his battle and making sure his ship stayed at long range while giving the order and getting damage assessments. He felt terrible for the men in Georgia but had to continue sailing at the best speed if he didn't want to be overtaken by the Japanese ships.

California, Colorado, Bretagne, Lorraine, and West Virginia each reported successful hits on the enemy. The unlucky battlewagons on the receiving end were Hiei (one main turret destroyed), Kongo (hit below the waterline, major damage), Mutsu (superstructure hit), and Yamato (bow damage and one 155mm gun turret destroyed).

The Imperial Navy also got busy with battlecruiser Amagi, battleships Mutsu and Nagato; they straddled Maryland (bow, waterline), California (main armor belt, another hit center of the ship, and West Virginia (two primary and three secondary gun turrets destroyed) with several powerful shells. Kongo and Hiei concentrated their fire on stricken Georgia to finish it off before its sailor could bring its guns back online. The old lady exploded catastrophically after over fifteen shells hit it in succession, as it could no longer move nor defend itself.

Now over an hour old, the battle slowly ebbed as dusk settled on the Pacific Ocean. While the burning ships on both sides would be spottable from a great distance in the dark, Nimitz proficiently disengaged his fleet from the long-range shelling so that by 1842 (roughly twenty minutes before sundown), the American ships were out of range. The battle of the Pacific was over.

The struggle ended in a Japanese tactical victory, with the Imperial Navy in control of the sea after the battle and with an advantage in the loss ratio. Two light carriers sunk on each side, and one battleship sunk on the Allied side.

Strategically, it was also a win for Yamamoto since he'd wrecked the Boeing factories in Seattle. The Grand Admiral, who ordered his ships back toward Pearl Harbor, finally felt satisfied for the first time since his successful invasion of Pearl Harbor. There were losses and much damage to repair, but he was victorious and holding the American juggernaut at bay.

EPILOGUE

Back to square one
The un-improving situation August 17th, 1942

Roosevelt was inhaling a long drag from his cigarette while General Marshall and Admiral King sat on their respective chairs on the other side of his Oval Office desk.

"So, gentlemen. Let's have it." The American president dropped his butt into the ashtray and looked at the two commanders while they started their description of the last two disastrous days.

"Mr. President," started the General, clearing his throat. *"The initial report from the Boeing Factory No. 2 is that they have been able to put down the fire and save a lot of the city in the process. The damage to the plant remains to be assessed, but the Boeing executives think they should be able to resume production within a month. After all, they have other buildings, and they are even considering re-opening Boeing Factory one and moving the equipment that survived the destruction there."* Marshall paused since he knew Roosevelt by now. The man had a question. *"General. How many dead?"* *"So far, over 123 confirmed dead. The raid was during the day, and the factory was full of workers. Some civilians living near the factory were also caught in the inferno. We expect the final number to climb over 200."* *"Damn Japs. Damn Yamamoto."* Roosevelt was angry. *"Ernest, what of our fleet and the result of the Battle?"* *"Mr. President,"* started King with his usual coarse voice and shitty tone of voice. *"The battle was hard-fought. Battleship Georgia is sunk, plus light carriers Bogue and Long Island. The rest of the ships are damaged to different degrees. The fleet is currently just arriving in San Diego harbor and will need a lot of repair work."* The Admiral stopped for a moment, fishing out two folders that he gave to the other two men in the room. *"I have issued orders to sprinkle the ships along the West Coast to get them repaired as soon as possible. The good news is that the Japs also lost two carriers and have incurred heavy damage as well."*

"Okay," answered Roosevelt, heaving his chest loudly. *"We'll just have*

to go with that, gentlemen." The President knew that these men were doing their best under challenging circumstances. The Japs had a significant superiority in terms of fleet assets. The U.S. production would eventually offset that balance, but the war was only six months old. *"What news of General MacArthur and the SWPA front?"* Marshall shifted uneasily in his chair. *"The situation is critical, Mr. President. Douglas is mounting a counteroffensive on the Western Coast as we speak, and it should be launched within the month since it takes time to move the troops up north with the bad roads. The real problem is with Port Moresby and our whole position in the Coral Sea. Admiral Leahy's fleet is worn down, and almost every ship is damaged to different degrees. The town has been destroyed by the japs, and it's now encircled by the 67th Imperial Division and being bombed daily. We've landed supplies, military engineers, and workers to work on getting the harbor repaired o we can resupply them, but nothing is certain at this point. We would need a fleet to increase our chances."*

At that, Admiral King decided to talk about Admiral Nimitz's proposal. *"As we all know, we have an operation set for next month on Pearl Harbor. Admiral Nimitz proposed that we should surprise the japs and transfer most of our fleet to the Coral Sea after that battle. They would not be expecting such a move."* The President sat backward in his chair, obviously showing that he liked the idea. *"That's not a bad idea, Ernest. Not bad at all. When do you think we should do this?"* King hesitated for a moment, seemingly thinking about his answer. *"Well, Mr. President, once we've got the ships repaired and our Hawaii operation in September is over, we could send what doesn't need repairs through the milk run and arrive in Brisbane sometime in October. I believe that we could be in sight of Port Moresby....."* he paused for emphasis. *"Perhaps by mid-October."*

"Mmmm, the siege will be over at that point if the Japs have anything to say about it," answered Roosevelt. *"Those are exactly my thoughts, Mr. President. So, I worked to scrape the barrel a little more to find ships, and I have come up with something pretty decent in the short term. Battleship Indiana has just completed its refit in the Norfolk*

shipyards, so it can sail immediately. Saratoga and Enterprise were already being transferred to the Pacific fleet for the coming operation on Pearl Harbor, so that's that. As per your suggestion yesterday, we have also contacted the Free French authorities, and they have agreed to send the battleships Dunkerque and Courbet to the Australian theater. Both ships have just completed their refit after the French disaster in 1940 and were ready to sail. Canada will also sail down its small Pacific fleet, including the cruiser Ontario and five destroyers. New Zealand also agreed to send its two light cruisers." "Perfect. I have also had some correspondence with Churchill over the matter, and the Royal Navy also dispatched the carrier Indomitable and two heavy cruisers, the Frobisher and the Effingham."

"With these ships, Mr. President, my men will hold the line, and Douglas should do the rest," finished King. And indeed, he would.

Extract from General MacArthur's book, Reminiscences, 1964
The critical fight for Australia

The final stage of the struggle was now at hand. The defense of Northern Australia's last line of defense, Port Moresby, entered its most critical stage. Our forces were encircled all around the city, ringed by the enemy 67th Imperial Division and several other regiments and heavy artillery. The troops were under constant air attack as my forces struggled to gain the upper hand, facing overwhelming Japanese forces. We indeed needed to hold there, for it would be the invasion of Australia proper after that.

During the entire Papuan campaign, the enormous flexibility of modern airpower was constantly exploited. The calculated advance of bomber lines through the seizure of forward bases meant that a relatively small force of bombers operating at short and medium ranges could attack under the cover of an equally limited fighter force. Each phase of advance had as its objective an airfield that could serve as a stepping stone to the next advance. In addition, as this airline moved forward, naval forces under newly established air cover would eventually begin to regain the sea lanes, which had been the undisputed arteries of the enemy's far-flung positions. Ground, air, and sea operations were thoroughly coordinated. It was a new type of campaign—three-dimensional warfare—the triphibious concept. It was the practical application of this system of warfare—to avoid the frontal attack with its terrible loss of life; to by-pass Japanese strongpoints and neutralize them by cutting their lines of supply; to thus isolate their armies and starve them on the battlefield; to, as Willie Keeler used to say, "hit 'em where they ain't"—that from this time forward guided my movements and operations.

Such a strategy was challenging to implement in August 1942 as we were holding on to dear life in Port Moresby. But as a solution to the quandary, I started to look at the other side of the Owen Stanley Range and the bases from which the Japanese Army was getting its supplies from and where its air strength was based: Buna, Lae, and Rabaul.

If supply flow could be cut or severely hampered there while we re-established our own through our herculean efforts in Port Moresby proper, something could be done about the final victory in the theater. Our Flying Fortress numbers were regularly growing and reached a very respectable 325 units by the middle of August.

It was a far cry from what we had when I arrived in Melbourne to take my command a few months earlier. When he assumed command of the American air units in Australia, Major General George C. Kenney made a personal, plane-by-plane inventory of his available forces. Of bombers, he found we had sixty-two B-17s, but only five of them were in condition to fly. The rest were grounded for various reasons, either damaged in combat or awaiting replacement parts. There had been a failure to solve the problem of front-area aircraft maintenance. Nothing is more useless than a plane that cannot fly. A grounded air force is no air force at all. Kenney's soundness of concept was brilliantly evidenced in his ability to keep his planes flying. He also got things done to receive the parts from the States.

Of all the brilliant air commanders of the war, none surpassed him in those three great essentials of combat leadership: aggressive vision, mastery of air tactics and strategy, and the ability to exact the maximum in fighting qualities from both men and equipment. Through his extraordinary capacity to improvise and improve, he took a substandard force and welded it into a weapon so deadly as to take command of the air whenever it engaged the enemy, even against apparent odds. He brought with him as a field commander a leader of similar caliber, Brigadier General Ennis P. Whitehead.

The General had also organized a *"sky train"* through the *"milk run"* route. The B-17s flyable from the North American Mainland to Australia via an intricate series of stops on islands far away from the fighting. The bomber's range (3750 miles) did not permit it to fly nonstop to Australia, but it was sufficient to fly to newly built airbases in faraway islands that I had never before heard the names of. The aircraft would fly from La Paz in Mexico's Baja Peninsula, 3041 miles away in the remote Marquesas Islands. From there, it was refueled at a newly built Air Force base to the Kermadec Islands, another 2867 miles away. It would then be able to fly the last leg of the voyage to Brisbane, another 1750 miles away.

Thus, in this way, I was finally able to start thinking offensively, as in the next few weeks and months, I would employ my forces in several daring operations to destroy the enemy supply bases on the Northern New Guinean coast and kill Jap supply over the Kokoda trail.

The fight for Port Moresby's mastery was far from over, but I had the blueprints for victory.

Bridge of Battleship Yamato
The Combined Fleet enters Pearl Harbor August 17th, 1942

As supreme battleship Yamato slid into the protective embrace of Pearl Harbor, Grand Admiral Yamamoto surveyed the scene before him. It was a scene of damaged ships. Burnt, scarred, blackened. Mangled pieces of metal, gaping holes in armor belts. The telltale signs that a great battle was fought.

The Combined Fleet was back in its new adoptive home port. Isoroku's forces were damaged, but the Japanese strategic mastermind was happy regardless. The operation was an Imperial strategic and tactical victory. It wasn't a war-winner, but it was something to rejoice. The Navy had struck at the heart of American aircraft production, completely wrecking the Boeing factories in Seattle.

He would have been happy with only that result, which, according to the last air recon, would leave the city and industrial area utterly desolate for a while. But his forces also accomplished a lot more. They'd sunk a U.S. battleship (the Georgia) and destroyed two light carriers (the Long Island and the Bogue). The Nipponese big guns ship had added a plethora of heavy damage on the enemy. In addition, three heavy cruisers had been sunk.

Japan paid the price for the battle as well, but one that Yamamoto would gladly pay in a scuffle to have victory in exchange. Two light carriers were gone. The Hosho (a 15-plane aging carrier) and the Chiyoda (a converted seaplane tender) were not what you could call the Imperial Navy's backbone, so while it hurt to lose them, it wasn't a strategic disaster.

He'd reviewed the list of damage. Most of his capital ships were okay. The two most critical were the Shokaku and Zuikaku, damaged below the waterline (Zuikaku) and with a wrecked deck (Shokaku). Imperial engineers reported that they would patch up the ships within the next five to ten days. They wouldn't be perfect (their speed would be reduced) and would eventually need to go to Japan for lengthier repairs, but they would be battle-ready by the end of August. The Akagi had received some damage on its deck, but the damage control crews had already patched up the holes on the two-day voyage that the fleet did after the battle to get to the Hawaiian Islands. Hiryu and Soryu had only got superficial hits, so all was well there.

His dreadnought strength was a little more roughed up, but that was to be expected in any surface battleship battle. Sister ships Hiei, and Kongo would be the first in Pearl's drydocks as they had the most extensive damage; waterline armor belt heavy damage for Kongo and a destroyed gun turret for Hiei.

The Grand Admiral had also ordered the transfer of the second Imperial Navy repair ship, the Satsuma, to Pearl in order to keep up with the unrelenting repairs needed for the Combined Fleet's continued operating far away from the Home Islands. It would start working on two ships at a time, the Nagato and Mutsu, that only needed armor belt patch-ups since they'd been hit where their protective steel was thickest, so they were relatively unscathed from the battle.

The last ship that would be repaired was to be Yamato, The Grand Admiral's flagship. It lost a 155mm turret in the battle, and the rest was damage to its armor. The ship, according to the engineers, was in great fighting shape.

Yamamoto wondered what was next for the campaign and the war as a whole. The Imperial Forces were still reigning supreme everywhere, but he could see that Allied resistance was stiffening. The Navy had pretty much reached its operational limit, even if he would have liked to invade the rest of the Pacific Islands beyond the already occupied Japanese perimeter. He hadn't really been able to reinforce Samoa, New Caledonia, and the extreme outlying positions as he originally planned to. The needs of the war in Australia and everywhere else made for heavy competition for resources within Japan's military, and far-away islands seemingly under no threat did not come high on the priority list. He wondered if the Empire's inability to reinforce those bases while it had the time to do so would become a problem. Of course it would, he thought darkly.

But the men leading the country into its greatest ever war did not understand the sheer scope of it, nor Japan's capabilities to win it – or lose it all.

THE STORY WILL CONTINUE IN BOOK 3 OF THE PACIFIC ALTERNATE SERIES:

STRUGGLE PACIFIC

Thank you very much for reading my work.

I HAVE A NEW FACEBOOK PAGE! PLEASE GO AND VISIT: https://www.facebook.com/profile.php?id=6155877008234
4

*** Please review my book(s) on Amazon and Goodreads.com and try not to be a troll.

.

*** Send me an email at **souvorov@hotmail.com** if you feel like chatting with me. **I respond to every email.**

Some of the books that I have unpublished are for sale on:

www.maxlamirande.com

THE BLITZKRIEG ALTERNATE SERIES

BY MAX LAMIRANDE

Book 1: Blitzkrieg Europa – 2nd Edition
Book 2: Battle Europa 2nd Edition
Book 3: Battle Russia
Book 4: Struggle Europa 2nd Edition – winter 2024
Book 5: Fortress Europa 2nd Edition – winter 2024
Book 6: Stalemate Europa 2nd Edition – winter 2024
Book 7: Staggering Europa 2nd Edition – spring 2024
Book 8: Faltering Europa 2nd Edition – spring 2024
Book 9: Crumbling Europa 2nd Edition – spring 2024
Book 10: Falling Europa 2nd Edition – TBD
Book 11: Soviet Europa 2nd Edition – TBD
Book 12: Red Europa 2nd Edition – TBD
Book 13: Climax Europa 2nd Edition – TBD

THE PACIFIC ALTERNATE SERIES

BY MAX LAMIRANDE

Book 1: Blitzkrieg Pacific
Book 2: Battle Pacific
Book 3: Struggle Pacific
Book 4: Staggering Pacific
Book 5: Burning Pacific
Book 6: Sallying Pacific
Book 7: Siege Pacific
Book 8: Faltering Pacific
Book 9: Crumbling Pacific
Book 10: Collapsing Pacific
Book 11: Shattering Pacific

THE NAPOLEONIC ALTERNATE SERIES
BY MAX LAMIRANDE

Book 1: *Austerlitz Alternate*
Book 2: *Friedland Alternate*
Book 3: *1809 Alternate – Winter 2025*

THE AXIS ALTERNATE SERIES
BY MAX LAMIRANDE

Book 1: The Bear and the Swastika
Book 2: World War
Book 3: Axis Triumphant
Book 4: Axis Victorious
Book 5: Axis Overwhelming
Book 6: Stalemate
Book 7: Axis Resurging
Book 8: Axis Siege

THE GREAT WAR ALTERNATE SERIES
BY MAX LAMIRANDE

Book 1: *Schlieffen Alternate*
Book 2: *Great War Alternate (Summer-Fall 2024)*
Book 3: *1915 Alternate*
Book 4: *Weltkrieg 1915*
Book 5:
Book 6:

Also, from the same author:

BLITZKRIEG PACIFIC

The year is 1942.

The world is at war. Almost every major nation has declared for the Allies or the Axis. Europe is occupied by the Third Reich, and the British Islands have been invaded and conquered by the Germans. Metropolitan France has fallen, along with its North African colonies. Spain and Turkey have joined the Axis. The Middle East is Axis. The USA and Soviet Russia are also at war with the Third Reich.

Only one major power is still on the sideline. Imperial Japan, already busy in its war of conquest in China, dawns on the idea of conquering the Pacific and Southeast Asia following German successes in Europe and the subsequent weakening of the resource-rich Franco-British and Dutch colonies.

The United States, following Japan's occupation of the French colony of French Indo-China in 1940, froze all of Tokyo's assets, stopped scrap metal deliveries, and is just about to stop delivering oil to the hungry Japanese military machine. A move certain to trigger a reaction from the warmongers in Tokyo.

President Roosevelt's decision to do so is about to have dire consequences for America. The Imperial Navy has set its sights on the main US base in the Pacific, Pearl Harbor. And all across the Japanese-held islands of the Pacific, the forces of the Rising Sun prepare for a full-scale invasion that they hope will give them control over the resources the country needs to continue on its expansion.

This is the story of the War in the Pacific.
Also, from the same author:

Also, from the same author:

AUSTERLITZ ALTERNATE

DECEMBER 2ND, 1805

The War of the Third Coalition rages in Europe. Battles have been fought, and Napoleon Bonaparte's Grande Armée sweeps everything before it. After a big victory over an Austrian Army in Ulm, the French occupied Vienna, the capital of the Austrian Empire.

The Russians entered Austria to come to the help of their Allies and under pressure from the British. The Austro-Russians and the French are about to clash in a small, unknown town called Austerlitz.

And then everything changes. The French stop trying to retake the Pratzen Heights, and the day's battle ends in a stalemate for both armies. Kutusov, the allied army's leader in the absence of young Tsar Alexander (who fell ill and is still somewhere in Galicia), decides to retire the army northward with the Austrian Emperor's approval.
The news galvanizes the Revolution's enemies and of the Empire, jealous of Napoleon's success and wanting him gone. The Prussians decide to join the war and move their troops into Austria to link their forces with the two other powers. The German states and other countries like Naples rethink their stances in the conflict. And the French Emperor's internal enemies, ever-wishing the old regime's return, start plotting to overthrow the government in Paris.

All the while, the Ottoman Empire, convinced by the French several months earlier to enter the war, has decided to intervene in favor of Bonaparte and invade southern Hungary with an Army. Austria is on the brink of annihilation, but Napoleon's Grande Armée also has a big challenge ahead since it now needs to defeat three major powers simultaneously.

Everything will come down to either Napoleon's genius to overcome the odds and win regardless of the troops arrayed against him or his defeat and the end of the French Empire.

This is the story of the Napoleonic Wars.

Also, from the same author:

SCHLIEFFEN ALTERNATE

Europe, August 1914.

The World explode into war as Austro-Hungary declares war on Serbia following the assassination of the heir to the throne, Archduke Franz Ferdinand. Russia follows suit and mobilizes, while Germany supports its ally and declares war on Russia. France then joins the conflict as it is Russia's ally.

The British intervene when the Germans execute their Schlieffen Plan and attack through Belgium to outflank the French defenses. And then pandemonium explodes everywhere. The Austro-Hungarian attack in Serbia and Galicia, the Russians invade Prussia, and the Germans smash into France. In the Middle East, the Ottoman Empire declares for the Central Power, while Italy stays neutral.

The German Army is unstoppable and closes in on Paris as the Allies retreat in disarray all along the front. The fate of the World hangs in the balance as a big battle looms for Paris. However, no gains come without giving something away. While the German Army is busy conquering the French and beating the British Expeditionary Force around, the Russians storm Prussia and roll over the German 8th Army. The Reich has all of its remaining troops fighting in the West and nothing fresh to put in front of the Russian steamroller. Koenigsberg fall and the Austro-Hungarians fail before Belgrade and in Galicia. Something will have to be done, or else Berlin will fall to the Russian Imperial forces.

This is the story of a war that might have been.

Also, from the same author:

THE BEAR AND THE SWASTIKA

The year is 1939.

The World rocks with the news of the signing of the Germano-Soviet pact. A dark veil soon falls on Europe as Poland is invaded and destroyed by the overwhelming forces of the Wehrmacht and the Red Army.

France and the United Kingdom can only sit by and watch the two military juggernauts obliterate the Polish state. No one believes the two totalitarian regimes can agree in the long term as their ideologies completely contradict each other.

Russia wants influence in the Balkans, has eyes on Finland, and wants an opening to the Mediterranean. Germany needs Romanian oil to keep its war machine operational, and Hitler is adamant about not letting the Bolsheviks gain another inch of ground in Europe. At least not more than he has already given out in the treaty of non-aggression signed before the Polish campaign.

The year is 1940.

The French campaign then unfolds with a disaster for the Allies, and the Germans win an incredible victory over the combined forces of the United Kingdom and France. British forces narrowly escape to their island with the remnants of their armies, and France surrenders. Half of the country is occupied by the Germans. It seems that the swastika will conquer the world, especially with the Russian bear watching its back.

Germano-Soviet Axis talks were organized in October 1940 concerning the Soviet Union's potential entry as a fourth Axis Power during World War II. The negotiations include a two-day conference in Berlin between Soviet Foreign Minister Vyacheslav Molotov, Adolf

Hitler, and German Foreign Minister Joachim von Ribbentrop. The two powers will try to agree on a formal alliance to divide the world.

The fate of liberty hangs in the balance.

Also from the same Author:

BLITZKRIEG EUROPA – 2ND EDITION

September 1st, 1939.

Germany invades Poland, igniting a major European war. A few months later, the French are also invaded, and the allied armies are utterly defeated. Then the Dunkirk disaster happens, and the United Kingdom loses most of its land army. Soon, the British Isles are also attacked, and the British are hard-pressed with a serious German invasion. The French struggle to resist the Axis forces bent on conquering all of their mainland home country and West African colonies. Watching from its safe shores, America cannot stay still while Western Europe and all of the Mediterranean fall to the forces of the Axis. And when the Afrika Corps plunges over the Suez and invades the Middle East, the Soviet Union finally decides to join.

And through it all, a hero emerges. Erich Walder, tank commander, will have to fight on all fronts and attempt to survive what the enemy will throw at him.

This is the story of the Second World War.

Also, from the same author:

SPACE WAR, An Empire Divided

The Empire built by Haakon the Great is no more. It's 4124, and the Human race has spread to the stars in four different star clusters by discovering light speed and wormholes. A civil war has broken out between the different human enclaves to see who will be the next emperor of humanity.

The Ptolemy and Hadesian Star Nations are invading Elysium, allied with New America from the Alpha Perseis Cluster. Large battles are being fought in star systems between former comrades of the Imperial Fleet. In space, battleships unload their powerful weapons at each other while giant battle mechas fight for control of the ground.

The opportunity is too great for the evil Cybernetic forces in the Caldwell 14 Star Cluster. Having fought – and lost – a terrible war against the Empire two hundred years ago, they are gathering for a return engagement against humanity.

A thousand years before, Haakon has dreamed and foreseen a terrible time for humanity. The Black Death is coming to consume all, and his Empire will not be there to fight it.

www.ingramcontent.com/pod-product-compliance
Lightning Source LLC
Chambersburg PA
CBHW070441120726
47910CB00003B/873